MUSIC MAN

Romance in Rehoboth #1

K. L. MONTGOMERY

MOUNTAINS WANTED
PUBLISHING & INDIE AUTHOR SERVICES

Printed in the United States of America

Paperback ISBN 978-1-949394-15-3

Mountains Wanted Publishing

P.O. Box 1014

Georgetown, Delaware

www.mountainswanted.com

Cover design by the author

Editing & Proofreading by Mountains Wanted Indie Author Services

❀ Created with Vellum

To all the music men I have known—and women too—for filling our lives and hearts with beautiful melodies. It's hard to imagine life without music. It's not a life I'd want to live.

Jack's Singer-Songwriter Playlist

Runnin' Down a Dream - Tom Petty
Higher Ground - Stevie Wonder
Piano Man - Billy Joel
You Were Always on My Mind - Willie Nelson
A Change Would Do You Good - Sheryl Crow
Ring of Fire - Johnny Cash
Hotel California - The Eagles
Heaven - Bryan Adams
Jack & Diane - John Mellencamp
Dreams - Fleetwood Mac
A Change is Gonna Come - Sam Cooke
Don't Let the Sun Go Down - Elton John
Coat of Many Colors - Dolly Parton
Glory Days - Bruce Springsteen

1

"Do you like this dress?" I spin away from the mirror, turning to face my boyfriend, Jack, who is six years my junior and one delicious piece of tall, dark, bearded man candy.

"Is it new?" Jack's eyes trail up and down my body, soaking in the view.

"Yeah…" I sigh as I whip back around to face the mirror, smoothing the skirt of the dress over my wide hips. "I gained back some of the weight I lost during my Reinvention, so I had to buy some new clothes. I got rid of my size eighteens and twenties when I got into a sixteen. Coulda used those clothes right about now."

"I think you're hot as hell," Jack confirms, bending down to press a kiss to my bare shoulder.

"Thanks, honey." I smile at his reflection in the mirror. "I think, for the first time in my life, I've come to terms with being a fat girl. And I'm okay with it."

His brows nearly collide as he twirls me around to face him. "You know I don't like it when you use that word."

"What? Fat?"

He nods as I turn back toward the mirror.

"Jack, we've been over this a million times. It's not a bad word. It's just an adjective."

"You're not fat, Claire. You're beautiful." He spins me around again and catches me in his arms.

"The two are not mutually exclusive," I remind him. How many times did I include that statement in my *New York Times* column? How many times have I included it in the book I'm currently writing?

"You can be both fat and beautiful." I grab his chin and force him to meet my gaze. "I'm both, and proud of it."

"I know you say that, but I—"

"You don't get to choose what word I use to describe my body," I cut him off. "I'm reclaiming the word. It suits me, and I'm not ashamed of it—nor am I ashamed of my body. I'm never going back to that girl who hated herself and her body, Jack. I've come too far to regress like that. I love myself just the way I am, and that's the end of it."

Now he's grinning, looking at me like he wants to make me his next meal. "I guess I can get on board with that," he tells me, "because I love you just the way you are too."

"And I feel the same about you." I run my fingers through his thick, dark hair, then press a kiss to the spot where his beard meets his ear. I love that spot.

"Well, I guess we're on the same page then." His eyes flutter closed when I trail kisses down his neck.

"If by page you mean bed, then follow me, and we can make it happen." I beckon him seductively with my index finger.

He follows me down the hall to my bedroom. "I'm pretty sure I'm going to love this story," he jokes before he throws me down on the mattress and covers me with a combination of kisses and beard-tickles.

I am one beautiful, fat, happy woman.

JACK'S ARMS tighten around my waist as his breath fans my ear. "I don't know what's more beautiful, the view…or you?"

"Why choose?" My eyelashes flutter as my gaze darts up and down his ridiculously gorgeous face. "You can have both, you know."

"Can I now?" He nuzzles my neck, tickling me with the aforementioned beard. "And by that I mean *right now*."

"Mmmm, Mr. Reilly, we're in public!" I scoff and gesture toward the expanse of Nature that stretches beyond us as far as the eye can see.

"What, you afraid that heron is gonna see us?" His eyebrows furrow momentarily before he presses his lips to mine again.

He is pretty damn irresistible. And, for the record, we're actually not in *public*. We're on my deck, but living right on the river, there's always a ton of wildlife about: herons, eagles, hawks, raccoons, squirrels, turtles. You could film an episode of *Wild Kingdom* in my backyard.

I blaze a trail of kisses down his neck. "Hmm, I bet Mrs. Heron wouldn't mind if Mr. Heron brought home a few new moves."

"I might mind, though!" comes a screeching voice to our right.

Our eyes rocket over to my neighbor's property, and sure enough, there's a little old woman standing with a broom in her hand, casting us an extra-snarly glare.

"Oh, Mrs. Vandeveer!" I shoot up from my position on

Jack's lap, my spine so stiff and straight, I'm ready for inspection by a drill sergeant.

Still seated in the lawn chair, Jack begins to chuckle. I can tell from the sound of his laugh that he's looking forward to seeing how I will handle my Cantankerous Neighbor.

"Yes, that's right, I've been watching you two!" She points a stubby finger in our general direction. "I haven't had a man between these legs for going on three decades now, so I'd appreciate it if you'd keep your intercoursing to the indoors, please!"

OMG, WHAT?!

I don't know what I need to worry about first: my jaw dropping to the deck, my eyes popping out and rolling into the river, or my neighbor using the word "intercoursing." Even Jack is speechless.

I struggle to get my lips and tongue and all the other body parts required to formulate speech to all work together to push something—anything—out of my mouth as I stand there gaping at my next-door neighbor, all five feet of her with her scraggly gray curls and all the wrinkles around her...

All the wrinkles around her—oh, FFS, why does my imagination have to go *there*?

Now I'm not sure even Mr. Reilly can save me from self-imposed celibacy.

Jack stands up beside me in apparent solidarity, his chest expanding as he sucks in a sharp breath. "We're so sorry, Mrs. Vandeveer." His tone is surprisingly even and sincere.

"Just take it inside, you two. Keep those lips and groins *inside* the house from now on!" She throws her hands up in the air as she continues her mumbly rant. Then she shakes her head and takes hold of the broom to finish sweeping her deck.

Without another word, I make a mad bolt for the French doors and throw them open so hard, I'm surprised the glass didn't shatter. As soon as Jack enters behind me and shuts the door, the rumble of laughter bubbling up like magma inside a volcano about to blow its top can be contained no longer. It explodes out of my mouth, shaking every single part of me: my shoulders, wobbly thighs, flabby tummy—even my hair is shaking with uncontrollable chortling.

"How dare we offend your neighbor, Claire! Why didn't you tell me she has such delicate sensibilities?" Jack joins in. Now he's trying to keep a straight face, but I can see his lips twitching with amusement, even under his beard.

"*Three decades!*" I repeat, howling so loudly that if the neighbor can't hear me, I'm sure every dog in Slower Lower Delaware can.

As my hysterical laughter finally starts to die down, Jack's smile fades. "So, I guess I'm not getting laid, am I?"

I grab his hand. "Oh, honey, I'm so sorry."

"It was the word 'intercoursing,' wasn't it?"

I shrug. "Well, it certainly didn't help!"

I'm still in recovery mode when he collapses on the sofa in a defeated heap and grabs the newspaper off the end table beside him. "I guess I'll get over it." He lets out a long, pitiful, dramatic sigh.

"Oh my god, Jack, we did it this morning. Don't be acting like you're all deprived over there!" I shake my head with disbelief. He's been quite a horndog lately—not that I'm complaining!

"Sorry! It's the first day of spring break, and I think

I'm channeling my inner college student." His eyes dart up from the paper. "We should go out for drinks tonight."

Hmm…that idea has merit. Who knew teachers get as wild as students on spring break? Thinking of drinking apparently brings my best friend to mind. "We could invite Jean-Marc and his new boyfriend. What do you think?"

"That sounds like a plan. Maybe we can find some good vegan grub for dinner. Jean-Marc always knows the best places!" Jack's face lights up with the words "vegan grub," the way mine does when I think of a nice, succulent crab cake or juicy prime rib.

Okay, so Jack and I don't see eye to eye on *everything*, but we have managed to make this relationship work pretty well for six months now.

We're taking it slow.

Like slooooooowwwwwweeeeerrrrrr than slow.

No one's moving in with anyone just yet. We didn't get to the stage of practically spending every night together until after the new year. I don't know exactly where our relationship is going, but I'm having a hell of a lot of fun. And after fifteen years of being married to Jeremy, King of the Asshats, I deserve a hell of a lot of fun.

Though, I'll admit I have this sneaking suspicion that Jack is THE ONE.

I mean, not the *first* One, obviously, because that honor belonged to the aforementioned King of the Asshats. But I think he's the *real* One.

I think Jack may know it too. We both had our practice marriages, and now it's time for the real thing. Well, not literally *right this moment* now. But someday…I hope.

An hour later, after showers and putting on real clothes (being a full-time writer means I have Work Clothes and Real Clothes, and no one wants to see the former out in public), we head out to the driveway where we face our usual point of contention: which car to take. I have a little silver sedan, and Jack drives a VW Beetle. The latter is uncomfortable, and I don't like it, but I also don't like to drive us around. Then there's the question of who'll be the DD.

"Why didn't we just call an Uber?" He looks straight at me. And neither of us has opened our mouths to address to Car Situation, but we both know what the other is thinking.

"It's too late now. Jean-Marc is expecting us."

"I'll drive," Jack says, climbing in. "You can drink."

I shoot him a mischievous smile. "You're just trying to get me all horned up again, like I was before the neighbor said—"

"Don't say it!" Jack reaches over and presses his finger to my lips. "Please, for the love of god. Please promise me you'll never say that made-up word again!"

"At least I know how I can *really* irritate you now!" I waggle my eyebrows as he cranks the ignition. Next thing I know, we're flying down Route 24 behind a chicken truck with white feathers flying out in all directions.

Such is life in Slower Lower Delaware.

RADIO ON, top down, cruising with my girl. How could life be any better than this?

Okay, the top is not down. It's March. But the radio is churning out The Eagles, and my girl is next to me. And we are cruising down to the beach. So, yeah, life is pretty good.

I've always been a melancholy person, always thought of myself as living in a minor key rather than a major one. But since Claire Sterling came into my life a little more than a year ago, I've been hitting much higher notes. There's just something about this woman. She makes me laugh, first and foremost. I've never met anyone who is more themselves than Claire. She's brilliant and awkward and silly and self-deprecating and oh-so-wise all at once. I would do almost anything for this woman.

Because it's March, there's actually parking along Rehoboth Avenue, so I whip my VW into a spot, and we get out to go meet up with Claire's best friend, Jean-Marc, and whoever this mystery man is. Claire grabs my hand, and we stroll down the sidewalk until we spot her friend standing outside one of the local watering holes with a tall blond by his side. The guy looks like he just stepped off a Viking ship, and even Claire does a double take. He doesn't look like Jean-Marc's type at all.

"Claire, Jack, I want you to meet Tony." Jean-Marc gestures toward the blond with a huge grin on his face.

"I'm happy to meet you," says Tony. And even though he's smiling, he still looks kind of serious. He just has that kind of face.

Claire shoots me a look that I automatically read as, *This guy's name is Tony? He does not look like a Tony.* I nod my agreement. He looks like *Thor* or maybe *Magnus*. He's ginormous. I'm a tall dude, but this guy is towering over me, and his bicep looks almost as big around as my thigh. And I'm not a small dude by any means. Damn.

Jean-Marc elbows Claire, his eyebrows waggling with something that might be...pride? as I pull the door open and usher everyone inside. We head toward the back of the bar area where the restaurant section begins, and there's a small stage where they're setting up for a band or some sort of performance. I love live music, of course, as a musician myself, so I can't wait to see who's playing. My buddy Drew and I have been toying around with starting a band, but so far his friends we've tried to jam with aren't too reliable about showing up.

We settle into our table, and the server comes by to get our drink orders. Claire is practically interrogating Tony when a man jumps up on the stage and grabs the microphone so abruptly that the sound of Claire's voice is quickly swallowed up by blaring feedback. My ears still ringing with the screech, I crane my neck to the stage behind me to see what all the commotion is about.

"Sorry, ladies and gentlemen, can I get your attention?" The man clears his throat as he scans the crowd.

There are only about twenty people in the joint, all spread out between the bar and the restaurant. While the twenty whopping people's volume gradually drops off from a forte to a mezzo-forte, two other guys come behind the speaker with a banner they affix to the overhang of the stage. I read the colorful teal, green and purple text:

Rehoboth Beach Superstar—Benefiting the Support Art Foundation!

"Thanks, folks! Just wanted to let you know that we're holding open auditions for the Rehoboth Beach Superstar contest in an hour. It costs twenty-five dollars to enter, and all proceeds will be donated to the Support Art Foundation. Finalists will perform at the Rehoboth Beach bandstand in May, and the winner of that contest will go on to compete in the Mid-Atlantic Superstar competition this summer with a chance at a national tour and record deal. So get in touch with your inner rock star, folks; it's for a great cause!"

There are like four people applauding as he steps off the stage. I shrug and turn back to the table.

Claire's face is lit up with a beaming smile. "Go sign up, Jack!"

"What? Why would I do that?" I shake my head, thinking I'm saved from further debate when our server returns with our drinks.

"Because you're a good singer, and it's for charity! An arts charity, and you're a music teacher!" She doesn't miss a beat as soon as the server walks away. She picks up her drink, swirls the pink frothy mixture around with the tiny straw and raises her glass. "Who here thinks Jack ought to do the contest?!"

Jean-Marc and Thor—*I mean Tony*—don't miss a beat either, and their glasses shoot up to join Claire's. "Here here!" Jean-Marc exclaims, and his Viking-esque date echoes him in his gruff voice.

I roll my eyes. "I don't have anything prepared to sing. It's in an hour! I thought you wanted to drink and hang out tonight, not listen to a bunch of amateurs butcher cover songs."

"Oh, I can't think of anything more entertaining to drink to. We could even turn it into a drinking game. For every flat note, you gotta do a shot!" Claire laughs as she glances toward Jean-Marc and Tony for their approval, and they're nodding and laughing right along with her. That's the most animated I've seen Thor all night.

After the man made the announcement, he moved to a table near the stage. Now he sat with a clipboard and a cash box, just waiting for someone—anyone—to go register. I sigh because he looks truly pitiful just sitting there, his desperation for someone—anyone—to express interest in the contest broadcast so loudly, anyone could pick up on it.

My sigh gets a reprise.

It *is* to support the arts. If people didn't do that, I wouldn't have a job. Besides, a lot of schools are cutting their art and music programs, so supporting the arts has never been more important.

"Look at him over there," Jean-Marc notes as if he read my mind. "He looks so lonely and sad. Come on, Jack, go cheer him up. Just think, if no one else registers, then you win, and you can play at the bandstand in May!"

"But I don't *wanna* play at the bandstand," I protest in a fake whiny voice.

Claire smirks when she gets my "But I don't wanna be a pirate" *Seinfeld* reference. It's our favorite show.

Though…if Drew and I ever do get a band together, this might be great exposure for us.

I stand up and rub my hands down the legs of my jeans to dry them off from my sweaty drink. "Fine."

It's just one song, right?

And it's for charity.

"Whoo hoo!" Claire cheers, and there's that beaming smile I'd do just about anything to see.

I head over to the table and plunk down my twenty-five bucks in cash, then sign my name on the clipboard. There are three other names there, presumably people who signed up before the dude made his announcement.

"Do you need accompaniment?" the man questions. "We have a PA system if you have a CD or the music on a thumb drive."

"Oh, no, I have my guitar in my car. I'll just go get it before I sing."

I give the bar and restaurant a once-over, noticing a few people have shown up, but it doesn't look like it will be a super big crowd. That's a relief. I haven't performed for anyone but Claire and my students for some time now. I don't count messing around with Drew and his friends

—and besides, Drew almost always sings lead when we jam.

"Great, well, we're glad to have you on board." The man extends his hand. "I'm Chuck Peebles from the Delaware division of the Support Art Foundation, by the way."

"Hi, Chuck." He has a death grip on my hand. *I need that to play my guitar, buddy, geez.* "Are you expecting a big crowd?"

He smiles. "Yeah, just wait. People will start trickling in any minute. We're hosting a bunch more of these this month and in April too. We're hoping to qualify at least twelve for the bandstand competition in May."

"Wow, I had no idea this was even a thing." A slightly uneasy feeling comes over me as I notice about a dozen more people venture into the bar area, three of whom are heading over to the sign-up table.

"Oh, yeah. It's the first year for it, but we're already getting quite a bit of press and social media attention. This is going to be huge. Mark my words!" Chuck says with a wide grin spread across his thin lips, revealing a mouthful of teeth like a smiling cartoon shark.

"Alrighty. Thanks." I turn and head back to the table, where everyone is eager to hear what the deal is. My stomach has already started to churn. I have a feeling this was a terrible idea, but seeing the excited and proud look on Claire's face, I know I can't let her down.

MY HEART IS BEATING like a drum as I take the stage, my trusty guitar strap slung over my shoulder and the neck of the instrument in my hand. They've turned the stage lights up so bright, I can barely see the audience, but I can hear my girlfriend's voice rising above the crowd's din. She's got one of those voices that carries, you know?

She asked me about ten times during the last hour what I was going to sing, and I kept stalling because I couldn't decide. I'm not sure I'm even going to know until I begin to strum the first chord.

I'm waiting for the applause to die down and for Chuck to introduce me. I'm the fourth one to perform, and I guess there are twelve of us total. We have two minutes to win over the crowd.

The first three vocalists were all women. One sang "Amazing Grace" a cappella, which was a little strange to hear in a bar. The second one had an electric guitar and sang something original that was so screechy, I couldn't even tell you what the song was about. The third was so nervous, she rushed through and kept getting ahead of her accompaniment.

I hated the fact that their poor performances gave me a little more confidence, but I never claimed to be anything but human. Besides, between Claire's hoots and hollers and Jean-Marc's whistling, I'm pretty sure I have the loudest cheering section of any contestant.

"Okay, folks, you're in for a treat because tonight we have local music teacher Jack Reilly! Let's give Jack a round of applause!" Chuck announces, and my cheering section goes to town. It's almost embarrassing how loud they are, really.

I strum the first chord, and the song leaps into my mouth. "Jack and Diane." I mean, I *am* Jack, right? Besides, who doesn't like a little Mellencamp? Next thing I know, the entire crowd is clapping along in time as I belt out the bridge.

It's over before I know it, and everyone in the restaurant and bar area are on their feet shouting and clapping. I don't perform very often in public—other than singing a few bars for my choir here and there—and I'd forgotten how exhilarating it is.

Chuck thanks me, or at least I think that's what he says. His voice is swallowed up by the still-thundering applause. When I step off the stage, my adoring fans—and especially my personal cheering squad—are still going nuts for me!

I'll have to be careful not to get a big head after this. But no worries. I'll go back to school on Monday, and my adolescent charges will be less than impressed with me, just like they always are.

Claire is standing up to welcome me back to the table with stars in her eyes, a smile curving her lips, and her arms open wide. She grabs me by the hand and yanks me toward her body with such force, I nearly bowl her over—inertia and all that. I'm a big guy! I mean, I'm no Thor... but even he looks mildly impressed as I glance over at him and Jean-Marc, who shoots me two thumbs up.

Then Claire's finger presses against my chin, turning my attention to her waiting lips, which I bend to meet without another second of hesitation.

Oh, I'm so getting laid tonight. What chick doesn't want to do it with a rock star?

2

I've become somewhat of a Domestic Diva since moving into my own house and having Jack and my son, Elliott, to cook for. It doesn't hurt that Jack will eat almost anything —as long as it never had a face—and Elliott, in typical teenage boy fashion, can consume copious amounts of food. I've had to come up with vegan versions of all my usual dishes, but there's nothing I love more than a challenge.

Cooking is an excellent procrastination tool, by the way. They tell me my "real job" is supposed to be writing books, but I'm not sure I believe them.

My stupid cat jumps up on the counter for about the millionth time. I'm about to launch that sucker out the window and into the river. Maybe I'll just drive him over to Jean-Marc's and give him back since I didn't want him in the first place. *Evil cat.*

Elliott wanders into the kitchen. "Come here, Figaro." He scoops up the tubby little black and white beast and holds him like a baby. The only person Figaro likes is

Elliott. If I picked him up like that, I'd end up looking like a deranged tiger got ahold of me.

My son nuzzles the cat, then looks up at me. "What's for dinner, Mom?"

"Kohlrabi steak and cauliflower mashed potatoes," I answer.

"What the hell is kohlrabi?"

At least he didn't use the F Word, right? I'm feeling like Mother of the Year. I know his dad uses all sorts of colorful language around him, but he knows to tone it down a notch when he's here. Or at least I *thought* he did.

I still feel contractually obligated to ask, "Can you please not use that word?"

"First amendment, Mom. You might wanna study up on it," he tells me with a smirk that reminds me of his father. And not in a good way.

My hands fly to my hips. "This house is not subject to the U.S. Bill of Rights, Son. This is Claire's Castle. There is no first amendment here."

He rolls his eyes. "Is there anything actually edible being served?"

"Mac and cheese," I tell him.

"Not the fake vegan stuff though?"

"No, the real deal." I need my cheese too, after all. It's bad enough that we almost never have meat when Jack is over for dinner. Jack doesn't eat anything that had a face. I promised him cheese never had a face, but he still says no.

Elliott's mac and cheese anticipation warrants a fist-pump, which happens as Jack comes in from the garage. "Well, you won't believe who just called me." His eyes dart over to Elliott and then back to me.

"Who?" I haven't even looked up from my pot of fake mashed potatoes that I'm currently beating the crap out of with my mixer.

"Remember when I did the talent contest thingie last weekend?"

"Oh, yeah?"

"Well, I won!" He sounds surprised. And ecstatic.

My head whips up. "Really? That's awesome, babe."

"Yeah!" I haven't heard him sound this excited since his daughter last came to visit. "So that means I'm performing at the bandstand in May. I have to prepare!"

"Wow, well, I'm so proud of you, baby!" I turn off the mixer, and despite a super attractive smear of cauliflower on my boobs (because everything lands on them. I swear there are food magnets in there), I turn to him and press a big wet smooch on his mouth.

"Ewww," Elliott protests, his nose scrunching up in disgust.

"Oh, whatever, it's not like we haven't caught you and Jes-sie k-i-s-s-i-n-g four million times!" Jessie is Elliott's girl-friend of almost a full year now. And I always say her name like that: Jes-sie. Because he hates it.

He rolls his eyes at me and takes a seat at the table as I carry over a steaming bowl of mashed cauliflower. Jack dons oven mitts and grabs the roasted kohlrabi out of the oven, and then I return for the salads and mac and cheese. It all smells pretty good for being like seventy-five percent vegan.

Jack is really quiet as he fills his plate and begins to chow down. Uncharacteristically quiet. Wow, he's really absorbed in this singing contest. I didn't think it mattered that much to him—after all, he didn't even want to do it. I practically begged him!

He has a fantastic voice, but his confidence has never matched his talent. Evidently his parents never supported his music career. It wasn't until after his father passed that he pursued his first love, going back to school to get his education degree to teach music and band in high school. Before that he had some boring IT job he hated. I can't even imagine him being one of those IT guys. He's much too handsome and bearded for that. No offense to any IT guys out there.

He finally looks up from his food. "So, I'm thinking of having my band back me up."

"What band?" My nose wrinkles.

I don't mean to be negative, but…it doesn't seem like his friend Drew is the most reliable person on the planet.

"Well, Drew and I have been talking about holding auditions for new bandmates, and being able to tell them we have such a huge gig just a couple months out is sure to be a big draw." He holds his fork out, using it to emphasize his point. "I know musicians have a reputation for being flaky, but if we treat this like a real business—"

I'm so glad Jack isn't the flaky type. I thought he might be when we first started dating, but it turned out he just wasn't quite ready for a relationship yet. I thought *I* was ready—but I was *definitely* not. So I'm glad that, even though he was the first man I met from the dating site, we had a couple of false starts before we really got involved. I learned a lot about myself in the interim. A LOT. And it only took me one therapist, one body image coach, and approximately one hundred gallons of wine to do it!

"Hey, you don't need to convince me," I remind him. "It's the musicians you have to convince. Please tell me you're not going to post something on Craigslist this time. Or that Drew is going to just call up every other bartender he's ever worked with—"

Jack sighed. "I know Drew's track record isn't…perfect, but he really is a good guy. I wish you'd give him a chance."

"I don't have a problem with Drew. I know he's a

bright guy, but he doesn't really seem to want to apply himself. How many different bars has he worked at since you've known him?"

Drew was our bartender the very first time Jack and I went out. He made me some girly pink drink that I am still thinking about to this very day. I mean, that's what stands out most from that date because I did *not* think Jack was into me after that night. Talk about a *false start…*

"You're kinda a social media expert now, aren't you?" He looks at me with his big, dark puppy-dog eyes—a look that has only intensified in effectiveness since I've come to know him and henceforth fallen in love with him. *Henceforth* is a great word, isn't it?

"I wouldn't say expert." I have a Facebook page for my authory stuff. Pretty sure that does not make me a social media expert. Oh, I have an Instagram solely for stalking purposes. For stalking Elliott, of course. *Like I said before: #MomoftheYear.*

"What's Craigslist?" Elliott pipes up. He has eaten none of his kohlrabi and maybe a forkful of mashed cauliflower. However, the mac and cheese bowl is nearly empty, and I'm guessing the contents are now in my son's belly.

"I'm pretty sure only perverts use it." I turn to Jack. "So, you know, if you want a band full of child molesters, you're good to go."

He ignores my observation with the patience and concentration of a Buddhist monk. "Can you help me with Facebook? Maybe we can put out some feelers."

"That sounds pretty creepy after the child molester comment," Elliott points out.

"Maybe we shouldn't talk about child molesters at the table," I decide.

"You brought them up!" Elliott proceeds to pick up his plate and literally *lick* the surface of it clean.

I slap my hand down against the table. "Ewww! Were you raised in a barn?"

Jack is just watching, like this is Dinner and a Show, his lips slightly parted in a smirk.

"I'm still hungry! Kohlrabi is gross, and the mac and cheese is gone now!" Elliott whines.

"Go make yourself a sandwich, then." I palm my face. Yes, a *literal* facepalm. "Please go eat *anything* in the kitchen rather than licking your plate. *Anything* else."

He shrugs and ventures off to the kitchen to eat me out of house and home. And now Jack and I are alone.

"Yes, I'll help you," I agree. "Or I'll try to, anyway."

"And I have to figure out what song to sing," he says like he didn't even hear my very generous offer to fool around on Facebook with him. Then maybe we can fool around in other places. Not my deck though, obvs.

Now I have even more procrastination exercises to avoid writing my book. Lisa—my agent—is going to kill me.

Unless my editor finds me first. I'm sure she'd love to wring my neck at this point.

I AM PRETTY SURE my brain is in La La Land. Claire just said something to me, and I think she had to repeat it four times before I finally realized she wanted to know my thoughts on the kohlrabi.

"It was great, dear," I assure her. Wow, we already sound like an old married couple. Not sure if that's a good thing or a bad thing.

Just that mere thought summons a spirit hailing straight from the very depths of hell: my ex-wife. As soon as I step away from the table, my phone begins buzzing, and I instantly have a premonition it's the Spawn of Satan on the other end.

I've never exactly admitted to Claire just how much I detest my ex-wife. I guess it feels like a bad move to disrespect the mother of my child, especially in front of a woman I'd like to, you know, like me. What is it they say? *Chicks before dicks*? What if Claire took offense to me calling Anita the Spawn of Satan? She might not appreciate it and take her side—which would be a huge mistake, because her side is right beside the Prince of Darkness.

I try to surreptitiously sneak into the other room so she won't hear my side of the conversation. I have a real attitude problem when it comes to this woman. Her mission is to make my life as hellacious as possible, a mission she seems quite capable of accomplishing even from several states away.

Fortunately, I don't have to deal with her very often. I FaceTime with Mariana, my daughter, at least once a week, and she spends two or three weeks a year with me here in Delaware. I make all those arrangements through Anita's sister, Camellia, who is a lot less demonic. She's actually fairly tolerable.

Knowing Claire might be eavesdropping—totally wouldn't put it past her—I start off as pleasantly as possible. "Hey, Anita, how's it going?"

"I don't believe your child support check has cleared

my bank account yet this month," is how she starts the conversation. I mean, that's her *opener*. No pleasantries. No small talk. Straight to hell.

"Oh, sorry about that. I will get it deposited tomorrow," I promise her.

"The fifteenth of the month, Jack. Or have you forgotten how to read a calendar? Get your head out of your ass and take care of your daughter," she spews.

I've never missed a payment. *Ever.* I usually send more than I'm supposed to because I feel guilty about being so far away.

"I'm sorry, Anita. It's just I don't get paid till tomorrow, and I was going to include a little extra for Easter—"

"That's not why I'm calling," she snaps.

Oh, so that was only the *prelude* to the raging bitchfest. *Good times.*

I don't even get a chance to ask her to reveal the real reason behind her call before she starts in again, her nasal voice grating on my every last nerve. "I have an opportunity with my current company that I want to explore. It means working out of their London office for a year—"

"London," I interject, then immediately bite my tongue because now I'm going to get my head bitten off for interrupting her.

"Yes, London," she snarls. "I didn't stutter."

Does my daughter have any hope for turning out normal when this is her role model? *Sigh.*

"I would prefer to take Mariana with me, of course," she continues, "but I could possibly be talked into allowing her to come live with you instead—for the time I'm gone."

My heart almost leaps out of my ribcage. I never thought in a million years that having custody of Mariana —even for a brief period of time—would be on the table. It's all I've ever wanted as a father and a human, to have my little girl with me 24-7-365! Maybe 365 would be all I'd get, but I haven't had more than a week or two at a time with her since she was a baby. I never considered fighting Anita for custody because I knew it would turn into a battle of epic proportions and wouldn't be good for Mariana to witness.

"Yes," I blurt out without giving it even a moment's thought. "Yes, I want her."

There's silence on the other end.

"Did you hear what I said, Anita?" I repeat, "I would love to have my daughter here while you're in London. For however long you are gone or want me to keep her."

"Oh," is all she says.

Oh?

Did I actually surprise her?

She has this narrative built up that I'm a bad father because I'm not with her anymore, but the truth is that Anita is the one who wanted to move back to Texas to be near her family. My dad was sick, and I had a job here, and I didn't want to go. Not to mention the fact that we were never the same after Mariana was born. I may have been a selfish jerk, but she is the one who left. Not me. She's the one who took our daughter away from me.

"Is that okay?" I scrub my hand down my face. I have some rights. I can't forget that, and I can't let her have all the power. Our agreement states that if she wants to move Mariana out of state, our custody arrangements will be revisited with the judge.

"I said I would consider it. I asked you if you wanted her, didn't I?" Her tone is dripping with snarkiness.

"Yes, but now you're acting surprised that I actually want to take care of my daughter. Of course I do, Anita. I love her. I want to be with her as much as I can be."

How many times have I flown down to Texas to see her

in the past several years? How many plane tickets have I bought for both her and her aunt to travel to see me?

"When are you going?" I ask when I'm met with continued silence on the other end—I'm pretty sure this is the quietest Anita has ever been in her entire life.

"Next month," she says. "I need to be there April fifteenth."

"Tax Day," I retort, because that's the first thing that comes to my mind.

"Yeah, whatever. Will you be able to fly down and pick her up?"

"I will make it happen," I promise her. "Whatever I need to do."

"And you'll need to get her enrolled in school right away," Anita continues, like I wouldn't know that my daughter needed to be enrolled in school. "I don't want her to miss anything."

She's in kindergarten, not a junior in high school, but, yeah, okay.

"I will take care of everything," I vow.

"Alright. I'll be in touch with more details."

She sounds disappointed. Like she didn't think in a million years I'd actually agree to take our daughter. Of course, she still didn't say I can have her. Only that she'll consider it—

"You know our custody agreement specifies that if you move out of state, we have to renegotiate custody," I remind her.

"I'm well aware," she fires back.

"I will fight to have her stay here with me," I promise her.

"Okay."

That's it. That's all she says.

Then: "Goodbye, Jack."

And click.

That's the end of that.

I slip the phone back in my pocket and look up to see my girlfriend staring at me with wide eyes. I've got some 'splainin' to do.

3

"So how are things going with Thor?" I ask as Jean-Marc scoots out the chair in the coffee shop, scraping against the concrete floor in a way that nearly obliterates my hearing. *Eh, didn't need that sense anyway.*

"Thor?" He crinkles up his nose as he stares at me, blinking slowly. "Do you mean Tony?"

I shrug. "Look, you know as well as I do that he looks like a Thor."

He cocks his head for a moment, then nods. *Yeah, that's what I thought.*

"He's magnificent!" He takes a sip of his fancy frothy coffee, getting just a little bit of the foam on his mustache. He licks it off a little too suggestively. "He's magnificent in *all* areas, Claire. Not just his…*stature*…"

"Oh, I do *not* need to know about your boyfriend's penis," I assure him. "Trust me on this."

"He really could have done porn," Jean-Marc continues like he didn't even hear me. "Maybe he did, even?" He stares off wistfully.

"Look, I have important stuff to talk about, and Thor's

Hammer is not on my list of discussion topics, alright?" I shoot him a little glare but then burst into laughter because, come on, that was hilarious.

My best friend is smiling too. "So what's up? We haven't had one of our morning coffee dates in a while, especially not on a weekend. Isn't Jack home?"

I lean in because it's a good position for divulging lots of juicy info. "He's home, but he's auditioning band members because he won that singing contest he participated in last week in Rehoboth."

"What?" Jean-Marc's eyes bug out. "Really?"

"Yup!" My brow furrows. "What, you didn't think he was good?"

"No, it's not that," he assures me. "I'd just already forgotten about it, that's all… I may be a little preoccupied with a certain Norse god…"

"Mmmhmmm," I mutter before taking a sip of my coffee. "But that's not all my news."

"Do tell," he urges me on.

"Right after he found out about the contest, he got a call from his ex-wife. She's going to be working in London next year, and she wanted to know if their daughter could come live with him while she's gone."

"Oh, wow, really?" He swallows down another gulp of his frothy concoction. "And what did he say?"

I give him one of my "duh" looks. "Well, he said yes, of course. Jack's a family man. He loves his daughter."

"How old is she?" Jean-Marc looks past me at someone coming in the door of the coffee shop, but then looks away, hiding his face with both hands. "Don't let that dude see me."

I roll my eyes. "I'm fat, Jean-Marc, but I'm not a human shield."

"Can you try? Please? For me?"

I grab the newspaper off the table next to us and unfold it, making a big show of snapping it into position upright and opening it to cover Jean-Marc. I think every eye in the joint is now on me, and sure enough, that dude is approaching our table.

"Jean-Marc?" comes his husky voice. He's quite an attractive silver fox.

My bestie doesn't say anything, so I slowly, dramatically lower the paper to reveal him sitting there in all his glory, legs crossed with his perfectly groomed goatee and styled hair, hands cradling his coffee mug like a holy grail.

"Oh, hi, Marty," he gushes in an overly polite tone. "Nice to see you."

"You didn't call me back," this Marty character accuses. He's no Thor, but if Anderson Cooper ever needed a stunt double…

He makes a *tsk* sound and shrugs. "Sorry about that. Just got super busy."

"Uh huh. I was hoping to go out with you again sometime…"

I decide to step up to the plate. I mean, what are best friends for if not warding off unwanted beaus? He'd do the same for me. "Jean-Marc has a new boyfriend. His name is Thor."

"Oh." Marty's lips purse. "Whatever. Nice to see you, Jean-Marc." When he turns toward me, apparently noticing me for the first time, a look of rapture overcomes his features. "Oh, are you Claire Sterling?"

My lips spread into the biggest smile. I love being recognized. It doesn't happen very often, but when it does, I milk it for all it's worth. "I am!"

"Oh, I have a paper with your column in it in my car. Can I run out and get it so you can autograph it for me?"

"Of course!" I give him a humble nod. I just finished

up a contract for writing a syndicated column for a little paper you may have heard of: *The New York Times*.

Marty steps away to retrieve the newspaper, and Jean-Marc's mouth has transformed into a definite scowl. "Thanks a lot. I thought you were supposed to be my best friend."

"You're welcome!" I flash him an innocent smile as Marty returns with the paper. I find the Lifestyle section, my article and scrawl my name in pen across the top. "Here ya go!"

"You're awesome, thank you!" He presses the paper to his chest like it's Extra Special and practically skips away from the table.

"Anyway…" Jean-Marc lifts his head from the facepalm he was executing and glances around to ensure Marty has vacated our immediate area.

"Jack's daughter might be coming to live with him," I remind him.

"And how do we feel about this?" he jumps right back into the prior discussion. "Is this the daughter I met at your house last summer?"

"How many kids do you think he has?" I laugh. "Yes, same one. Only one. Mariana."

"How old is she?"

"Five."

"And how do we feel about this?" he repeats.

I shrug. I have been thinking about it ever since Jack told me a couple days ago, and I'm kind of…ambivalent. I hate that I have any sort of trepidation at all, but in case you haven't noticed, I'm human, and, as such, I'm a bit neurotic.

"I'm super happy for him, of course," I finally answer. "She's a real sweetie. A bit spoiled, but that's because she's around adults all the time, and they dote on her."

"Well, that's not exactly going to change here," my friend points out.

"No, it won't. I mean…Elliott is here, but compared to her, he *is* an adult." Ugh, I hate that thought, but it's true. He just turned sixteen.

"So…you don't sound Super Happy," he observes, and I can hear the capital letters he puts on those two words, just like I would. He knows me too well.

"It's just that I've gotten used to Jack being able to come and go as he pleases. You know, because Elliott is older and because he goes to his dad's sometimes, Jack and I can do Adult Stuff."

"Is that like straight code for butt stuff?" Jean-Marc's facetious smirk shines at me across the table.

"Haha, no. I mean like going to concerts and bars and art galleries and…you know, things you can't do with a five-year-old in tow."

"Right."

"I'm sure we'll figure it out," I assure him. "Maybe Elliott will get some babysitting experience this summer. I know he wants to earn some cash…"

"There ya go. He and Jessie could watch her—"

"The only thing those two would be watching is the clock for her to fall asleep so they could mess around." I sigh. It's true, though. I don't think I'd trust them to babysit together. In fact, it might be time for a refresher on me being too young to become a grandmother.

"Well, I'm happy for him," Jean-Marc pronounces. "And you better figure out a way to be happy too—happier than you seem to be right now, anyway. If he doesn't think you're supportive, he may just kick you to the curb. You know he's probably thinking of you as stepmother material…"

I'm being a selfish biatch, aren't I? It's going to be a big adjustment, and I haven't taken care of a little kid in a hot minute. But *stepmother*? It conjures up images of Cinderella and her evil stepmother, and I have no interest in becoming the villain in Jack's fairy tale.

"You really think he sees me in a stepmother role?"

Jean-Marc squints at me in disbelief. "Uh, yeah, Claire. You've been dating a while now."

"Only a few months," I protest.

"You two were meant for each other," Jean-Marc insists, then he licks his lips before adding, "just like me and Thor's Hammer."

MY HEAD HURTS.

So far we've had eight people audition for the band, which is actually a lot more than I anticipated. But one of them was Elliott, and he can't even play an instrument. Another was his girlfriend Jessie—and, yeah, same. And a third was a dude I'm pretty sure is the homeless guy who flashes unwitting tourists on the boardwalk every summer.

That leaves five actual auditions. Three are Drew's friends, one of whom also does not play an instrument. Except the tambourine. No wonder my head hurts!

Did I mention that hardly any of them actually play instruments? That's kind of a prerequisite for being in a band, believe it or not. I'm a high school band director, and I deal with kids who don't know how to play their instruments all day every day—but I get *paid* to do it. I don't want to teach people in my spare time. Actually, I do that as well; it's called giving lessons. But I get paid for that too.

Unless it's Claire. I'm pretty much teaching her piano for free. But there are certain fringe benefits to that arrangement…

It was nice for Claire to let us use her garage for auditions. She's a little more isolated than I am on a semi-busy street in Milton. Though I wouldn't put it past her neighbors, Red or Mrs. Vandeveer, to storm over here all irate. I keep expecting one of them to poke their heads in at any moment.

"Well, Luke and Russ stuck around for the verdict," Drew tells me as we're starting to pack up our stuff. "Not sure what happened to Sam."

"Wait, they stuck around? Like they went in the house?" *Ugh.* Claire is not gonna like that.

"Yeah, Elliott was gonna show them some video game they were talking about."

"We better go make sure everyone's okay." I roll my eyes as I pack away the last mic cord.

"They're adults, Jack, geez." Drew purses his lips. "But yeah, we better."

I throw open the garage door and step into the laundry room, then lead Drew down the hallway that opens into the living room with a gorgeous view of the river. There are Russ and Luke sitting on Claire's couches drinking my beer. Yeah, that's just about what I expected.

Russ and Luke have played with us before. They're just super flaky. I wanted the *opposite* of flaky for this venture. They don't seem to understand what's at stake here—we want to actually start playing some gigs and making money. It's hard to make money as a musician if you're a flake or a hack.

Which is why I'm a teacher—a job where the focus is taken off the soul-crushing doubt of whether I have any actual talent and more on whether my band students are going to gang up and bludgeon me with their instruments.

But it would be fun to do it on the side. A little moonlighting gig—while I'm still young enough to do it.

Drew's friend Sam bursts out of the bathroom in the hallway before I get a chance to say anything. "Do *not* go in there!" he warns everyone, shaking his head emphatically.

I roll my eyes again. No wonder I have a headache. It's probably eyeroll-induced.

I perch on the arm of the couch and run my eyes over these four guys. They're all in their twenties. They're in a very different stage of their lives than I am. "Look, guys, I know you want to play with us, but we have an honest-to-God gig, and we need to have several consistent practices with everyone showing up in order to get ready for it, okay?"

"Yeah, we know!" Luke insists. "You're playing at the Support Art Foundation contest at the bandstand in May, right?"

We hadn't told them the exact gig—or at least *I* hadn't. Drew must've spilled the beans.

When I didn't answer, Luke continued, "Look, I've been wanting to play that bandstand since I was a kid. I remember going down to the boardwalk with my parents in the summer to hear the concerts, and I always wanted to be up there on stage myself. This is my chance. Are you gonna kill a little boy's dream?"

I sigh. *Really?* We're gonna bring guilt into this equation?

"I want to have at least six practices before the contest." I look around to gauge their reactions.

"Can I play tambourine?" Sam pipes up.

"I need you all to take this seriously!" My tone reveals my growing agitation. These three guys, Luke, Sam and Russ, seem about one step up on the maturity ladder from my high school students, and that's not saying much. They make Drew Clark look like Mr. Rogers…like someone who is super responsible, adulty, and an all-around good human.

"We promise you," Russ says. "We're ready to take this seriously too. It really helps to have an actual gig, to have something to work toward."

"So what song are you going to sing at the contest?" Luke interjects. "One with a drum solo, I hope?"

I scrub my hand through my beard and adjust my glasses on my nose. "I haven't decided yet, but I was thinking about doing an original song."

"Oooh, I can write one," Drew offers.

"I have one written already, but thank you," I reveal. "I wrote a song for Claire."

"Awwww!" Drew coos at me in a high-pitched voice. "That's just so precious!"

I roll my eyes. "Come on, guys. Is this really the best we can do?"

Russ stands up and walks over to Claire's piano. He sits down and cracks his knuckles before placing his fingertips on the keys. Then his hands start flying up and down the keyboard a million miles an hour. It's "Solfeggietto." Not the hardest piece to play, but he's really flying—and it's flawless. He finishes with an emphatic, resounding chord. "Well?"

"That was pretty good." What he played for his audition wasn't that complex, but I try to hide any signs that I might be impressed.

"I had ten years of lessons, dude," he tells me. "Trust me, I got this."

"And so do I," Luke promises. He picks up a pair of pencils from the end table next to the couch and proceeds to drum out a complicated rhythm on the coffee table.

"Please don't damage Claire's furniture," I warn him. "She might kill you."

"Fine," he finishes up, using a metal vase as a cymbal, nearly knocking it off the table, "but just so you know, I played in my high school's band back in the day."

"We're all committed to this," Drew vows, glancing from Russ to Luke to me. "We wanna make this happen."

I sigh. Judging from the talent—or lack thereof—we attracted today, this is probably the cream of the crop. And there's not much time to keep searching before the contest.

"Alright, guys, but if you let me down…" I shoot them a sharp glare, "well, trust me, you don't want to see an angry Jack Reilly. It's not pretty."

"Now we just need a kick-ass band name!" Drew chimes in.

"One step at a time," I cut him off. "Show up at practice on Tuesday night at seven, and we'll discuss a band name then."

One by one, the guys file out, but not before shaking my hand and promising me again that they won't let me down. I don't know why I have a bad feeling about this, but I do.

Claire

4

"What are you doing?" Jack's deep voice bellows from the doorway. "Are you spying on the neighbors?"

I straighten up and turn from my perch in front of the window. "*Neighbor*. Singular."

"Is that Red?" Jack steps closer, trying to get a look at what I've been staring at.

"Um…maybe?"

My neighbor on the left-hand side of my house is a man named Red. He keeps to himself, so I don't really know much about him. I'm not even one hundred percent sure what his last name is because even his mailbox simply says "Red."

Glancing at him, you might wonder where he got a nickname like "Red" because he has a long snow-white beard à la Santa Claus, and his hair probably matches, but I couldn't say for sure because he always wears a baseball cap. The one he wears all the time was possibly black or navy at one time and had some sort of logo on it, but both the logo and the color have been ravaged by time and the sun.

"What do you mean, *maybe*?" Jack presses. "It's either him, or it's not."

Well, it's *definitely* the neighbor; it's just that I'm reluctant to admit I've been gaping at him for much longer than what might be considered neighborly. I mean, I don't have a Santa fetish or anything, but the guy has a much more muscular physique than I ever could have imagined. He's planting some shrubs along the side of his house that faces mine—and he's shirtless.

Jack pushes past me to take a gander out the window and almost immediately scoffs. "Oh, I see what's got you all twitterpated."

"What?" I scoff right back. "You think I'm ogling the neighbor?"

Jack's eyebrows arch. "Pretty sure." He flexes his muscles, making the band of his t-shirt tighten around his biceps. "If you want a hunky guy to look at—one who's more in your age range—I can take off my shirt."

"I'll definitely look, but that's not what I was doing." Okay, I'm lying. But it was more the element of surprise than anything else. Red apparently works out.

"Uh huh." He strips his shirt off and stands before me, all muscles and chest hair. And the beard. Don't forget The Beard—he could practically get a trademark on that puppy. And Jack's is not at all Santa-esque—which is a good thing. A great thing, actually.

"You know what?" I glance out the window again and see Red's muscles flexing as he pounds into the hard ground with a shovel, scooping out a hole for the next shrub. "Mrs. Vandeveer said she hasn't had a man between her legs in how long?"

"Oh, for Christ's sake, Claire, don't remind me about that! I'd already scrubbed my brain of that conversation!" Jack protests. "I do not wish to relive it."

"Right, but…what if the only thing standing between those two making a love connection is my house?" I stare at him, my mouth gaped open and eyes wide with delight at my Brilliant Idea. I am known to have one from time to time.

"So, what, you're going to play matchmaker between your neighbors now?" He rolls his eyes and laughs at me. "Don't you have a book to write?"

"Book schmook," I fire back. "I'll get the book done. I've made considerable progress already."

"Like how much?"

"That's not what we're talking about." I trail my eyes across his manly chest. It's really hard to argue with him when he's standing here half-naked. There are so many other, better things I could be doing with my mouth right now.

Like *kissing* him, you pervert. What did you think I meant?

"Well, I like to make people happy," I continue, taking a step toward him. "And maybe Mrs. Vandeveer wouldn't get so bent out of shape when we're making out on my deck if she's getting some action of her own, you know?"

"Or maybe we just shouldn't make out on the deck," Jack suggests.

Perfect segue. "Well, we could make out right here, right now…"

He wraps his arms around my waist and pulls me close to him, so close I catch a whiff of his sandalwood cologne. It's just so manly and swoon-worthy…

He strokes a finger down my cheek. "Did Elliott leave?"

"Why yes he did," I confirm, a wicked smile curling my lips.

"So we're here all alone?"

"That's what I said…"

"And I could kiss you if I wanted to?"

"Quit teasing me and get those lips on me now!"

And then they land on me, all soft and warm and wet. His hands thread through my hair as he deepens the kiss, stroking his tongue against mine and making my knees buckle, but he holds me firmly in his strong arms.

I've fallen for this man. I never thought I could be this happy or this excited about the future. Jack is everything I never thought I deserved. Especially if I stayed fat.

But here I am, rockin' this Fat Girl body, and he loves me.

HE LOVES ME.

Twenty minutes later, after a quickie that rumples both my sheets and my hair, we lay naked in my bed. I'm curled into the crook of his arm. It's so cozy and safe, and I never, ever want to leave.

So, naturally, his phone rings.

In the other room. *Crap.*

"Is that Darth Vader's theme from *Star Wars*?" I ask as the sound filters into my ears.

He bolts up in bed. "Yeah, 'The Imperial March,'" he confirms. "My ex. Gotta go grab it…sorry, babe." He slides out of bed and rushes into the living room, where his phone is resting on the coffee table. I remember seeing it earlier.

He walks back into the room, holding it to his ear. "Yeah, okay… Yeah, fine. Alright… I already told you I would." There's a pause, and I can hear a woman's voice as Jack's eyes roll back so far in his head, I'm not sure I'm ever going to see his eyeballs again. Oh, there they are. *Whew.*

My heart is pounding, and it takes me a moment to

figure out why. He's talking to his ex, and it sounds like he's confirming arrangements for Mariana to come.

"Anita, we went over this. Yes, I am aware," he says, his tone turning sharper by the second.

Jack has always spoken highly of his ex, but he doesn't usually talk to her on the phone, at least not when I'm around. He says she's a really smart lady, works for some global logistics company doing stuff that sounds over my simple little writer's head. I know they grew apart in their marriage, and after their daughter was born, she wanted to move to Texas. Jack didn't want to leave his family or job here. So...they split up. But I thought it was amicable. Using Darth Vader's theme for your ex's ringtone doesn't sound that amicable.

Also, why didn't I think of that for *my* ex??? Jeremy could give good ole Darth a run for his money.

"Okay, Anita. Yes. I will be there. Okay, I will... I understand. Fine. Goodbye." He hangs up, and the first thing he does is take a deep breath. I kinda wish I had a cocktail poured and ready to hand him, because he sure looks like he could use one.

"Well?" I lift my gaze to him from the bed, then wave him off, knowing I'm being far too impatient. Patience isn't exactly my strong suit. "When you're fully recovered, I mean."

"She is really..." He stops himself before he says something negative. I can see it on his face. "Demanding," is what he settles on. "But it looks like Mariana is coming. I'm going to Texas to pick her up in two weeks."

"Wow, two weeks," I repeat.

He sits down on the bed and strokes his hand down my blanket-covered thigh. "Are you okay with this?"

"What?!" I scoff. "It doesn't matter if I'm okay with it.

She's your daughter, Jack. I would never get between you and your child."

"I know, but…" His eyes trail across my face like he wants to say something but can't quite spit out the words. "Everything has been going so well…"

I straighten my spine and look at him with a half-smile because it sounds like he shares the exact same concerns I do. And that really relieves me in many ways. I want him to understand my reticence has nothing to do with his daughter. I really adored her when I met her over the summer and then saw her again at Christmas.

I'm more worried about Jack and I still having time together. Or whether we'll grow apart after getting so close.

But this great man has walked into my life, and I've known the entire time that he's a dad. And I'm not going to let that fact interfere—because it's actually a very good thing, him being a father. He's an amazing dad, and a wonderfully caring and compassionate man, which I am sure he owes, in part, to being a dad. So I'm not going to let this change have a negative impact on our relationship.

I grab his hand that is still resting on my thigh and squeeze it in my own. "We are going to make this work, honey. No matter what. Mariana is welcome here, any time, of course. I know we probably won't get as much time together, but every minute we do get will be pure magic as far as I'm concerned."

He leans over to press a kiss against my cheek. "Thank you, Claire. I am really excited about this, and I know we can make it work. You're right, we'll have less time together, but it will just make the time we do have even better."

"Exactly."

There's a tiny voice in the back of my head that wishes he'd spring the moving in or the marriage talk on me—

because then we really *would* be together all the time. We are still maintaining two households even though right now we're together at my house almost all the time. But it's too early for that, and he has enough on his plate without making other Important Decisions.

"Will you come shopping with me?" His eyes light up with excitement as he locks them with mine. "Help me pick out things for her room? I never did much with it since she wasn't here very often, but I want to fix it up for her. Make it special."

"Of course I will! Sounds like fun." I brush a kiss against his lips. "I will help in any way I can."

"ONCE AGAIN FROM THE TOP," I call out from center stage. With my fingers poised on the frets and my other hand ready to strum, I wait for Luke to count us off.

This is our second go at "Runnin' Down a Dream" by Tom Petty. I mean, it's not sounding *horrible*. But I think there's still plenty of room for improvement. I haven't broken out my original song yet because I want us to get a little more comfortable together—among other reasons.

I start to croon the lyrics into the mic, but it sounds like I have an echo.

"Drew, you can't sing!" I shoot him a sharp glare over my shoulder. "I mean, not for the contest. It has to be a solo endeavor—no backup."

His lips stop moving as his fingers continue to work the

bass. "Sorry, man," he apologizes. "I'm just so used to singing."

When we've jammed in the past, I've let him sing lead. I don't mind singing backup, but this is about me...for once.

The door cracks open, and the first thing I see is Claire's auburn hair. She's coming to check us out. She's heard me sing plenty of times, but I still get a little nervous when she's around. I always want to impress her.

She sits down on the dilapidated loveseat by the over-flowing storage shelves, and I catch a glimpse of her toes tapping in time with the beat. That's a good sign. Oh, she's got a little head nod action going on too. I keep singing, giving her my best sultry rock star stare as I start the second verse.

The guitar is ripping; the bass is thumping; the keyboard is giving us a solid foundation, and the drums are keeping us all together. Oh, yeah, this is the high I've been chasing. This is it!

Oh, yeah... I might as well admit it. There's another reason I've been saving the song I wrote for Claire. I wanted to do something super secret and super special with it, but now that Mariana is coming to stay with me, I don't think the timing is right.

I thought about writing a different song—because I think an original tune will impress the contest judges more than a cover. Then I can save Claire's song for its original intended purpose, whenever the timing might be right. But I haven't decided yet.

Writing a song is no easy task. No wonder Claire is dragging her feet at writing a whole book. A song is easy compared to that!

Just looking over at her, her beautiful turquoise eyes filled with love and admiration for me, I know I want to spend the rest of my life making her happy. She is everything I've always wanted but didn't know I deserved, especially after my first marriage turned out to be such a shitshow. And a lot of it was my fault. I married Anita before I really knew her well enough. I didn't know she'd become a controlling pain in the ass, and we had Mariana before we were ready. And I was also stuck doing that awful IT job where I was so miserable.

My life is completely different now than I could ever have imagined back then. Yes, I still have the scars of a failed marriage and losing my dad when I wasn't ready to say goodbye, but now I have a job I love, a daughter I adore, and a girlfriend who is quickly becoming my everything.

I'm a lucky man.

Now if I can just whip this band into shape, I'll have the perfect hobby too.

We finish out the last chorus, and when the sound dies out, Claire leaps off the loveseat, clapping her hands like a madwoman. "Bravo! Bravo! Encore! Encore!"

I love that she's humoring us. I take a deep bow, and as I rise, I flash her my broadest, most appreciative grin.

"So…band name?" Drew reminds me from his spot to my right.

"Oh, yeah. I've been toying with a few ideas." My gaze roves over my bandmates, briefly resting on each one as I prepare to share my thoughts with them.

Drew is a burly guy of German and Irish descent with a head full of curly, sandy-blond hair, and his skin stays tan all year long. Despite being smart and good at lots of things, he's one of those guys who flits from bartender job to bartender job, the classic underachiever. He's wearing a Star Wars shirt that says "I had friends on that Death Star" and features a crying stormtrooper.

Russ is tall and gangly with an unkempt, scraggly brown beard and dreadlocks that hit his shoulders. He's wearing a tank top in the middle of March, and, no, it's not warm here. Sometimes he wears contacts, but today he's got his thick glasses on, which make his eyes look like two pointy black beads on either side of his pale face. He's a sanitation engineer—someone's gotta do it, right?

Luke has a mustache—yes, a mustache, which is perfectly waxed and pointed at the ends at all times. He is of Indian and European descent, and he looks vaguely like Freddie Mercury except for his rapidly receding hairline. You wouldn't know it to look at him, but he's a marine biologist, so that's pretty cool.

Finally, Sam—whom we keep telling is *not* in the band, but he doesn't seem to be listening—is the only one of us who actually looks the part of a rock star. He has shoulder-length black hair and skin the color of bronze, reflecting his Native American heritage. Boasting a solid, athletic frame, he's also in the best shape of all of us due to playing rugby in a local league.

Other than Sam, we're all sort of misfits. I'm this huge, hulking lumberjack of a dude with glasses and a beard. Drew looks like a cross between a surfer and Comic Book Guy from *The Simpsons*. Russ's dreadlocks look like he may have lost his keys in there. And Luke—he looks like he belongs in a different century. Sam doesn't count because, like we've told him, he can't really play an instrument. However, I'm tempted to throw him on stage to serve as eye candy for any judges who happen to like attractive athletic-looking dudes. In Rehoboth Beach, that could be all of them.

"We're all a bunch of misfits," I tell them. "And I mean that as a compliment, by the way. We don't look like your stereotypical rock stars, and I think we can play off that. I was thinking of calling us The Melodious Misfits. What do you think?"

I expect Claire to pipe up immediately—this potential name is one she hasn't been privy to yet, and she always has lots of opinions on everything. But she's uncharacteristically silent. Her expressions usually give her away, but I can't tell her reaction based on her face, either.

Everyone is rolling the idea around in their minds and on their tongues. Each pronouncing it aloud a couple of times as they try it on for size.

"No." Drew shakes his head. "Too many syllables. Too much of a mouthful."

"Mighty Misfits?" Luke suggests, looking from me to Drew for a reaction.

"That's not bad," I agree. "Fewer syllables."

"The alliteration is too cheesy," Drew complains. Who knew the classic underachiever was going to be so difficult when it came to choosing a name?

"The Gallant Misfits," Claire finally says, rising from her loveseat cushion. "Gallant Misfits. It's like a positive and a negative. They balance each other out."

"Gallant?" Russ says. "What do you mean by that?"

"It means brave, chivalrous," Claire explains. "It's a good thing."

"I like it," Drew says, continuously mouthing it but without any power behind his voice.

"Gallant Misfits," Luke repeats.

Then Sam says it too, though I'm not sure we're going to count his vote.

"It's growing on me." I shoot Claire a smile.

She grins back, and I have this feeling she's going to be pouty if we don't go with her suggestion. "Does anyone have any other ideas?" I check, feeling like an auctioneer about to bang the gavel.

"I really like The Gallant Misfits," Drew says, nodding.

"Me too," Luke agrees.

"Me three!" Russ contributes.

"The Gallant Misfits it is!"

Now we need a toast. Claire has already cracked open the old refrigerator out here, which she's stocked with beer. She takes out a six-pack and begins to pass the bottles around. See what I mean about this woman? She's truly extraordinary.

And she just helped name our band.

Claire

5

I was surprised when Jack asked me to fly to Houston with him to pick Mariana up. But then he said his ex wanted to meet me since I'd be spending time with her daughter, and now I'm a nervous wreck. It's silly, too, because what's she going to do, take one look at me and decide I shouldn't be around her daughter? I mean...

Oh, crap, what if she takes one look at me and decides she doesn't want me around her daughter?

I squeeze Jack's hand in the seat next to me, though I'm practically on top of him because we're flying economy—and I'm a fat girl and he's a big guy, and we're all crammed together on an airplane. Yay for togetherness! At least on the way back, we can put Mariana in the middle seat. She's a tiny little thing.

He looks over at me, giving me that gorgeous grin. "Are you nervous?"

"Me?" I scoff. "No, I've got ice in my veins, babe. *Ice, ice, baby.* Cool. Calm. Collected. That's me."

He throws his head back and laughs. "I know you're full of it, but I love you anyway."

"Your ex scares me," I tell him. "I didn't realize until I heard the Darth Vader thing. Now that's all I'm going to be able to hear when she's headed toward me." I do my best rendition of "The Imperial March" using "*dunts.*"

"Sorry I didn't warn you before, but I worried if you knew how my relationship was with my ex, you might not like me as much." He shakes his head. "I know, it sounds silly to me now. It's not my fault she's the female version of Darth Vader."

"Oh, screw that. Have I told you about *my* ex? He's a total asshat."

"But you hardly ever complain about him," Jack points out. "At least around me. Maybe you save your rants about the ex for Jean-Marc?"

I thoughtfully chew on my bottom lip for a moment. "No, I guess I don't complain about Jeremy... I always imagine Elliott can hear everything I say."

The plane touches down with a bump that makes me dangerously close to losing my lunch. Then I realize the other reason I'm so nervous. I don't even know what this Anita character looks like. I'm guessing she doesn't actually *look* like Darth Vader? Probably no long black cape or mask. What if she's Super Gorgeous? How will I handle that? I'm just this plain, chubby middle-aged chick. I can't compete with Super Gorgeous.

Jack loves me, I tell myself as the plane coasts to our gate. I just keep saying it over and over again. Besides, what is it my mother always said (before she fat-shamed me)? *True beauty is on the inside.* Uh huh. Sure, Mom. Tell that to the rest of the beauty- and thin-obsessed world. Oh, and youth-obsessed. Let's not forget our culture's endless fascination with youth.

Jack grabs my hand when it's our turn to deplane, and we head down the aisle, me twisting sideways so my hips don't hit the armrests of the seats. He's carrying a single overnight bag. We're staying one night, then flying back with Mariana in the morning. But first we have to make it through dinner. It seems like a formal interview for the position of stepmother, even though Jack and I haven't committed like that.

We walk the plank, I mean bridge, to the terminal, my heart pounding in my chest. Why am I making such a big deal out of this? It's so silly! It doesn't matter what Anita thinks of me. I'm Jack's new woman. She better just get that through her big black helmet-covered head.

I'm trying to keep up with his long-legged stride, but he's a lot taller than me, and I'm falling behind. "Whoa there, Mr. Reilly. Can a girl go pee before we try to set a land speed record to Ground Transportation?"

"Oh, sorry." He stops and looks at me, nerves painted all over his face. He's nervous too. Normally Mariana's aunt brings her to Delaware and stays for the duration of her visit. This may be the first time Jack has ever cared for his daughter unsupervised—plus maybe he's just as nervous for Anita to meet me as I am to meet her.

I duck into the women's restroom and do my business, taking Deep, Calming Breaths like my body image coach, Mandi Shine, taught me. I've graduated from body image camp now, but Mandi's voice now resides inside my head. And that's a good thing.

As I look in the mirror, I remember the session she told me what she saw when she looked at me: my clear skin; my beautiful, bright eyes; my thick, shiny hair; and my warm, glowing smile. I wink at my reflection, confirming, yep, they're all still there.

I got this.

As soon as I return to Jack's side, he leans down and plants a kiss right on my lips, right in front of the hundreds of people rushing by. "In case I forget to tell you later, you're beautiful, and I'm proud to have you by my side."

My heart melts at his swoon-worthy words. He's like a fantasy man in so many ways. Sometimes I have to pinch myself to remember he's real. I take his hand, and we walk to the escalator, then descend to the lower level where we'll be meeting Mariana and The Ex. Now there's a band name.

I'd asked about taking an Uber to the hotel, then meeting them later at the restaurant for dinner, but Anita insisted on picking us up from the airport. I don't know if it's a control thing, or if she just wanted to save us from having to pay for a ride. Judging by what I know of her, I'd say it's definitely a control thing.

I see a petite woman wearing a business suit standing by one of the concrete pillars outside Door 7. Her phone is pressed to her ear, her back to us. A waterfall of almost jet-black hair cascades nearly to her waist. It swishes slightly as she taps her foot, and I'm mesmerized.

"There she is," Jack says, tilting his head in her direction.

Oh, of course that's her. It has to be some size-zero woman with the most gorgeous hair I've ever seen in my entire life. When she turns to face us, I'm not actually shocked at all because she looks exactly like I imagined. She is absolutely exquisite and doesn't look a day over twenty-nine. Flawless topaz-colored skin, the most gorgeous milk chocolate brown eyes I've ever seen, and lips that any supermodel would covet.

"Anita, this is Claire," Jack introduces us, forcing her to put her phone down. "Claire, this is Anita."

"Hello, Claire!" She grabs my hand in both of hers and shakes them firmly but warmly. "I'm so glad to finally meet you. Mariana is really excited about coming to

Delaware, and all she can talk about is getting to see Miss Claire."

"What? Really?" I glance at Jack and then back to Anita. "Wow, that's…that's really great. She's a special little girl for sure." Did I really make that big of an impression on her?

Jack is smiling, but when he grabs my hand this time, his grip is like a vise. I purse my lips and give him a sideways glance, trying to communicate that he's about to break my fingers. He doesn't look back, but his jaw visibly clenches. I see his beard move.

"Where's my daughter?" he says in a tone that is barely more pleasant than a seethe.

Darth Anita doesn't seem the least bit fazed by Jack's attitude. "She's at home with Camellia, and I figured we'd stop there first so you can help me load up her stuff."

"Stuff?" Jack narrows his eyes at her, stopping on the curb before climbing into the car next to me.

"Yes, *stuff*. She has several bags. You'll either have to ship them to Delaware or pay to check them on your flight back."

"What could she possibly need other than a suitcase, Anita? I can buy her anything else she needs."

"She has an entire bag full of stuffed animals, Jack," she hisses.

Oh, there it is. There's the Darth coming out. *Dunt dunt dunt dunt-dunt-dunt,* I hear "The Imperial March" in my head.

THIS WOMAN IS IMPOSSIBLE! I know we're only going to be in Texas for approximately twelve hours, but I may not survive. Claire is giving me her *calm down, honey, you're starting to scare me* look, and I hate being like this in front of her, but I just want to take my daughter and go. I don't want to lug a crap-load of kid stuff back to Delaware. It's a small state. There's no room for a million stuffed animals and Barbies!

We pull into Anita's driveway, and, of course, she lives in a mansion. She's a single woman, and she has a freaking mansion. I swear she bought this house just to rub it in my face that I never could have given her a place like this when she was a stay-at-home mom during our marriage. Not on an IT guy's salary, and most certainly not on a high school teacher's salary. And here I am paying her child support. *Sigh.*

Her sister Camellia opens the door and gives me a hug, then Claire. She lives with Anita and helps take care of Mariana, and as far as I know, she doesn't have another job. So I have no idea what she's going to do this year while Anita is in London.

"Oh, in case you're wondering, Camellia is coming to London with me!" Anita shares as she enters the room. "She'll help me get settled in."

Of course she will.

I make the necessary introductions, and Claire impresses me by how warm and gracious she is toward my ex-wife. I know in the back of her mind, she's still humming "The Imperial March."

As my ex starts to ramble on about our daughter's schedule, my gaze falls on the wide barrel-ceiling hallway that stretches beyond the foyer area that's open to the second floor above us. There are stacks of suitcases and a massive trunk piled on the marble tiles. I count six bags in total.

Six. Freaking. Bags.

There is no way in hell we are dragging all that on the plane tomorrow. As I'm trying to figure out a diplomatic way to break that news to both my ex and my daughter, I hear footsteps thundering down the polished oak stairs. "Daddy! Daddy!" comes a shrieking voice.

"Hi, baby!" I scoop my precious little girl up into my arms and swing her around while her hands clasp around my neck in a chokehold. She smells like cotton candy and perfection, and I drink it all in, reminding myself that this is what it's all about. This is what I live for, this little princess in my arms.

"Put me down, Daddy!" she squeals, wiggling away from me. And then: "Miss Claire!" She throws herself at Claire so hard, I think she might knock her over.

"Hi, Mariana!" Claire gasps, surprised to have an armful of five-year-old to contend with. "Don't you look pretty in your ball gown!"

"Oh, right," Anita pipes up. "I forgot to tell you. Mariana is going through a princess phase. She wants to wear a gown and a tiara just about wherever she goes."

"Um, you know, she's five. You can decide what she can and can't wear, especially outside the house," I remind her. She won't be playing dress up anywhere but at home, that's for sure.

Anita shoots daggers at me. "Well, we'll see about that." She turns toward her daughter. "Sweetheart, show Daddy your luggage we packed with all your things."

"Look, Daddy!" She prances into the hallway and does a ballerina-esque twirl so the skirt of her gown swirls around her little body. "These are my suitcases. I like the pink one best. Which one do you like?"

I see what they're doing here. Not gonna work.

"Sweetie, this is too much stuff to take on the plane. They don't have room for all this stuff. I'll tell you what, you can bring three bags, okay? Let's prioritize what you need most at Daddy's house, and then we'll buy you anything else you need."

I look over at Claire, hoping she'll back me up, but she has her mouth clamped shut. So I send her an S.O.S. kinda look, and she just ignores me. *Nice.*

"No, I need *all* my things, Daddy," Mariana says, wrinkling up her little nose. Then she puts her hands on her hips. "I don't want new stuff. I want *my* stuff!"

"Oh," Claire says, stepping out from the shadows like she might actually be coming to my rescue. *Maybe. Hopefully.* "If it were me, I'd want all new stuff for sure."

"Why?" My daughter purses her adorable little lips, her hands still firmly fisted on her hips.

"Because you can have Mommy's House Stuff and Daddy's House Stuff," Claire explains. "And that means you can have *twice* as much stuff!"

Mariana looks closely at Claire, intrigued by the concept of double stuff.

She continues, speaking like the world's authority on "double stuff." *This is where she'd insert a funny quip about Oreos...* "Remember Elliott, my son?"

Mariana's hands remain on her hips as she takes in Claire's brilliance. "Yeah?"

"Well, he has Mommy's House Stuff and Daddy's House Stuff—he even has two gaming systems, one at each house!" Claire's eyes grow wide with excitement, and her voice rises in pitch and volume as she really tries to sell it. "He has two bookcases and two beds and two toothbrushes. Double everything!"

I can see the moment it crystallizes on my daughter's face. "Oh…"

"Miss Claire is *really* smart," I interject, flashing my lovely girlfriend a grateful smile. "You should really listen to her. And I know she'd love to take you shopping. Wait until you see how we decorated your room!"

"Does it have princesses?" Mariana asks, rising to her tippy-toes to do another twirl.

"Hmm, does it have princesses, Jack? I can't remember…" Claire answers, shooting me a wink.

Claire gravitated right to the princess stuff in the store. She loved it and pronounced it the very perfect thing. She claimed it's what she would have wanted when she was a little girl. Sounds like she was right on the money.

"It does have princesses!" I confirm, and without any hesitation, Mariana leaps into my arms and squeezes me tightly around the neck again.

"Yay! I can't wait to see it!"

6

I barely heard the pounding on the garage door over the blaring drums and guitar. I'm not sure how I became the band's de facto manager, but here I am. I thought Sam was going to take that role, but so far he just shows up and drinks beer. He's waiting for a good tambourine solo apparently.

It's my neighbor. *Oh joy.* She better not tell me anything about her sex life this time. I steel my resolve and gird my stomach just in case.

"Oh, hi, Mrs. Vandeveer, what can I do for you?" I say in the absolute sweetest voice I can muster.

"Claire," she huffs out. I love that she's on a first-name basis with me, but she has never once invited me to call her Harriett, which I only know is her name because I've gotten her mail in my box before. I guess it's a generational thing. *Okay, Boomer* and all that.

"Yes?'" I step out onto the concrete pad, holding the door open about an inch behind me. It blocks a little bit of the noise, but we're still shouting over it.

"What is that ungodly racket coming from in there?"

She tries to peer past me into the garage, which is dark except for two overhead lights aimed on our makeshift stage to simulate spotlights, and some Christmas lights strung up across the rafters for…ambiance, I guess?

"Oh, Mrs. Vandeveer, that's Jack's band! Did you know Jack is singing in the Rehoboth Beach Support Art Foundation charity contest next month?"

Her thin gray brows furrow as she scans my face. "Is that so? Well, he's a celebrity then! Where's that gonna be at?"

"It'll be at the bandstand by the boardwalk on May eighth." The guys finish up "Ring of Fire" by Johnny Cash, and…now I'm shouting. *Volume modulation, Claire!* I smile as persuasively as possible at her. "You should really come out and support him!"

"Oh, honey, you know I don't leave this house except for Friday night bingo and to go to the market. And even then my daughter Trish has to come and roll my weary old bones out of here." She rubs at her hip to emphasize her statement.

Looking at her, there doesn't seem to be one physical thing wrong with her. She walks just fine without assistance. I think the *weary old bones* thing is only in her head—or perhaps she just milks it for all it's worth. Then again, I shouldn't judge. There could be something I can't physically see.

"Claire?" comes a small voice from behind me, pushing the door open. The guys are now arguing about—I mean, debating—what to sing next.

I turn around to find Mariana standing there in one of her princess dresses, a sparkly tiara perched on her head. "What's wrong, sweetheart?"

She huffs out a breath and gives me a most indignant

look. "Are they almost done practicing? They're giving me a headache."

"And who is this young beauty?" my neighbor asks, her gaze falling on the five-year-old in her fancy dress.

"Mrs. Vandeveer, this is Jack's daughter, Mariana. She was here over the summer; do you remember?"

"Oh, sweetheart, my memory isn't very good these days." She waves me off. "Well, she's a pretty little thing. Where'd she get such tan skin in April?"

"She has good genes," I tell my neighbor before she says something racist or offensive about Mariana's Latin heritage.

Well, now I'm even more curious about Harriett Vandeveer's health issues. Is she actually falling apart or is she just a hypochondriac? She doesn't look much older than sixty-five or seventy. She knew how long it'd been since she's been with a man…so how bad could her memory be?

The band strikes up again with a pulsing beat and a pounding drum.

"When are they going to stop that godforsaken noise?" a deep, raspy voice bellows across my front yard. Red appears out of nowhere, glowering. At least he has a shirt on this time.

"Hello, Red," Mrs. Vandeveer coos from her spot on the concrete pad. She straightens her posture and pushes her gray curls out of her face, suddenly appearing rather vibrant and healthy.

Red strokes his fingers through his white beard. "Harriett," he acknowledges her.

Oh, they know each other! And they're both standing here preening like teenagers. Maybe a love connection between these two isn't so far-fetched after all?

"It's a horrible racket, isn't it?" Mrs. Vandeveer sighs. "I just came over here to complain!"

"Miss Claire, I have the *worstest* headache ever!" Mariana whines and tugs on my shirttail.

"Okay, hun, we'll go inside and get you something to drink in a few minutes, okay?"

"I wanted to take a nap this afternoon." Red folds his arms across his chest. "How am I gonna do that with all this *goddamn* cacophony?"

I gesture toward Jack's daughter as I shoot him a glare. "Uh, little ears are about, so could you please watch your language?!" Then I turn to Mariana. "Run inside, and I'll be right there."

"Can't they find someplace else to practice?" Mrs. Vandeveer crows.

Two minutes ago, she was excited about Jack being a minor local celebrity, and now she's complaining again. Though…if she and Red can unite against a common enemy, it might bring them closer together. I don't mind being that common enemy. It's in the name of love, after all.

"Sorry, guys, but this is the best place for them to practice. Jack's house is in town, and the other bandmates don't have their own houses." I turn to Red to explain, "Jack is performing in the Support Art Foundation contest in a couple weeks. They need to get some solid practice time in if he wants any chance of winning. The winners go on to represent Rehoboth Beach in the Mid-Atlantic regional contest."

"I wonder what the police would say about all this racket?" Red growls, looking from me to Mrs. Vandeveer with furrowed brows.

"There's no noise ordinance out here," I tell him. "So they probably wouldn't say anything at all; they'd just be annoyed at being called out for no reason. Besides, one of Jack's bandmates is best friends with a state trooper."

Red spit on the ground. "Well, I don't like it. This music is horrible."

"That's fine. You don't have to like it. Maybe you can choose a song for them to practice that's more to your liking…or maybe you and Mrs. Vandeveer can commiserate together?"

Mrs. Vandeveer just *tsks tsks* and starts to walk back to her house, mumbling something about how that was "a damn waste of her time."

Red's pitch lowers to a gruff rumble, "This is not the end. Not the end by far."

"Okay, toodle-doo!" I shoo him away with a wave of my hand. I think he means to be scary, but that would be like Santa Claus being scary, well, if Santa Claus had buff arms and abs. Still…not very scary.

Oh, Jack's going to love hearing about this interchange later.

Jack

"SO WHO ARE THESE JUDGES?" Drew looks from me to Luke, Russ and Sam and back again. "And why are they such jerks?"

Jack shrugs. "Sorry, guys. I don't know them personally —but I will call and ask them to reconsider their decision."

"You can't plug our band name at the contest?" Luke throws up his hands. "Then what are we even doing here?

Why even perform with a band if you can't mention our name? What's in it for us?"

"We'll hopefully pick up some local gigs out of this," I explain, trying to sweeten the deal. "This charity contest is supposed to be a solo affair—I told you guys that from the beginning. And it's going to be exposure either way, even if we can't say The Gallant Misfits in the program and from the stage."

"My wife is gonna come with a huge banner that says Jack and The Gallant Misfits," Sam says from his corner near the fridge—i.e. close to the beer.

"One of the judges is the mayor, right?" Drew pipes up from his stool. "My mom's cousin's husband is the mayor's brother. Maybe I can put in a good word for us?"

"Is anyone else even performing with a band?" Russ asks. "I mean, won't people like Jack better anyway just by virtue of us being on stage with him. I mean, we make you look good, Jack."

Can't help my eyeroll on that one, though I'm sure there's a kernel of truth to it. "I'm not sure. I think most of them are just solo artists accompanying themselves on one instrument or with a track."

"How many contestants are there again?" Luke lays his drumsticks on his snare. I think that means we are done practicing for the day.

"Ten," I answer based on what I remember from my phone call with Chuck Peebles, the Rehoboth Beach SAF director. "I thought they were going for twelve, but as it stands, eight different bars in the area hosted the preliminaries in March, and two of them had ties. I think there are six women and four men. And lots of different genres represented: country, pop, folk, rock, gospel, from what I understand."

"How is it judged?" Russ asks.

"There's a panel of five judges, who will all score the performances, and those scores are averaged together. But then there's also the fan voting. That counts for half the final score."

Luke scrunches up his nose. "Wow, half? How do they calculate that?"

"Fans can vote on the charity's website for a buck per vote. So it's a fundraiser for the SAF as well."

"Oh, so we need to do some serious campaigning!" Drew rubs his hands together.

"Will your students vote?" Luke asks me.

"I hope so. A lot of them are coming." My students were so excited when I told them—and it takes a lot to get high school students enthused about something that doesn't involve them directly.

Sam's eyes brighten. "You need to get them on social media and have them get all their friends to vote!"

I shake my head. "Look, I want to win because I'm the best singer and entertainer, not because I have the most connections. I don't want any special treatment."

"Alright," Drew concedes, pursing his lips. "I think that's a mistake, but it's your funeral…"

I'm confident I shouldn't go out of my way to drum up support. This is for charity. And for fun. I decided to participate on a whim, and the best thing that's come out of it so far is that I've gotten a solid band together. Well, semi-solid. Like Jello.

We've practiced five or six times now, like real, productive practices. And, hopefully, if we can get some exposure and start a fan base here in Rehoboth Beach, then we can get some local gigs. That's the ultimate goal.

The biggest concern I have about this contest and the potential band thing is my daughter.

Now that Mariana is here, I won't be able to play every

weekend. Once or twice a month. That's what I'm thinking. But this contest will get us started, get our foot in the door.

I CLIMB into bed next to my love, and she immediately turns over and snuggles into my side. We've had a busy day, and it's the first time we've gotten a chance to talk without little or adolescent ears around.

I let the stress of the day soak into my pillow. The biggest thing on my mind has been my daughter. So much so, I feel like my job and this contest have really taken a back seat. But I really want to know how I'm doing so far, so I suck in a sharp breath and ask, "How do you think Mariana is adjusting?"

"Well…" Claire's voice trails off, and I know right then and there she's trying to figure out how to deliver negative feedback gently.

"Well, what?"

"Well, she's been over here so much, I'm not sure she's really adjusted to living with you at your house yet. She's basically moved into my guest room, you know?" Claire takes my hand into hers and pats it with her other hand. "I'm not complaining, because it means I've gotten to spend a lot of time with you, almost as much time as I did before she came."

I fight off the frown creeping onto my lips. "But?"

"Well, I just worry she's going to tell her mom she's living at my house instead of yours, and Anita's going to flip out. You know, go all Darth on you. Or me."

I scoff, "Are you scared of my ex?"

"Well, not *scared*…not *physically* scared," Claire explains. "I mean I could sit on her, and I'd probably crush her instantly. But I don't want to cause problems between you and her or between her and Mariana."

I'm quiet for a moment, just breathing in and out and soaking up her thoughts. She's right. I know she's right, and I know it's not what Anita had in mind.

Not that she has a problem with Claire—if she did have a problem with her, I'm *sure* she would let me know. Repeatedly. And loudly.

But I decorated this beautiful room for Mariana, and she's hardly slept in her new bed since we returned from Texas. We've spent a lot of time at Claire's. And I have to be honest, it's been nice, with her and Elliott and Mariana and me—it feels like we're a family.

It feels like home.

Her voice softens, "I hope you're not upset, Jack…"

"No, I'm just…" I gulp down more air. "I'm just kind of at a loss on how to entertain her…how to just be with her, day in and day out."

"It's not like you haven't taken care of her before, though."

"No, but Camellia was always with us, and my mother would come down and spend a few days with us." I feel like a total jerk for saying this, but it's the truth. "I'm not used to being alone with her. And it just feels awkward…"

"She's your daughter, Jack." She presses a kiss to my chest and looks up at me with her luminous turquoise eyes.

"I know…" I've told myself a million times that I'm being completely ridiculous. And I'm sure she doesn't feel like it's awkward. I mean, she's five. "I just don't know what to do with her for all those hours we're together. I'm not into princesses, and I can only watch *Frozen* so many times."

"Jack," Claire's voice turns stern, "I have a son. Do you think I've always known what to do with him? Do you think I've always had the same interests as him? When he was five, he was obsessed with trucks and dinosaurs and Legos, none of which are exactly my cup of tea. But you better believe my ass was on the floor building Legos and racing trucks, and I don't know what the hell you do with dinosaurs, but I'm sure I did that too."

"Really? But you get what I'm saying, though?"

"I do, and you're gonna have to get over it. I guarantee you she doesn't think any of it's awkward."

"No, she probably doesn't…" I sigh because I hate that we're having this conversation, that I even feel this way. Especially with how badly I wanted Mariana to come stay with me.

"And I'm not telling you this because I don't want to see you and spend time with you both," she explains. "I just want what's best for you guys. I don't want to stand in the way of your father-daughter bond."

I love this woman. She is so damn selfless.

I wanted to sing the song I wrote for her for the contest. I wanted to tell her I'd love nothing more than to spend the rest of my life with her. But Mariana coming really threw a wrench in things. I can't ask Claire to commit when we're in the middle of this crazy year. At least not until things settle down and seem normal again.

"You're right," I tell her.

"Jack, I know you're an amazing father. You're going to figure this all out. It's only been a couple of weeks now." She buries her face in my chest. "Mariana is a lucky girl to have such a great dad."

"You think so?" I tilt her chin up just enough to brush my lips against hers.

"Trust me, I was a daddy's girl, so I know…" Her voice trails off a little wistfully.

I know she lost her dad a year ago, and it still feels

fresh. I lost mine several years ago now, and it still stings sometimes, sometimes when I least expect it. He was a good dad, but fatherhood was different then. Different than it is now, I think.

I don't know if my dad ever felt an urge to make me proud—I'm guessing he didn't—but I have the strongest urge to make Mariana proud. It's not enough to provide for her or take care of her needs. Or to love her unconditionally. I want her to see me up on that stage next month and think, "Wow, that's my daddy, and he's the best!"

7

It's here. Finally here. The contest.

I'm currently trying to keep from hyperventilating in the bandstand's backstage area. There are a lot of performers, so we are all squeezed together. Luke, Drew, Russ and I are practically on top of each other. But my job as the leader of this motley crew is to be as cool, calm, and collected as humanly possible. With great beard comes great responsibility. I need to be worthy of it.

I'm performing next to last. I guess that's okay, especially considering the recency effect that I vaguely remember studying in college—namely that people tend to remember the first items on a list and the last, due to the primacy and recency effects. Or maybe I'm just mentally scrolling through all the stuff I learned in college so I don't freak out, I don't know.

Claire gave me a kiss and wished me luck, then she, Mariana, Jean-Marc and Thor went to sit in the audience. No matter what happens, she'll be proud of me, but winning this really would be a feather in my cap. And she has no idea which song I'm singing. We moved our practices to Sam's house for the past few weeks. One, he lives closer to me, and two, I really am trying to stay home with Mariana more. Sam's wife loves hanging out with Mariana while we practice, though Sam is afraid she has baby fever now. That's not my problem! *shrugs*

The PA system crackles, and Chuck Peebles' familiar voice carries out across the boardwalk. I know from standing on the beach that there's a point where you can hear the sound from the bandstand perfectly, but if you take a few more steps toward the water, the sound is swallowed up by waves crashing on the shore.

"Good evening, everyone, and welcome to Rehoboth Beach Superstar, a contest to benefit the Support Art Foundation. You're in for a real treat, ladies and gentlemen, because we have a great lineup of local artists here tonight who all secured their spots in the preliminary rounds hosted by local bars and restaurants throughout Rehoboth Beach. How many of you here tonight attended a prelim?"

Chuck pauses while a round of applause and hoots and hollers rise up from the audience. I think I might actually hear Claire and Jean-Marc above the din. I can't wait for her to hear the song I wrote for her. It's not the one I originally planned to do—the romantic ballad. This one is up-tempo and will really get the crowd pumped. At least that's what I hope.

Drew looks over to me. "You ready for this, buddy?"

"I'm as ready as I'm ever gonna be," I tell him. "It's cliché, but it's true, man."

"I hear you," murmurs Luke.

The four of us put our hands together, piling one on top of the other like we're in a team huddle. Sam is in the audience with his wife. "Gallant Misfits on three," I say in a low voice.

"One, two, three…"

"Gallant Misfits!" we all bellow, and the sound echoes out around us, annoying some of the other contestants waiting nearby.

From what I can tell, I'm the only one performing with a band. There's a really diverse group of singers back here, and as I glance around, I try to figure out how I fit in, what bracket I fill.

There's a young girl who doesn't look older than twelve who is with her extremely anxious-looking parents. There's a teen boy with a guitar slung over his shoulder. His jaw is so sharp, it looks like it might cut glass. If there are any teen girls in the audience, they're all definitely going to swoon over him. And there's a brunette woman who's maybe in her late twenties to my right wearing a bohemian dress and carrying a tambourine. *Oh, look, she must have finally found a tambourine song. Sam will be so jealous!*

It's so crowded, my chance to analyze my competition ends with that third contestant, and next thing we know, the stage manager, some short woman named Deb with a surprisingly loud and deep voice, comes down to bark out orders. The first contestant is already waiting in the wings, so she must be telling the second one to get ready. Sure enough, the bohemian brunette makes her way to the stairs, trying to silence the tambourine at her side as she goes.

And now…we wait.

Claire

"WELL, is Jack ready for this or what?" Jean-Marc asks as he scans the stage. He doesn't even wait for me to answer before turning to Thor, "Do you know this Chuck Peebles person? I feel like I know him from somewhere. I think he might be a realtor."

Thor shakes his head. He's a masterpiece to look at, but he doesn't say much. Actually, that might be part of his allure. The strong, silent type. I can definitely see why Jean-Marc is into him.

My best friend's head whips back to me like he's shocked I didn't answer his question, even though he changed the subject a millisecond after asking it. "Well?"

"They moved their practices to Sam's house," I explain. "I think I got fired as the manager."

Jean-Marc's brows knit together. "Huh. Well, that's kind of rude."

I shrug. "My neighbors were complaining anyway."

He nods as Mariana grabs my hand. "Miss Claire, I need to go potty."

"I asked you if you needed to go before we sat down, honey." I try not to show my irritation, but let's face it, hiding my feelings—particularly irritation—has never been my strong suit.

"We'll save your places," Jean-Marc offers.

Oh, by the way, Mariana is decked out in what looks like a mermaid's dress. It has a long, shimmery teal train that swirls around her feet, and the top half is purple satin. She asked me today if she could make her hair the color of mine—presumably to look more like the Little Mermaid. *Sigh.* Remember when Jack said he wasn't going to let her wear costumes outside the house? Oh, yeah, he folded fast on that.

"Can you guys keep an eye out for Elliott and Jes-sie?

They weren't going to sit with us, but they're supposed to stay on the boardwalk."

"Yeah, no problem." Jean-Marc gives me a nod and lifts Thor's arm, making it seem like it weighs a hundred pounds—and it very well may—so he can wrap it around his shoulder. He shoots me a smile. "That's better."

I can only laugh at my crazy best friend as Mariana pulls on my hand to urge me to hurry it up. I'd forgotten how fickle the bladder of a young child is. The first act is taking the stage, and I'm a little annoyed that I'm going to miss it, but what are ya gonna do? Let your boyfriend's kid pee all over herself?

We head over to the little building in front of the band-stand, which is where the ladies' restrooms are. Naturally, there is a line extending out the door and halfway down the boardwalk. Okay, maybe not that far—I'm a *tiny bit* prone to exaggeration. Now I'm recalculating, and I think we'll miss the first two or three acts. Good thing Jack is going next to last.

It's May but still chilly at night, and a cold breeze whips my sundress around my legs, making my freshly shaved skin prickle. *That's the worst feeling!* I notice as Mariana and I grab a place in line that she's bouncing from one foot to the other, and I don't think it's in time to the music—I think the girl legit has to pee. Too bad you can't go to the bathroom in the order of urgency. Then it would be pregnant ladies, then toddlers, followed by women who've had three or more children and have reached a *certain age*.

I bend down so I can speak directly in her ear. "You gonna be able to hold it?" Then I immediately regret asking that because I have absolutely zero plan in place for if she says no.

She bites her lower lip and nods, but I can tell she's got

ants in her pants. At least I hope it's ants and not something stinkier. Actually, ants would kinda be *no bueno* as well.

"You gotta go number one?" I ask.

"Number one?" Her beautiful dark eyes flash up at me.

"Oh, your mom didn't teach you about number one and number two?"

She shakes her head.

Well, leave it to me to corrupt the poor girl with potty talk. "Number one is if you gotta pee," I enlighten her. "Number two is if you gotta poo." She giggles as soon as I say the "p word." "It rhymes, so you can remember it easily."

"Number one," she tells me with confidence. Then her lips purse. "I think."

Well, I don't like the sound of that, but what can I do now?

Speaking of not liking the sound...

The first act on stage is country. Anyone who knows me knows I despise country music with the fiery passion of a thousand suns. I don't even know why! I just hate it. Is it the twang; the steel guitar; the preponderance of guns, trucks, and beer (I don't like beer either)? I can't rightly say. I hope you won't stop reading if you like country, though. 'Cause you're gonna miss a good story if you do. Though I doubt there will be much in the way of guns, trucks, or beer, if that's what you're into.

I grit my teeth and try to imagine better, happier sounds. Like really anything would be better than this, because, not only is it country, but she's really pitchy too. If I were Simon Cowell back in the *American Idol* glory days, I'd say, "It's a no from me."

We have moved approximately four feet by the time the horrible song is over. Chuck Peebles comes back on stage to remind everyone how to vote, and then he introduces the next act, which is a gospel singer. She takes the stage, and the recorded track starts up. The song is very slow and dramatic at first, and I have to say, her voice is pretty amazing.

We move another few feet, almost to the doors of the restroom now. I just know it's going to be gross in there, and I'm bracing myself. It's Saturday night; there are a ton of people down here, and it's going to be nasty. *Ugh.*

"You ready?" I ask Mariana. I see she's making faces at some little boy who is standing further down the line with his mother.

"Why is he in here?" she spits with her little hands on her hips.

"Well, if his mommy is the only one with him tonight, then *someone* has to take him to the bathroom, and the mommy can't go into the men's room," I explain.

Then I realize that if I wasn't here, Jack would have to either take her into the men's room or try to get some strange woman to keep an eye on her. I wouldn't really feel comfortable with him doing either one of those things. I never felt weird about taking Elliott into the ladies' restroom. Jeremy was never with us, so I had to do it all the time.

Our whole society is set up to handle moms and their young sons, but it is not set up for dads and their young daughters at all. You know what? That sucks.

"We're next!" she cheers, jumping up and down, and I'm standing behind her praying the impact of her little feet on the floor doesn't make her lose control of her bladder.

It just so happens the big stall at the end opens up next. It's like a miracle when that happens, especially if you're a big girl like myself and need to put another human in there with you. There's not much room for standing outside the door either, not without taking up the whole aisle.

Okay, so restrooms aren't designed for men with young daughters *or* for fat girls. I need to talk about that in my book. Which I need to write, by the way. I'm on like chapter three or something.

I slip inside and lock the door, then manage to get one of the covers on the toilet while also holding my nose. I hope she's fast because I might just run out of oxygen before she finishes.

She looks up at me. "You're not gonna watch me, right?"

"No, but do you need any help with your clothes?"

She glances down. She's wearing this damn mermaid dress. There's way too much material, and I have a horrible premonition about it falling into the toilet.

"Let me hold your dress up while you go, okay? I don't want it to get wet."

"Fine, but don't look at me!" she protests. "I mean it! Close your eyes!"

"Well, I need to help you up here and gather up your skirt first!"

"Miss Claire, you promised!" she whines.

I do my best to convince her I have my eyes closed while I position her on the toilet and hold her dress up behind her, trying so very hard not to touch anything but the dress. That means I'm leaning forward in this awkward position that probably has some sort of yoga name, and every muscle in my body begins to scream at me, reminding me how out of shape I've let myself get since Jack came into my life—oh, and since I began writing this blasted book. You gotta sit to write. *Them's the facts.*

My ears are poised to hear the tinkle of urine hitting the water.

And I wait.

And wait.

"I don't know if I have to go," Mariana's little voice squeaks into the small, tiled space.

I huff out a breath, trying to keep my jaw from clenching up, but it's a failed attempt. "Try harder, okay? We waited in line a long time."

She grunts and strains like she might be trying to pass a bowel movement, and I cringe at the thought of helping her clean up and avoid getting anything on her dress. Meanwhile, I can tell the music has stopped out on stage, which means the third act is over, and the fourth is about to begin. Jean-Marc probably thinks we both fell in at this point.

"I'm trying!" she insists and starts to put her hands on the toilet seat.

"Nooo!!! Don't touch anything!"

"You told me to go potty!"

"I want you to potty, but I want you to do it without touching anything," I explain.

"Are your eyes closed?"

"Yes. Yes they are," I lie from my weird yoga perch behind her.

"How did you know I was gonna touch something?"

Damn it, this kid is too smart for her own good.

And then...

Then I hear it. Not the next act starting, though that's happening too. No, I hear the glorious sound of pee hitting the water. The beautiful tinkling sound I've been longing to hear.

"All done!" She launches herself off the toilet so fast, I nearly *do* fall in. Fortunately, I let go of her dress just in time to avoid making her snap back into me.

"Whew! Come on, let's get our hands washed!" I flush the toilet and usher her out of the stall.

The bathroom is so vile, I feel like we need showers instead of a simple hand-washing, but we'll have to make do. We finally get back to our seats. It's growing dark now; that's how long we were gone. The act on stage is a rapper of some sort, and he's dancing and hopping around the stage more than he's actually rapping. *Okay, then.*

"Well?" I take my seat next to Jean-Marc.

"Oh, he's a shoo-in at this point. Gospel lady was pretty good though." He turns to Thor. "Didn't you think so?"

"I'd vote for Jack," Thor assures me in his soft-spoken way.

Mariana is relatively quiet during the next few performances. There's one teenage boy with a guitar who was pretty nervous to perform, but I could see some of the girls in the audience really liking him. And if an army of teen girls voted, then he could probably win.

The closer I get to Jack's performance, the faster my heart beats. I think I'm more nervous for him than is healthy. I just want him to be proud of all his hard work and have fun out there—so there's not really any reason for me to feel like a thousand butterflies just took flight simultaneously in my stomach.

Finally, Chuck Peebles comes out on stage. "For our ninth and next to final act, we have Jack Reilly and his band. Jack is a music and band teacher at the Delmarva Academy. He'll be singing an original song he wrote called 'Firecracker.' Let's welcome Jack Reilly to the Rehoboth Beach bandstand stage!"

My heart is pounding so hard, I hear it in my ears over Luke clicking off the drumbeat. Jack wouldn't tell me what he'd chosen to sing, and trust me, I tried every trick in the book to get him to spill it.

The guitar, bass and keyboard kick in with a driving rhythm as Jack steps up to the mic. Halfway through the intro, I realize I haven't heard this song before. Then he sings,

When we first met
there were definitely sparks
Some of them shot
outta your mouth
There was a real danger
I'd go up in flames
If things started to go south

I just didn't realize at the time
How red-hot your candle burned
But when we kissed for the first time
That's when I finally learned

You're my firecracker
Setting my world ablaze
Making my mind a haze
You're my firecracker
You keep me burnin' for days
In a million different ways
You're my firecracker
You're always sparkling; you're always bold
You're my firecracker with a heart of gold

My heart and body
explode for you
As soon as you detonate
You're a stick of dynamite

with a short fuse
Shoulda known you'd be my fate

You're my firecracker
Setting my world ablaze
Making my mind a haze
You're my firecracker
You keep me burnin' for days
In a million different ways
You're my firecracker
You're always sparkling;
you're always bold
You're my firecracker
with a heart of gold

I don't realize until the second verse that he's singing about me! Even though he's looking right at me as he belts out every word.

Holy cow! This man wrote a song for me, and I think I'm going to swoon right off this wooden bench. At the key change when the chorus repeats, I leap to my feet along with everyone around me. The crowd is loving it!

A woman behind me shouts, "Oh my gosh, that guy is hot!"

I want to turn around and scream, "He sure is, and he's ALL MINE!" but I don't want to miss any of the song. Jack's getting into it, swaying his hips and tapping his foot in time with the music as he goes into another guitar solo after the bridge, followed by the chorus one more time. Everyone in this place is rocking, clapping their hands with the beat. I can't believe how amazing it feels to be a part of this!

And just like that, the song is over. I'm beaming, tears stinging at my eyes as I lift Mariana up over the crowd to see the stage. She's yelling and cheering so loud (right into my ear, of course), letting everyone around us know that man up there who just brought down the house is her daddy.

I don't know how either of us could be prouder of him than we are right now.

Jack

BY THE TIME we get to the bridge, I'm owning it. I'm finally in my element; my vocal cords have relaxed, stretching into the pitch instead of tightening around it. My fingers light up the guitar, and the solo after the bridge is a thing of beauty. The best part is I look out into the crowd as the third chorus starts up, and Claire is holding Mariana up to see. She is clapping her little hands and screaming her head off, "Daddy! Daddy!" I can tell by the way her mouth is moving.

Claire looks like she's about to fall over with a mixture of pride and surprise. I made the right choice in not telling her about the song.

We finish the last chorus to a thundering round of applause, punctuated by screams and shouts. I can hardly believe it! It sounds louder than after the other performances, but I was in the dressing room for those, so I may not be able to accurately gauge it. But one way or another, I'm stoked.

Chuck comes out to usher us off and introduce the last act. Once we get our bodies and guitars off the stage, I realize my legs feel like jelly. I think all the blood in my body has pooled in my throat and fingers so I could give my all to that performance.

Now to wait for the judging…

After the last act finishes, there's a mass exodus with people tripping over each other to get back on the board-walk. The tall streetlamps illuminate the area around the bandstand, and it's so bright where I'm standing, I can't see a damn thing. It is the longest fifteen minutes of my life, waiting to find Claire and my daughter. Okay, maybe not the longest—that was probably when Anita was in labor with Mariana, and I thought I might lose my fingers due to her squeezing my hands so tight.

Finally, little arms wrap around my legs, and I bend down to scoop the petite mermaid-costumed creature up. Then I do a quick check to make sure this little creature is, in fact, mine. It would be mighty embarrassing to find out she was someone else's kid! And there's my Claire, beaming from ear to ear.

"Was that song about *moi*?!" She gestures to her chest and gives me a wide-eyed innocent look. She looks closer to twenty than forty the way she's batting her eyelashes at me.

"What makes you think that?" I fire back, deciding to tease her.

She scoffs at me, but before she gets a chance to fire off a witty retort—which I know is on the tip of her tongue—Jean-Marc throws his arm over my shoulder and squeezes my trapezius muscle hard. "Nice work, man! Really great song!"

Thor is standing there looking rather tall and Viking-like. "I liked it," he says in his normal stoic manner.

"Well, now we wait!" I look over my shoulder, and my

bandmates have packed away their equipment and are about to head our way to join our little gathering.

"So how will you know? Will they announce it?" Jean-Marc sweeps his gaze around the pandemonium of exiting fans. Some of them are still punching stuff in on their phones, presumably voting for the last contestant, though it's possible my voting window is still open. I've completely lost track of time at this point. That's how crazy and surreal this moment is.

I shrug. "I think everyone's waiting around to see." I tilt my head toward the stage where some of the singers are starting to gather in front of the scoring table. The five judges all have their heads bowed over clipboards, and I know they're deciding our fate. It's only slightly nerve-racking!

"So I guess we'll go wait over by the stage now that the crowd has thinned out?" Drew suggests and begins to lead my entourage in that direction.

I feel a little sick to my stomach as we wait for the results, but I keep repeating over and over again how this was just for fun—and for a good cause. And the outcome doesn't matter at all. I'm holding Claire's hand and probably squeezing it much too hard when Chuck Peebles makes his way to the microphone. Most of the crowd has dispersed, but there are still a few people on the white benches in front of the stage. And, of course, all the artists gathered around anxiously awaiting the results.

"Thanks for your patience, everyone!" his voice booms over the PA. It sounds way louder now that there aren't a thousand people absorbing the noise. He unfolds a slip of paper in his hands. "I have the results right here. Now remember, only the top act is moving on to the Mid-Atlantic Superstar round, which will happen in Philadelphia next month."

"Hurry up already!" Claire grits out between clenched teeth. I think she's at least as anxious as I am, maybe even more so. She turns to me, "That song was about me, right?"

I laugh at her persistence, then lean down to whisper in her ear, "Of course it was, baby."

"Third runner-up in our contest, with an average score of 8.5 from our judges and 315 votes from our audience, is Madison Glenn!" he announces, and the young woman in the bohemian dress with the tambourine rushes up to the stage to claim a small trophy. Everyone claps and cheers.

"Second runner-up, with an average score of 8.8 from our judges and 378 votes from our audience, is Peter Newton! Congratulations, Pete!" He looks around, but Peter, the young man who rapped, doesn't seem to be in attendance.

"He already left!" someone yells from the crowd.

"Alright, then, let's announce our first runner-up, with an average score of 9.2 from our judges and 433 votes from our audience, Jacklyn Durham!"

My heart about leapt out of my chest when I heard "Jack." The lovely gospel singer who performed early in the night makes her way onto the stage to claim her trophy. I'd forgotten her name was Jacklyn.

"And now, the moment we've all been waiting for!" Chuck begins, though the pounding of my pulse in my eardrums might drown out his words. I hope I can actually hear if he calls my name. "With an astounding average score of 9.6 from our judges and a whopping 547 votes from our audience, our winner, our Rehoboth Superstar is none other than Jack Reilly!"

I'm so stunned when I hear my name, I'm frozen in place for a moment until the slaps on the back and hugs around my neck snap me back to reality.

"Go on, Jack!" Claire yells. "Go claim your prize!"

I rush toward the stage, my knees feeling like jelly, completely bowled over that I actually won. I wonder what my father would say if he were alive to see this. If he'd be proud, or if he'd just shrug and seem indifferent, like he did about so many of my accomplishments.

As I clutch the shining gold trophy in my hand and gaze out from the stage into the loving eyes of my girl-friend and daughter, I realize it doesn't matter what my dad would have said or thought. All that matters is that the two most important ladies in my life are clapping so hard and shouting so loudly, showing they couldn't possibly be prouder of me in this moment.

Claire

8

My half-sister Nora and her family are on their way down here from Pennsylvania, and Jack's mom is coming as well. We're having a little party to celebrate Jack's win last weekend in the Support Art Foundation's contest. I've also invited my mom and my other sister, Eliza, but I think Eliza had something with her kids or her in-laws this weekend, so she's not coming. It's pretty obvious she doesn't approve of Jack, but screw her, not everyone can get swept off their feet by a doctor like she did.

And that's just our immediate families. The band is coming, of course, with plus-ones, if they have them. It goes without saying that Jean-Marc and Thor will be here. Jean-Marc is more of a family member to me than a friend, anyway.

So I had an interesting conversation with Drew after the contest. We all went to grab pizza afterwards at Nicola's, and Jack took Mariana to the restroom. Yay, I didn't have to do that again! But I haven't been able to get what Drew said out of my mind ever since.

"Jack was going to sing a different song he wrote for

you," he told me, "but he said the timing wasn't right." He'd shrugged. "'Firecracker' was better anyhow, at least for this venue."

"Another song?" My eyebrows had probably flown up my face because I was rather intrigued at this revelation. "What kind of song?"

Drew rolled his eyes. "He wouldn't even let us rehearse it. He said he was saving it for a very special occasion."

Well, if *you* heard that, and *you'd* been dating someone for a year, what would *you* think? It sounds like a proposal is about to go down, does it not? So, I did what any self-respecting control freak would do and got a manicure today because, well, heaven forbid some sexy bearded rock star puts a rock on my finger and my nails look like crap. We couldn't have that, now could we?

It was his idea to invite everyone over to celebrate, so what if…what if tonight's the night?

I think I may have to keep up this manicure thing until he pops the question. I don't want to be unprepared. Everyone who knows me knows I hate surprises, but this might be one surprise I'd be willing to make an exception for.

As soon as Jean-Marc arrives, I pull him into the kitchen with me, where I'm hastily scooping watermelon balls into a hollowed-out watermelon containing clumps of various other fruits. Just call me Martha Stewart. I hold up my fingers, waving them in front of his face. "Notice anything different?"

"Your fingers are stained?" He glances down at them and then back up at me.

"What?!" I shriek as my eyes dart down to my fingertips. They are tinted purple on the ends. "Oh no! The blueberries!"

"Your nails look nice, though," he tells me with a shrug.

"Oh no, how could this happen?" I rush over to the sink and plunge my hands under the cold tap water, willing it to wash the purple away.

Jean-Marc furrows his brows. "What's the problem? It's just a little blueberry stain!"

My sister Nora walks in while I'm standing there with the cold water running over me. "You okay? Your face is all red."

My fingers are blue; my face is red. Now I just need my hair to turn green or something, and I'd be a real prize. Why does this stuff only happen to me?

"Did you cut yourself?" she continues to guess when I don't answer.

"Her fingertips are stained from blueberries," Jean-Marc explains.

"Oh! Use some lemon juice." Nora walks over to the refrigerator, grabs the bottle from one of the shelves on the door and hands it to me.

"Will this work?"

"If not, at least your hands will smell all nice and lemony!" she assures me.

"Oh, wait…" Jean-Marc glances back down at my hands, then up to my face, which I'm sure is reflecting my abject horror. "I know why you're freaking out about your fingers and nails!"

He looks at Nora before both pairs of their eyes rocket to mine. "You think Jack is gonna propose?" Nora gasps.

Well, I didn't really mean for anyone else to know what I've been ruminating about for roughly a week now, ever since my conversation with Drew. But I guess the cat is out of the bag. And I mean that literally, because Figaro just climbed out of a grocery bag I accidentally dropped on the floor. He turns to look at us in his usual unimpressed manner, then pivots, flipping his tail up in the classic "talk to the butt" maneuver that all cats do.

"Claire?" Jack's voice reaches the kitchen before his body does. "Do you need any help with anything?" He takes one look at the three of us and laughs. "You guys look like you're having a super-secret meeting or something."

Nora chuckles. "No, we're just trying to help Claire get the blueberry stains off her fingers," she flashes me a wink, "you know, in case anyone wants to look at her fingers later."

I clench my jaw and shoot daggers at her. *Why would she say that?!*

"Why would anyone want to look at her fingers?" Jack asks, his eyes circling the room and landing on each of us in succession.

Jean-Marc huffs out a laugh and puts his hand on my shoulder. "Good luck, Claire." He then sashays out of the kitchen to find Thor. I mean Tony. *His real name is Tony, right?*

I dry my hands on a kitchen towel and hand my water-melon boat masterpiece to Jack. "Here, you can take this out to the deck with the other snacks."

"You sure you're okay? Did you cut yourself or some-thing?" He squints at me, trying to read my expression.

"I'm fine, honey. Just pretend you're Baby from *Dirty Dancing* and carry that watermelon, alright?"

He gives me a smirk and a headshake, and then he's on his merry way. I hear him shout, "I carried a watermelon?" as he opens the door to the deck.

Well, at least he gets my jokes. So there's always that.

"What made you think he was going to propose?" Nora asks.

I think I'm probably jinxing myself big time, but I decide to tell her what Drew said about the other song Jack wrote for me but didn't think it was the right time to perform it.

"So you think he wrote a proposal song?" she verifies.

I nod and bite my lower lip. "Is that stupid?"

Her eyes grow wide as a smile enraptures her face that looks so very much like mine. "I did see the band setting up in the garage."

"You did?"

"Uh huh." She squeals and grabs my hand. "I hope this is it for you!"

"I know, me too! I didn't think I was ready after Jeremy, but—well, I've grown and changed a lot in the past year."

"I think we both have," she says, squeezing my hand. "And I better be your maid of honor, or you're never gonna hear the end of it!"

I throw my arms around her. Between her, Eliza, and Jean-Marc, there'd be an epic battle for the maid of honor spot. But that's a problem I'm willing to tackle if it means walking down the aisle and saying "I Do" to the man of my dreams.

MY GIRLFRIEND sure knows how to throw a party. I've barely talked to her in the past few hours, but I keep seeing her flit about, bringing out more food and conversing with everyone in attendance. I want to grab her and tell her she's the hostess with the oistest, but she's pretty caught up telling Nora and her mom what it was like to see me on stage singing a song I'd written for her. Naturally I'm across the room basking in the glory while Drew and Luke are making fun of me for the way I braided Mariana's hair today.

"Hey, I don't think I did half-bad for having zero experience in hair braiding!" I protest. They didn't think I was paying attention, but *surprise!* I was.

"It looks like a kindergartener did it," Sam's wife, Kayla, says. "Look, if you need some help, I can show you a few different braids: French, Dutch, fishtail…"

"What? There are different kinds?" Sam pipes up. He turns to me. "I think she's making that up."

I throw my hands up defensively. "I know I'm relatively clueless about this fatherhood thing, so I'll take all the advice I can get!"

"Well, bring Mariana over sometime, maybe next time you guys get together to practice, and I'll show you how!" She smiles warmly at me, and it might be patronizing, but I've had a couple beers now, so I'm not entirely sure.

Just then, Mariana runs over to me and throws herself into my lap. "I made a new friend, Daddy!"

I turn toward the hall, and Claire's sister Nora's daughter, Emily, is heading toward us with a huge grin on her face. She's a few years older than Mariana, and I'm thrilled she's not annoyed by having a little kid tagging along.

"Are you having fun?" I kiss the top of her head. Yeah, those braids are pretty crappy. They're falling out.

"Yes!" She smiles so wide, I can see all of her teeth, which are stained reddish-purple from juice.

"Good!"

"Hey, Jack?" Claire walks into the room empty-handed for the first time tonight.

"Yeah?"

She's wearing a really excited look on her face, so she must be having a good time too. "I thought you and the band might want to perform your winning song for everyone? Nora said you guys set up in the garage?"

"Oh, yeah, sure. Just give us a few." I turn to the guys, who are within shouting distance. "Let's go warm up."

When we get out to the garage, I find the door open, and Claire's neighbor Red is nosing around her workbench. "Uh, hello? May I help you?"

"I'm looking for my pliers," he says, his voice deep and gruff.

Claire is the least mechanically inclined person I know. I love her to pieces, but I doubt she even knows what pliers are, let alone how to use them. Thankfully I'm pretty handy and have been able to do a few things around the house for her. Hey, it usually leads to a thank you of the sexual variety so I'm A-OK with it.

"I don't think you'll find them in here." I try to keep my voice at a friendly level, but he's literally rifling through her things now. "Hey, do you mind? This isn't your house."

"I need my pliers!" he insists.

"Maybe you lent them to another neighbor?" Drew suggests, looking on with growing concern.

"Nah. I don't like anyone else on this block. I wouldn't let a soul on this whole street touch my tools with a ten-foot pole."

Well, there are only five houses on this gravel lane. It's not even a street, but okay.

"Mr. Red, I don't know what to tell you, but I am positive your tool isn't in Claire's garage. Now, we're setting up to do a song or two. You're welcome to stay if you want. There's even food and drink out on the deck." *Oh yeah, I'm diplomat of the year. *fistpumps**

Claire comes around the corner from the front of the house. "Oh, hi, Red! Coming to join the party?"

He grumbles something about his pliers and beer (I think, but I'm not quite sure.)

"There's beer on the deck in the blue cooler," she tells him. "Hey, do you want me to invite *Harriett* over?"

Red's lips purse. "That crazy old bat? No thanks." He folds his arms over his chest. "I will take a beer though."

I know exactly what Claire is doing with her two neighbors, trying to hook them up, but I don't think it will ever happen. It's funny and sweet that she's trying, though.

We all take our places on our makeshift stage as the crowd gathers around. Luke counts off the beat, and we break into "Firecracker." If we ever cut an album, this is going to be the first track, I can just feel it.

"Wow, that was very…energetic!" Claire's mom, Nancy, praises us once we finish. That *was* a praise, right? With her, you just never know.

"He wrote that song for me, Mom!" Claire beams with pride, just like she did the night of the contest. "Is there anything else you want to play, Jack?" She looks at me pointedly.

I glance around at the guys. "Do you want to do that Sheryl Crow cover we've been working on?"

There are some murmurs of agreement and nods, and I look back at Claire, whose face is now crestfallen. "We're gonna do our rendition of 'A Change Would Do You Good.'"

"Okay." She doesn't say another word, just leans against the workbench wearing a look of disappointment.

It's almost midnight by the time we get everyone out of the house and things picked up enough to go to bed. I'm beat. Mariana passed out on the sofa around ten, and I had to pick her up and put her in Claire's guest room. This is the first night we've stayed over for a while, and I have to admit that, despite my sheer exhaustion, I'm hoping to get a second wind so I can show Claire how much I appreciate her throwing this party for me.

She comes to bed shortly after me. "I finally remembered to feed Figaro. I think he was about to starve judging by the way he was crying and rubbing against me."

I stroke my fingers down her shoulder and back as she settles into the bed. "I promise not to cry, but I would like to rub against you if I may."

She purses her lips before she reaches behind her to turn off the lamp on her side of the bed. But she doesn't say anything, and now it's dark, so I can't see her expression.

"Everything okay?"

"I'm just tired," she says on a combination of a sigh and a yawn. "Long day."

"Tell me about it." I pull her body closer to mine, but I feel her stiffen as soon as she's pressed against me. "Are you sure everything's okay?"

"Yeah," she insists. "I'm just tired. I'm gonna turn over. Night." She plants a chaste kiss on my cheek and then turns over, taking most of the blankets with her.

I have no idea what I did to deserve the cold shoulder, but at the moment I'm hoping a) she feels better in the morning and b) Mariana sleeps in.

Claire

9

We arrived in Philadelphia last night for the Mid-Atlantic Superstar contest. It's convenient that my sister Nora lives so close because we were able to drop Mariana off with her last night. They'll be here at the performance today, but Jack and I stayed in the city last night—alone. It was one of our first nights with no kids in ages. I had forgotten what it's like to parent young children and then get a much-needed reprieve.

Elliott is so independent now, and he's typically sucking face with Jes-sie, so he really doesn't demand much from me at all except for food and the occasional twenty. Though soon I guess he will also be asking for the car keys with some regularity. *God help me. And God help all the other drivers.*

I did have a talk with him before we left. I mean, not the Basic Birds and the Bees Talk because he got that at like age ten or something. It was more like the Advanced Birds and the Bees Talk. I think he was properly horrified when I gave him a package of condoms and stressed how angry I will be if he makes me a grandma before I'm fifty.

I got over the disappointment of not getting a proposal at the victory party I held for Jack last month after he won the Rehoboth Beach contest. I really thought it was coming. He'd even been acting a little strange in the few days leading up to the party. I figure he'll ask me when he's good and ready, though I would be lying if I denied leaving a few hints here and there. I may have point-blank told him I wear a size seven ring, but whatevs. I'm not exactly known for my subtlety, folks. (See above reference to the Advanced Birds and the Bees Talk.)

"You ready for this?" I ask Jack as we walk into the venue. There are rows and rows of black seats, the theatre type that fold down, and from where we're standing at the back, the stage looks a mile away. I happen to know it only seats 2500 people—but that's a lot more than the Rehoboth Beach bandstand.

Jack murmurs something that I can't quite understand and continues to press forward down the aisle, his guitar strapped over his back. His focus is pinned on the spotlights and red velvet curtains hiding the backstage from view. Finally, he turns to me. "I can't believe I'm here. That this is happening."

"When are the guys going to be here?" I'm looking around too, taking in the classical architecture, the plaster embellishments around the proscenium, and the brass fixtures with frosted glass globes set to emit a dim glow along the walls. It's a classy joint.

"Any minute, I think. Hope they can find a place to park."

Parking in Philly, like any big city, is pretty dicey. Hopefully they can find a spot in the back to unload their equipment. "How many acts are there?"

"Twelve," he answers. "It's an all-night show. Everyone

gets two songs, and there's an intermission between the first six and last six contestants."

"Okay. Wow, this is really cool." I shoot him a smile. "No matter what happens tonight, I'm glad we're here. That I talked you into performing at that first contest all those months ago."

He returns my smile, his dark eyes twinkling in the house lights. "I thought you were nuts, but I'm glad you did." He shakes his head as if he still can't believe we're here. "The Gallant Misfits are already getting calls about performing in Rehoboth Beach. If that's the only thing that comes out of all this—"

"Then you already won, right, baby?" I take his hand, and he pulls me into his strong chest, where I breathe in the scent of his sandalwood cologne as my heart swells with pride.

He kisses the top of my head. "I've already won. No question about it."

We make it to the front of the auditorium, where several other contestants are milling about or waiting in the audience for further instruction. There are two men and a woman on stage; the latter is clutching a clipboard and seems to be the one in charge.

He waits for my eyes to land on his again after sizing up the competition. "Shall we sit?"

"Yep." I rub my hands together. I think I'm more nervous than he is.

He takes my clammy hands into his and squeezes them. "Even if nothing comes of tonight's performance, and I don't go any further, I just want you to know that I love you so much, Claire, and I never could have done this without your support."

"Well, you were a pretty good sport when I dared you

to enter the contest that night we were supposed to be drinking and having fun?" I joke.

"I'm glad you pushed me a little out of my comfort zone. I always wanted to perform—I've wanted to my whole life, but I never thought I was good enough, or that anyone would want to listen to me. Between you and the reaction we got at the bandstand, I finally have some confidence."

"You're a really talented guy, Jack." I lean over to rest my head on his shoulder. "*My* really talented guy," I correct. "And you are more than deserving of all of this." I gesture around the space.

Before I can fawn over him any further, the white woman with short, spiky black hair wearing denim overalls and a bright neon-yellow t-shirt and clutching the clipboard to her chest makes her way to the front of the stage. She's also wearing a body mic—*fancy*—and it's loud! So loud that everyone stops chattering as soon as her mouth opens and her first two words fly out, "Welcome, everyone!"

She has enough enthusiasm for about ten people. *This is gonna be a long night.*

"We're gonna kick off the contest in T minus two hours!" Her hands fly up in front of her face as she speaks, almost like she's performing spoken word poetry and mime at the same time. She actually kicked her foot out when she said the word "kick." It's the weirdest thing I've ever seen, and I've seen some pretty weird stuff in my forty years on the planet.

"Who's getting pumped up?!!" She makes a motion like she's pressing down on an air pump when she asks for the crowd's pumped-up status. *Just wow.*

Just when I think I've recovered from her gratuitous enthusiasm, again her voice screeches from all the speakers. "We're gonna have a rockin' good time tonight, boys and girls!"

Jack is taking it all in with a smirk on his face, which you can barely see due to his beard. *Gosh, he's so gorgeous.* I need to calm myself down. I think I'm having a hot flash.

"We've got an incredible lineup tonight, and, by the end of the evening, we're going to crown our Mid-Atlantic Superstar!" She runs to the edge of the stage on the left. "Will it be you?" She points to a young man with long dreads in the front row, who kind of shrugs and smiles. Then she leaps across the stage to the other side and points to a middle-aged woman. "Or will it be you?"

The middle-aged woman clutches her neck, shaking her head. Oops, I think that's a contestant's mom, maybe.

The extremely hyper lady calls over one of the men who is still standing with her on stage and hands him the clipboard. Then she does a drumroll impersonation, drumming on the clipboard and making a trilling sound with her lips. "This is our assistant, Eric! He'll be coming around to pass out the schedule for the night." She does another drumroll as she points to the other guy, who is large and balding. "If you have any questions, please direct them to Steve, our stage manager."

"Oh!" she squeals. "I almost forgot! I'm Reee-neeeeet-aaaaa Whiiiii-stlerrrrrr!" She sounds like a pro wrestling announcer or something. She does a twirl and jump in the air, landing solidly on two feet in the center of the stage. This lady needs a chill pill stat!

"We invite you to come wait backstage now. There are four main areas down there, and we have twelve acts tonight, so there are three acts in each room." She actually managed to get through that without jumping around. Maybe because it involved math and therefore sucked up some of her energy.

She is finally quiet as she scans the crowd, possibly looking to see if there are any questions. No one says anything, so she claps her hands so loud, it sounds like she just cracked her own bones. "Alright then! Head on back, and Steve will be by later to give you a target time."

She makes some more hand gestures—no idea what those are supposed to mean. "This contest *will* be televised on a local channel, so we must stick to the schedule. You have two and a half minutes for each of your songs. Five minutes total on stage with five minutes between acts. Don't make us come out there and yank you off the stage!"

She wags her finger so hard, I think it might fly off into the audience and smack someone in the face. "Don't make us! I swear we will! And—there will be a fifteen-minute intermission between acts six and seven. You keep your behinds backstage during that. No ifs, ands, or buts! Got it?"

She laughs so loud into her mic that it pierces my skull, then she turns toward the backstage area. I think she's heading out, but, much to my dismay, she whips around, her voice shattering the Guinness Book of World Records for loudest, most obnoxious human: "And most importantly, HAVE FUN!!!"

Everyone in the first two rows of the audience cheers before forming a herd to move backstage. Jack and I hang in the back, still waiting for the others to show up. "Let me text Drew," he says, scanning all the doors at the back of the auditorium to see if they arrived during the director's extremely loud and vivacious—and acrobatic—speech.

We both stand there waiting for Drew to text back. It feels like a lifetime before Jack's phone finally buzzes. I hold my breath as Jack looks down to read the text.

His hand flies up in an instant facepalm as he turns the phone so I can read the text:

Drew: *Dude, we're lost. I think we're in New Jersey?*

I'M NOT A VIOLENT PERSON. I'm not even an angry person. But right at this moment, holding this phone with Drew's text announcing he's not only late, but he's in an entirely different state has triggered every single one of my anger receptors. Pressing the button to call him, I struggle to remain calm as Claire puts her arm around my waist and squeezes, trying to console me.

"Where the hell are you?" I bark into the phone much less amicably than I intended to.

"Camden, I think?" Drew sounds completely nonchalant and unaffected.

"No, you're past Camden now," Luke's muffled voice filters down the line. "You need to turn around!"

"I guess I need to turn around?" Drew parrots.

"If you're in New Jersey, then YES you need to turn around! What the hell, Drew? You said you knew how to get here!"

"I thought I did?" He lets out a long sigh. "Sorry, man. We'll be there as soon as we can."

"It's less than two hours till showtime. You better get a move on."

"Will do, Captain!" I can almost see him mock-saluting me.

"Stay in your lane!" comes Luke's exasperated voice.

I want to say something else, but I'm so furious, I'm

afraid I'll mouth off something I'll later regret. After pushing the button to end the call, I quickly slide the phone back in my pocket before I launch it across the auditorium.

Turning toward Claire, I plant my livid gaze on her. "You heard all that, right?"

"Yeah. Screw those guys," she says, patting my arm. "So what if they don't show up? You can just play your guitar and do an acoustic jam. Jack Reilly Unplugged, like old school MTV."

I swallow down the lump in my throat as I try to conjure up a mental image of myself on stage alone. By myself. Just me and the guitar.

"I know what you're going to say," I tell her before I admit I'm scared. I'm a real man, right? I'm not supposed to get scared or have stage fright. Nope, it's toxic masculinity at its finest to suck it up and not admit I'm actually quaking in my boots at the prospect of performing alone.

Her eyebrows draw together as her eyes bounce between mine. "What do you mean?"

"You're going to say I performed by myself just fine at the bar in Rehoboth Beach that night you talked me into entering the contest."

"Okay?" She squints at me.

I scan the theatre, the crowd milling about. I imagine all the seats filled with bodies, and all those bodies with two eyes planted right on me. Well, except for pirates. They might just have one eye planted on me. But it's still a butt-load of eyes. *Okay, not the best choice of words.* It's a lot of damn eyes!

"Wait, are you nervous? Scared to go out there by yourself?" She isn't making fun of me. Her tone is soft, like a warm blanket wrapping around me. When I don't answer, she puts her arm around me again. "It's okay, Jack. It's okay to have stage fright."

My eyes lift to hers, which are like aqua pools under the theater house lights. "There'll be a lot of people in the audience…and it's going to be on TV…and I can't sing 'Firecracker' without my band. It just wouldn't sound the same."

She taps her index finger against her lips as she ponders my predicament. "Don't you have any other songs you could sing? Any…songs for special occasions?" She looks at me with wide, sincere eyes, but there's something deeper there, a little sparkle of knowledge I can't help but pick up on.

She knows.

She knows about the other song.

Drew must have told her, that freakin' bastard. Now I'm gonna have to kill him twice. Once for ending up in New Jersey, and once for spilling the beans to Claire about her special song. The song that's *specialer* than "Firecracker." That's what Mariana would call it.

But I'm not ready for that other song. There's still too much up in the air with Mariana and this contest.

My phone starts to ring just then, and it saves me from having to admit to the "specialer song." I grab my phone and answer the call in one swift motion. "Hello?"

"Hey, it's Russ." There's a pause and some muffled cursing in the background. "I wanted you to know that we just got pulled over for speeding. And the officer is taking his time—especially after Drew told him his best friend is a Delaware State trooper, and he should be let go with a warning. We're definitely getting the maximum fine, whatever that is."

Facepalm. Yet again. I'm going to end up with a bruise on my face before the night is over.

"Would you guys quit goofing off and just get here? And tell Drew not to get into a fight with the cop!" I don't even wait for a response before I hang up and turn to Claire. "So, Drew just got pulled over for speeding."

Her face meets a similar fate as mine when her palm flies up to smack it. "What is that dude's problem? See? I told you he was unreliable!"

"I thought he was becoming reliabler," I tell her.

She blinks slowly. "Reliabler?"

"That's what Mariana would say," I explain.

"Right." Claire looks around for a moment, sweeping the room for apparent inspiration. And then: "You know, Mariana will be in the audience with me and Nora. Just focus on us," she tells me. "Focus on your two girls. Just pretend like you're singing to no one else but us."

I shake my head, wishing it could be so easy. "I'll try…" I blow out a breath and rake my fingers through my hair. "Better head backstage. You're going to wait out there for Nora?"

She nods. "We still have ninety minutes. Surely Drew and Company can get their heads out of their butts before then."

I huff out another frustrated sigh. "I'm not holding my breath."

Chinese water torture? Nope, the newest, most effective way to slowly drive someone insane is to make them wait in a little tiny room with a bunch of obnoxious people.

I'm normally a people person, but the contestants I've been grouped with backstage are truly making me want to pull my hair out. One of them is egregiously flatulent, and by that I mean he is farting up a storm. I want to tell him there's a restroom right around the corner, and he might want to take care of that issue before he goes out on stage, but I can't seem to talk myself into getting within ten feet of him.

Another guy has been on his phone speaking very loudly to someone who must have a hearing impairment. That's the only reason I can think of for his outrageous volume. He's run through his song at least four times as well. Each time it's in a different key—or three.

The remaining act is a dude who has taken over the middle of the room to do lewd yoga poses. If this guy sticks his crotch in my face one more time, my boot is likely gonna make contact with it—and hard.

According to the stage manager, I should go on in five minutes. Apparently the cure for stage fright is being stuck in the green room with these aforementioned acts. Now I can't wait to get the heck out of here, even though it means performing in front of thousands of people.

I make my way toward the wings as I check my phone one more time to see if the band has arrived. It's too late now anyway because they don't have time for a sound check or to set up their equipment. But it would be nice if they could at least see me perform.

Last I heard, the cop who pulled Drew over suspected he was drunk, so he ran him through a battery of field sobriety tests, which Drew passed, but it took a while for them to even get on the road again. Then they took a series of wrong turns trying to get into downtown Philly, and then when they got close to the theater, they couldn't find a place to park.

So either there's a giant conspiracy against me, or I was meant to be a solo performer tonight. I'm mostly bummed because I won't be able to perform "Firecracker," which I think the audience would really love. Instead, I'll be forced to sing two cover songs, and I'm really hoping I don't screw them up since I didn't get to practice. I'll do "Jack and

Diane" like I did at the bar in Rehoboth Beach, because it went well, and I felt comfortable with it, but I've only practiced the other song in private—well, mostly private.

Mariana heard me sing it the other day, and she told me I sounded like the "bestest singer" she has ever heard. Now if that's not a ringing endorsement, I don't know what is. It's "Heaven" by Bryan Adams, one of my favorite singer-songwriters of all time.

Now I'm just trying to figure out whether to go fast, then slow or slow, then fast as I step out onto the stage to the thundering applause of the audience. The lights practically blind me, but I spot Claire, Nora and Mariana in the fifth or sixth row, front and center. Mariana is sitting on Claire's lap to get a better view.

"Heaven" isn't the "specialer" original song I wrote, but it *is* romantic, and I think Claire will like it. I take a seat on the stool after the obnoxious lady from earlier, who is apparently the Regional Director of the Support Art Foundation, introduces me. I would rather have good ol' Chuck Peebles any day, but I guess Renita Whistler will have to do.

The crowd's applause dies as the spotlight shines down on me, making it almost impossible to see my girls in the audience if not for Claire's bright auburn hair and pale skin. I lift my guitar and begin to strum out the intro, closing my eyes as I center myself. My heartbeat steadies as I start the first verse, trying to modulate my pitch and keep it soft but strong.

I know Claire's holding her breath. I can see it on her face, and soon she's the only thing I can see. She's the one filling my lungs with oxygen and forming the lyrics on my lips.

When I hit the chorus, Claire's swaying in time with the beat. I don't know if she's the only one swaying, or if the whole audience is—I can only see her. I don't even know if Mariana is still on her lap because now it's just her and me in this room. It's her, me and this song about heaven—a heaven I found there in her heart.

When the last chorus ends, slipping off my tongue like a feather, I swear there's a collective sigh of "aww" from the audience. I'll take that as a positive sign as I switch gears to "Jack and Diane." The intro is pretty sparse with just the acoustic guitar, but as soon as the first line comes out of my mouth, the crowd realizes what song it is and jumps to their feet, clapping along.

The lights either dimmed, or I got used to them, because now my baby girl is standing on the seat next to Claire, clapping and cheering. When I get to the bridge, everyone's really rocking out with me. And as soon as I finish, four people in the back are hooting and hollering like their pants are on fire. One is doing the whistle-through-his-fingers thing, and one sounds like a human air horn. The amount of noise they're generating is unreal!

When I squint, I realize it's Drew, Luke, Russ and Sam. They made it just in time.

10

Jack told me that waiting backstage was cruel and unusual punishment, but how could it be any worse than this?

Most of the crowd has filed out of the auditorium, and the only ones who remain are the twelve contestants and their entourages, each sitting in clumps throughout the theater. On stage, a crew is deconstructing the sets and taking down the huge banner that reads "Support Art Foundation's Mid-Atlantic Superstar." Directly offstage, near the pit area, a panel of judges is deliberating, and up in the sound and light booth, I see the silhouette of Renita Whistler talking with the stage manager and a few others. I'm surprised I can't hear her all the way down here.

They've told us they hope to have the results in an hour. So for now, we wait.

"It doesn't matter if I win," Jack says as he looks around to our small group. Drew and the guys finally showed up—right before Jack went on stage—and they've offered all manner of conciliatory gestures to boost their apologies. "I really appreciate everyone's support. Just having you all here to cheer me on is amazing."

I watched all twelve contestants this time, and if I'm being objective, I admit the judges have their work cut out for them. The top two performers will advance to the national competition next month in Washington, DC. The other cities hosting contests are New York, Atlanta, Miami, Indianapolis, St. Louis, Minneapolis, Dallas, Phoenix, Las Vegas, Portland, and San Diego. Twelve cities with two contestants each, so twenty-four finalists will compete in a two-day competition. Yay for math simple enough, even I can do it!

"So, how much do you owe the Great State of Pennsylvania for your speeding ticket, Andrew?" Jack asks, training his gaze on his bassist.

Drew purses his lips. "A hundred and eighty, but I'm hoping Everson can help me get out of it."

"Um, Everson is a Delaware cop. I am pretty sure he has zero pull in PA," I point out, shaking my head.

"I can't believe he thought you were drunk!" Jack chuckles.

"He couldn't do his alphabet backwards from W to M," Russ pipes up.

Drew scoffs, "Whatever, that's hard, man! You gotta be sober to do that!"

"You supposedly were!" Sam teases him.

"I don't mean sober; I mean smart!"

Everyone laughs, then Mariana stands up, putting her hands on her hips. "I can sing my alphabet!" And then she proceeds to do so—very loudly.

Out of the corner of my eye, I catch a woman leaning toward us as she walks past. "Is that your daughter?" she asks, looking right at Jack.

"It is!" He grins with pride.

"She's so cute!" the woman gushes. She plops down

right next to him like I'm not even here. "You were brilliant up there. Love Mellencamp!"

"Thanks," he answers humbly. "I enjoyed myself."

"I think you're a shoo-in to win," she says, fanning her chest like he's made her all hot and bothered. *Puh-leeze!* She's practically throwing herself at him.

"Oh," Jack dismisses her prediction with a hand wave. "I'm just lucky to be here."

"I'm serious!" the woman continues. "My brother performed right before you—Neal Gadway. I just got kicked out of my family's encampment because I said you were better." She giggles. "Hi, I'm Natalie Gadway; nice to meet you."

He thrusts out his hand to shake hers, and my face is becoming increasingly flushed. "Hi, Natalie," my voice oozes with fake enthusiasm, "I'm Claire Sterling, Jack's girlfriend."

I hear Nora snickering beside me. *Whatever. No way is this skinny bitch sidling up to my man.*

"Hi, Claire," she turns a supposedly genuine smile in my direction, "your boyfriend was incredible."

"He sure was—and is," I agree, smirking.

Jack stands up. "Oh, look, the judges have packed up their stuff, and Renita is making her way back to the stage. Looks like it's announcement time."

"I can't believe everyone leaves and misses the winner announcement," Natalie complains as she folds her arms over her chest. "It's so anti-climactic."

What's anti-climactic is her attempt to schmooze with my guy.

"Yeah, this contest is scored really oddly. I wonder how it will be at nationals," Jack responds, still ignoring the stink-eye I'm giving him.

Renita makes her way to the stage, and in her usual

over-the-top fashion, she squeals into the microphone, "Ladies and gentlemen, we have our two finalists who are going to the national competition in Washington, DC!"

Everyone claps and cheers.

"We tally the votes from the audience and combine those with the average judges' scores to create a final score. And the two performers with the highest scores were Jessica Vicks and Jack Reilly!"

I'm shocked for a moment, can't even speak. I don't know whether I'm more shocked that Jack won or that Renita Whistler was able to deliver the contest results in such a calm and professional fashion. Both of these facts are currently blowing my mind. I feel suspended in some sort of goo, unable to speak or move.

"You did it, Jack!" Drew shouts and makes that obnoxious air horn sound he made after Jack's performance.

"Get up there and claim your trophy!" Luke adds.

My mouth finally decides to work again. "Oh my god, I can't believe it, honey!" I throw my arms around him and give him a squeeze before he briskly walks to the stage. Mariana is jumping up and down as she watches her father climb the stairs and stand next to Renita, who is holding out two trophies and posing for the flashing cameras.

And just like that, we're going to Nationals.

Jack

CLAIRE and I lucked out and got another night in the hotel room alone, with her sister Nora graciously and generously volunteering to keep Mariana. Mariana was thrilled to go back and hang out with her friend Emily. I can't tell you how glad I am those two hit it off.

Claire is already in bed when I sweep the covers back and climb in to join her. I feel wired and exhausted at the same time—such a strange, conflicting feeling. This whole day has been quite a roller coaster.

"Well, has it sunk in yet?" She turns toward me, her teal eyes glowing with excitement.

"I don't think so," I admit. "It's like I know I'm excited, but I haven't really begun to think of all the ramifications. Just wait until my students and the school find out about this. They already held a pep rally for me before today's competition. I wonder what they'll do this time!"

Claire's brows scrunch. "Well, school is out next week, isn't it?"

"Yes, I suppose you're right. Hmm, so maybe I'll just fade into obscurity. Everyone will forget about my fifteen minutes of fame by the time school starts again in the fall." I laugh as I trail my fingers down her bare arm. "Oh, what's this?" I peel back the covers again to reveal my beautiful girlfriend's ample curves highlighted by a sumptuous satin nightgown. It's an aqua color that almost matches her eyes perfectly with white lace along the edges.

"Still wanna talk about the contest?" She arches one brow as her eyes dart between mine.

"I do not," I quickly confirm before rolling on top of her.

"Good, I didn't want you to forget about me…" Her voice trails off.

"Never!"

She arches her back, lifting to meet my lips as my arms wrap around her waist. She's so soft, so voluptuous. I love the way her flesh presses into my body, melting into my thick, hairy dad bod. That something so silky and delicate feels like perfection against me proves the whole "opposites attract" theory.

"Are you ready for me?" My voice comes out in a rasp as it falls against the shell of her ear.

She shudders against me, whimpering slightly as her hands fold around my back, pressing me closer to her. "What do you think?"

"I think it's a yes…"

Afterwards, she lies in my arms again, her skin still flushed around her chest. I don't know what happened to that silky number she was wearing. I mean, it looked great on her, but I'm sure it looks even better in its current location, wherever that might be. I'm coming down from multiple highs, but the serious Type A part of my brain that I try to silence as much as possible because it tends to suppress my artistic, creative side is already poring over checklists of things I need to do for the national contest.

"Hey, where'd you go?" her soft voice echoes into the room.

I've switched off the light, and I guess my brain took that as a sign it could do whatever the hell it wants. "I'm still here."

"I can feel your thoughts drifting…"

She knows me all too well.

"Stay here with me?" she pleads.

"I'm sorry. I was already starting to think about Nationals. I can't believe they're in two weeks. I had way more time to prepare for Regionals than that."

"Jack, trust me, I am the worst when it comes to over-analyzing and ruminating on stuff—please just let your brain rest tonight. Get some sleep, and you can obsess tomorrow, okay?"

I can't stop a little chuckle from slipping out. "You're

right, babe. That's exactly what's happening. Thanks for helping me put things in perspective."

"Anytime."

"Now give me a kiss so we can get some sleep, okay?"

"As you wish…"

After her lips meet mine, the tension and adrenaline that have been coursing through me finally start to dissipate. My limbs relax, my muscles sinking into the pillow and mattress. Claire turns and snuggles her butt right into me, and I succumb to the siren call of sleep.

Claire

11

Jack has been busy with the band and Mariana, so I haven't seen him much since he won the Mid-Atlantic Superstar contest. Actually, he was the runner-up. We found later that the other contestant beat him out by a few points. That's okay. We're still pretty proud of the guy.

He's become a bit of a celebrity around here, recently interviewed by both the local paper and the TV station in Salisbury, Maryland, which serves our area. And the folks at his school threw a huge party for him, though even he admitted he felt like the students considered it more of an end-of-the-school-year party than a party in his honor.

I have to say, all this alone time has been a boon to my writing agenda. With Elliott gone at his summer job and then with Jessie the rest of the time, and with Jack and Mariana out of my hair, I've actually made some progress on this blasted book that's due to my editor by the end of the summer. My agent, Lisa, has been harassing me for the last eight months, basically since I found out the publisher solicited her after reading my *New York Times* column. I was given a year to complete the project.

Our conversations have gone a little something like this:

Lisa: *Hey, Claire, how's the book coming along?*

Me: *Pretty good! I wrote two pages today!*

Lisa: *Really? That's pretty good progress.*

Me: *Yes, I wrote two pages…*

Also me: *…but then I deleted everything except two sentences because I was suddenly overcome by rampant crippling and debilitating self-doubt.*

Lisa: *Oh. Well, are you going to have the first three chapters to your editor by your deadline next week?*

Me: *Sure thing!*

Lisa: *Are you* actually *going to have them for her?*

Me: *In spirit, yes.*

Lisa: *I am pretty sure she needs them in a Word doc format.*

So, I guess you could say I've pretty much nailed this writing thing. My contract is to write a bodypositive manifesto—oh, so my contract doesn't come right out and call it that, but the title I'm toying with is *Claire's Bodypositive Manifesto*. I may not use my name. I may call it *The Fat Girl's Bodypositive Manifesto* instead. You'd buy that book, right?

I've written and re-written the intro to this baby more times than I can count, and I was hoping today would finally be the day my muse would arrive and help me figure it all out. I've got my fingers perched on the keys, but I can't seem to make the words go.

I take a deep breath, a bolstering sip of coffee, and crack my knuckles. I funnel all my energy into this positive intention: *Okay, this is it. I'm gonna do this. Right now.*

As soon as I make up my mind and return my eyes to my document, my fingers start to fly. Words are flowing like the Nile River—or maybe the Amazon, whatever river is more flowy. I'm seeing sentences appear, paragraphs appear right before my very eyes. Holy crap, positive intentions work! It's like magic!

And then…

Pound. Pound. Pound.

Oh, you've got to be freaking kidding me!

My heart is thundering from the surprise knock on the door, and using that boost of adrenaline, I leap up from my extra roll-y executive chair and rush to the front door. I can see out the window that it's my neighbor, Red. At least he's wearing a shirt.

"Yes?" I pull the door open so only the screen door stands between us.

"Do you have a cat?" he seethes. He's always so angry!

"Um…yes?" I scan the immediate vicinity for the little butthole.

He's technically a tuxedo cat. You know, the black and white ones. I think it's supposed to make him seem refined and sophisticated, but instead he's a smug, pretentious prick of a cat.

Red's lips thin into a stern, straight line, his jaw clenching as he glares at me. "Do you mind coming over and getting it before he humps my female that's in heat?"

"Oh!" Welp, definitely didn't have *Figaro tries to impregnate the neighbor's cat* on today's bingo card. "I didn't know he'd gotten out."

"Yeah, he's gotten out, and he's over there strutting his stuff like he's Casanova!"

"Do you mean Cat-anova?" I quip, giggling.

He just continues to glare at me like he either didn't understand the joke or doesn't have a soul. Probably the latter. Maybe he's Santa's evil twin?

"Okay, sorry. I'll be right there." I close the door and run off in search of the cat carrier. I just don't know how I'm going to lure him in there. He hates me.

I'm pretty sure I left it in the garage, so I head out there and grab it off the shelf, where it's been since Figaro's last visit to the vet. I exit the door on Mrs. Vandeveer's side, and sure enough, the elderly woman is out pruning her rosebushes (and no that's not a euphemism for anything). I don't really have time to chit chat with her, so I try to sneak by. I mean, she's supposedly decrepit and has a terrible memory. Maybe her ears don't work very well either?

"Where are you going with that cat carrier?" Her words hit my back like a quiver of arrows.

"Figaro got out and is tormenting Red's female cat who's in heat," I explain, hoping that will express the urgency of the situation.

"I thought Figaro was a girl too," she says.

"Uh…no…" Figaro is a male cat in Pinocchio and a male character in Mozart's opera. So I don't know why she'd think that, but do I really want to stand here and pontificate about gendered naming conventions and fictional characters when my cat is trying to impregnate my neighbor's cat?

"I thought you told me she was a girl," Mrs. Vandeveer says.

Okay so her memory problem is *misremembering*. Got it.

"Sorry, but I have to run for now," I apologize and haul my fat butt across the lawn, over the driveway to Red's lawn.

He's standing there holding my cat by the scruff, and if I thought he was scowling before, this is like the super intense ramped-up version. Again, at least he's wearing a shirt. His snow-white beard is gently blowing in the summer breeze as I pace toward him slowly, trying not to freak Figaro out.

See? This is why I can't get any writing done. Because stuff like this only happens to me.

I tell the universe I'm going to write today, and the universe says, "Oh hell no. You're going to cockblock your cat instead."

I inch closer, trying to figure out how I'm going to get this furry beast into the carrier. "Okay, so I just open the door, and you put him in there?"

Red nods, holding the creature as far away from his body as possible, like it's a snake that might strike him at any time. I open the door to the carrier and position it so it faces Red at the same level he's holding the cat. All he has to do is gently stuff the feline through the door, and then I'll shut it.

So far, so good... He starts to insert the cat into the hole tail-first, even though Figaro is hissing at him like the afore-mentioned snake might. He's resisting, but Red's a pretty strong dude, as we've covered already. He shoves him a little more forcefully, pushing him inside the carrier up to his shoulders. One more push and...

I go to slam the door shut and...

Bam! Figaro shoots out of the carrier like a cannonball and springboards off Red's chest before flying across the grass toward Red's backyard.

Oh no!!!

I can't say that I exactly sprint after him because, well, it's me, but I hustle at a relatively fast pace in pursuit of my cat. Red is hot on my heels but passes me in no time because "fast" is probably not the best term for my rate of speed, after all.

"He went right!" I shout, though I'm sure Red is just as capable of seeing the streak of black and white shoot across my backyard as I am.

All the sudden, I hear, "Got 'er!" ring out from between my house and Mrs. Vandeveer's.

"Got him," I want to correct her. I jog over, and there she is with the basket she was using to collect her rose bush trimmings turned upside down on the lawn.

"He's under there?" If you think there might be a hint of disbelief in my tone, I can assure you it is actually *dripping* with it.

Red had run clear across the neighbor's yard but now jogs back, coming to a stop a few feet away, his chest heaving a bit as he sucks in some breaths. His eyes trail up and down Mrs. Vandeveer's frail body. "How did you do that?"

"She came, I mean, *he came* this way like a bat outta hell, so I just threw the basket on top of him. But I don't know how you're gonna get him home."

"Simple, I'm gonna pick up the basket and carry him there." I march over to the basket, which is deep like a trashcan. "Can I borrow that?"

My neighbor has a towel out there on the grass for some reason. Maybe she was sunbathing in the nude earlier; I have no idea, nor do I wish to have an idea.

She nods, and I pick up the towel, then turn the basket over, quickly putting the towel over it and threading the ends through the basket handles on the side. Without saying another word, I pick it up with both hands and march right back to my house, where I dump my asshole cat in my bedroom and shut the door.

Horny bastard.

When I glance out the window, Red and Mrs. Vandeveer are still standing there staring at each other.

"HEY, guys, I have some great news!" I walk through the door into Sam's garage to find my bandmates all sitting like dogs awaiting a command, instruments in hand and eyes trained on the door.

They're worried I'm going to fire them after they missed the gig in Philly last weekend.

While it's great to see them so contrite, not to mention on time—for once—my great news involves them, which means I need to keep them around. At least a little while longer.

"What is it?" Drew pipes up from a stool near the door to the house.

"Well, do you want the good news first—or the even better news?" If I sound like I'm glowing, well, I definitely am. It's hard to contain this much excitement all at once.

"Tell us the good news first, and then the better news," Russ suggests.

My gaze bounces between the four guys all hanging on my every word. "Okay, so the good news is that we have a gig next weekend in Rehoboth Beach. It's only an hour-long set, and we're not the main band with the prime timeslot, but it's a start, and I'm really excited about it!"

"That's awesome," Luke agrees. "So what's the better news?"

I waste no time spilling it, because this secret's been burning a hole in my pocket all day, so to speak. "I spoke with the director for the national Support Art Foundation, the one who's in charge of the contest in DC, and they told me we're allowed to perform with a band and to credit them. We can't perform as The Gallant Misfits, but I *can* perform as "Jack Reilly & The Gallant Misfits."

"Whoo hoooo!" Drew howls, then he does an impromptu celebratory riff on his bass. Luke joins in on the drums, and Russ performs a stunning glissando on the keyboard.

"If only I had my tambourine," Sam adds, his head hung in disappointment. "No, seriously, that's great news, guys!"

"It is great news," I agree. "And I have calls into a few other establishments in Rehoboth Beach. I'd like us to try to get a few more gigs down at the boardwalk before the crowds thin out at the end of the season. I wish Nationals was another month out because then we could remind everyone who comes to each gig to vote for us to win. But we can definitely do that next weekend when we play."

"Oh, it's going to be on TV, right?" Russ confirms.

"Not only that, but it's at the Kennedy Center," I reveal. "I don't know if you've ever been there, but it's an amazing venue."

"How many songs do you get?" Luke questions.

"Two again. I definitely want to do 'Firecracker,' but I haven't decided on the other one yet. I guess a ballad?"

"What about the other original song you wrote?" Drew looks at me with arched eyebrows. "Didn't you write it for Claire too?"

I shrug. I had kind of put that song on the back burner until things settle down. Now with Mariana here and Nationals on the horizon—I still don't know what to do, especially if I end up touring.

"Oh, that reminds me," I tell them, my eyes growing wide again. "There's a tour after Nationals."

"What?" Drew's practically salivating. I think I just saw a drop land on his bass. "We'd go on tour?"

"There are twenty-four performers in the national contest, and they're going to send the top ten on tour all over the country for six weeks to earn even more money for the foundation. Can you guys imagine us taking The Gallant Misfits on tour?"

"That would rock!" Russ agrees. "But what would we do about our jobs?"

"I guess the trash all over Rehoboth Beach would pile up with you gone for six weeks," Luke teases him. "But I'm sure my lab could give me some time off."

"What does that say about the importance of our jobs, huh?" Russ fires back. "The city would be buried under a mound of garbage without me, but they could get along just fine without a marine biologist." He scoffs and mumbles under his breath, "Like that's even a real job."

"We'll cross that bridge when we come to it, guys. For now, I want us to get a solid set list together for our Rehoboth Beach debut. We're going to close with 'Firecracker,' that's all I know for sure. We'll probably do 'Jack & Diane,' but what else?"

"That Bryan Adams song you did in Philly was nice," Russ suggests.

"The Sheryl Crow one we were working on is good too," Luke contributes.

"Okay, let's do those for sure, then I was listening to some Fleetwood Mac, and I was thinking of doing a Stevie Nicks tribute. She's always been my favorite female artist."

"Sounds good!" Luke crashes his drumsticks against the snare and then the cymbal. "Let's get this party started!"

As Luke counts us off to warm up with "Firecracker," I survey my fellow bandmates who are here, dedicated and committed. I'm looking forward to seeing our band grow in talent and opportunity in the next few months. This is everything I wanted and was missing. Now I have my girl-friend, my daughter, and my band.

Life is good.

I TIPTOE down the hallway as quietly as I can. It's Saturday night, and I made a bargain with Mariana. If she goes to bed early, we'll go out for Fractured Prune donuts in the morning, and then we'll head down to the board-walk. The donuts are made fresh when you order, and they have all these different toppings to choose from, and they're honestly one of the best things I've ever put in my mouth.

I've been so busy working with the band to get ready for my performance that I've hardly spent any time with Claire. Not to mention the fact that Mariana's been here, so we've been staying most nights at my house. A warm, content feeling fills my chest as I head into the living room and catch sight of Claire sprawled out on the loveseat with a bowl of popcorn. My baby girl down the hall. My beau-tiful lady all ready for movie night with me. I'm living the dream, honestly!

"Well, how did story time go?" Claire asks, sitting up and putting the popcorn bowl on the coffee table. There's quite a bit missing since I just spent the last twenty minutes coaxing my daughter to go to sleep. Claire's blue eyes flash up at me. "I can pop some more, sorry. I have the munchies."

I chuckle softly. "It's okay. I'll pop another bag. You stay right there."

Her eyes follow me into the kitchen. "So, story time?"

"I read Rapunzel to her, and she was a bit freaked out by it." I laugh, remembering Mariana's scrunched-up nose. "'The prince climbed up her hair, Daddy? For real? That's weird. And it would hurt,' she told me."

"Well, she's not wrong," Claire agrees.

I take a whiff of the buttery fresh popcorn, then pour the whole bag into the bowl before heading into the living room to sit next to Claire on the loveseat. With an arm around her and the bowl between us, I prop my feet up on the coffee table. "So, what are we watching?"

"Oh, you actually want to watch a movie?" Claire's brows draw together as her eyes bounce between mine.

"I thought you lured me over here with the promise of popcorn and a movie?" I tease her.

"Well, you do have popcorn." She waggles her eyebrows then leans over and drops a piece of popcorn down her shirt. "Oops…seem to have lost one—"

"Allow me." I lean close, running a finger over her smooth, soft collarbones and then down her cleavage, retrieving the "lost" kernel of popcorn, which I pop into my mouth. My lips trail up her neck, and a long, breathy sigh escapes as I nibble on her earlobe.

"See? This is way better than a movie," she moans, leaning back against the arm of the loveseat and pulling me down on top of her.

I stroke my hands down her body, her ample curves so soft beneath my touch. This woman makes my heart sing.

Before I can go any farther, I stop and look deep into her turquoise eyes. "Claire, I have to thank you…"

"Thank me? You popped the popcorn." She giggles, trying to lighten the serious mood I've just cast over us.

"You're always so good to me, and you're so good with my daughter too. You didn't have to help me co-parent her this summer, and yet you have. You've made space for her in your home and your life, and you've helped me take care of her when I've been so busy with rehearsals. You're so supportive of me, Claire, and I'm eternally grateful for you."

I think I see the beginning of a tear glistening in her eyes as her features soften and her lips curl into a smile. "Jack, I love you. Of course I'm going to do anything and everything I can to show you my love. We make a good team, you and I."

"We sure do," I agree, pressing a kiss to her lips. Her arms wrap around me, and the kiss deepens, our bodies merging together. The popcorn and movie idea has been officially abandoned, but I think we've found an even better way to entertain ourselves on this fine Saturday evening.

Like I said earlier: life is good.

12

Well, here we go again.

Nationals.

The entire town has been buzzing about it all week, and I haven't been able to get my mind to shut up about what happens if Jack places in the top ten. There's a national tour for the top ten. He'd be away from us for six weeks—if he goes.

Last summer, if he'd had this opportunity, it wouldn't have mattered at all. He and I were just hanging out here and there, and his daughter was in Texas. He's a teacher, so he's off work during the summer.

So literally any other summer in the past few years would have been better for him, would have been less disruptive. But here we are. You don't get to choose when life events happen. They come whether you're ready for them or not.

Well, you *can* choose your wedding day—something I've been thinking about, when I allow myself to.

But the exact timing of most other important life-changing events is almost completely out of your control.

So here we are. I asked Jack about his ex, and if she knows what's going on, and he said, "We'll cross that bridge when we come to it." And I asked him if he goes on tour, does that mean Mariana will go to London with Anita, and he said, "We'll cross that bridge when we come to it."

And all I can think is, when we crossed the Chesapeake Bay Bridge to go to Washington, DC today, we were crossing both the literal and metaphorical bridges he's been waiting for.

After all, he only has to make top ten out of twenty-four, and he's performing my song.

He's going to Firecracker his way right into the top ten —I can just feel it.

Tonight I'm sitting in the audience at the Kennedy Center with Mariana, Jean-Marc, Thor (we've completely forgotten what his real name is by now. I think even Jean-Marc calls him Thor), and Sam's wife, Kayla. We're all dressed up like we're at the Oscars or something. Actually, this is probably the closest we'll ever get to an actual red-carpet event.

Jean-Marc squeezes my hand as Mariana fidgets in her seat. I hand her my phone, open to one of the apps she likes to fool around with so I can have a moment of adult conversation.

"You nervous?" he asks, his dark eyes meeting mine. I know better than to lie, because my best friend will always be able to see right through me.

"Yeah, pretty nervous." I rest a hand on his thigh. "Hey, this is terrible, but…I think I'm more nervous for him to win than for him to lose."

Jean-Marc smirks and nods sympathetically. "I understand. I think Thor's job is going to take him away from me too."

"What do you mean? I thought he worked at the bookstore?"

My best friend rolls his eyes as he *tsks-tsks* at me. "Oh, there is much you don't know about Thor… That's not even his real name!"

I scoff, "Well, I know *that* much! I thought his real name is Tom. Or Tim. Or something with a T."

"Tony."

"Right, whatever." I shrug. *I was close.*

"That's not his real name either," Jean-Marc whispers dramatically.

Oh, so the truth comes out! I knew this Viking-esque guy couldn't actually be named Tony. "So what, is he like a spy or something? FBI? CIA?"

"Shhhh…" He presses a finger to my lips. "I've said too much already."

I scoff again. "I'm pretty sure you're making all this up."

"I'm just saying, if he leaves, I'll be able to commiserate with you while Jack is on tour. And at least if Jack goes, it will only be six weeks. That's nothing. And you can finish your book."

This is a rather scoff-y conversation apparently because another one hisses out of my mouth. "I'm already almost finished."

"Uh huh. How many pages have you written?"

"A lot," I tell him. "Too many to count."

"You better hurry it up before your publisher drops you." He shoots me a warning glare like he's some sort of expert on the publishing industry. The only things he's an expert in are real estate, fashion, and how to mix me the perfect martini.

No wonder I keep him around!

The lights dim, and a silver-haired woman in a classy

off-the-shoulder red gown comes on stage with two children. One looks about Mariana's age, and the other a little bit older. "Good evening, I'm Brenda Monnett, and these are my grandchildren, Walton and Bessie. We're here to show you a brief video of the kind of impact our Support Art Foundation has had in the DC public schools."

I learn over and whisper in Jean-Marc's ear, "What do you suppose they're doing backstage?"

"I don't know. Why don't you text Jack and find out?"

"I don't want to interrupt. What if he's all zenned out back there?"

My bestie's eyebrows fly up to his hairline. "Jack meditates?"

"Oh, yeah. He does yoga too."

Jean-Marc punches my arm, cracking up with laughter and trying to rein it in while still managing to blurt out, "You really did hit the *jack*-pot with him, didn't you?"

I can do nothing at this point but roll my eyes at his bad pun.

But, yeah, I suppose I did hit the jackpot.

The atmosphere here is a lot different than it was at the other contests I've done. These people are professionals. I've heard several of the contestants talking about the various shows they've done and audiences they've performed for all over the world. Some of them have even done stadium shows. I thought the point of this contest was to discover amateur talent, but what do I know?

I'm just a lowly high school band director.

I've been playing casual observer all evening until a woman with long, golden hair approaches me with a guitar slung over her shoulder and points to the sofa cushion next to me. "Is this seat taken?"

"Be my guest," I tell her.

She flashes me a warm smile and stretches her long legs out before crossing them at the ankle. She's wearing a layered skirt with lace underneath. Maybe she sings country? But she's not wearing cowboy boots...

"What do you sing?" she asks as if reading my mind.

"Rock," I answer. "Mostly classic rock. Seventies and eighties. Some nineties. And some original stuff."

"Nice!" She nods with approval. "I'm Bonnie, by the way."

"Hi Bonnie. Jack." I take the hand she's offering and give it a firm shake. "How about you?"

"Some rock, some folk stuff. I guess you could say I have eclectic tastes."

I kind of gathered that from her skirt, ankle boots, and form-fitting tank top. She's wearing a variety of necklaces too, from a choker around her neck to a pendant that hangs below her...whoa, I should probably not be looking there. I quickly avert my eyes, moving them right back to hers. But she clearly caught me looking, and she smiles and laughs.

"What number are you?" she asks, referring to what order I'll be singing in.

"I drew an eight. Which is pretty crappy." I shrug. *Oh, well—you win some, you lose some, right?* Half of the contestants are going tonight, and the other half are performing tomorrow. They have specified time limits on the audience voting so it's all fair.

"I hear you. That's rough. But I'm actually going last."

A brilliant smile lights up her face, and I notice how pearly white and straight her teeth are. Her honey-brown eyes are sparkling right alongside her grin. She's a beautiful woman. She has a great look. If she can sing, she's definitely going to go far.

"So, you play guitar?" I glance down at the instrument resting against her midsection.

"Yep. You?" She nudges her head toward my guitar case. I haven't even taken it out yet.

"Yeah, but I'm also here with a band. They went off to find a vending machine. They missed my regional performance, so if they show up even a half-second late, I'm probably going to kill them." I chuckle. "So if you see me on the news later, and it's not for the contest, it's probably for that."

She laughs. "What regional contest did you win?"

"Philly. You?"

"Portland."

"Okay, cool."

An awkward silence festers around us, and I get the urge to go look for my bandmates. I have to say I'm wildly curious about whether or not Bonnie's talent matches her looks and cool, easy demeanor. If so, she's definitely going to be in the top ten.

The staircase we ascend to get to the stage is narrow and dark. If there wasn't reflective tape on each step, I probably would have busted my ass by now. Or maybe it's just that my legs are made of jelly, like my bones have dissolved.

Performing in Philly was tough for me, especially

without my guys there to back me up. But I got through it. As soon as I sat down and strummed my guitar, I felt the panic start to fade and the adrenaline surge through me, taking over. I am sure that will happen again today, but this crowd is even bigger. There's a national audience, and viewers all over America will have to decide if they want to vote for the geeky bearded band director. I can only hope they fall in love with our geeky misfit faces and our sound.

The lights come up on us in our places, all raring to go. We're fresh off the energy from our gig last weekend in Rehoboth Beach, which went even better than we'd hoped. We have the whole state of Delaware behind us—even the governor tweeted today to wish us luck and told us to make The First State proud.

I start off with my guitar, strumming the first few chords of "Jack & Diane." We figured it's worked so well for me, why not keep it as our good luck charm? I'm sure Mellencamp would approve. I wonder if he's watching? I definitely want to do him proud.

The crowd is getting into it, clapping along, and their energy amplifies and bounces back toward the stage. It goes into my fingers, past my lips, wraps around my vocal cords. I feel it enter my body and soak right into my bones as I continue to belt out the lyrics. I feel this in my soul, being here, on stage.

I always wonder at this point in the song—why was I scared? What did I have to be afraid of? I've got this.

It feels like I was born to do this.

Maybe my parents couldn't understand, and they couldn't get behind me doing this as a career. I guess that's why I never even considered pursuing it. They were always pushing me toward something that would be easy. That would be steady. That would pay decently. My dad bought me my first computer when I was twelve and convinced me that was my destiny.

But I'd lie in bed at night, humming lyrics from the songs I'd made up during the day and think—would anyone want to hear this? Would anyone want to hear these tunes I wrote myself on the backs of napkins and in notebooks in class when I was supposed to be paying attention to the teacher? Would anyone want to clap along while I plucked my guitar strings and belted out my favorite tunes?

And now here I am, and it's happening—all because Claire had faith in me and pushed me just a little bit. She continues to support me—even though this contest and Mariana have taken me away from her so much in the past couple of months. I know things will settle down again when this is all over, and it will just be her and me again.

I hope she will wait for me. I hope she will wait for me to play out this dream, just long enough to see where it goes.

Claire

As Jack and the guys finish up the last strains of "Jack & Diane," I steal a moment to glance around me. The crowd is into it, clapping and stomping their feet. But they don't have a clue what's coming, because they'll do a fade out on this song, and then BOOM, the drums will kick in, and the bass will start driving, and then the keyboard and electric guitar will take over as "Firecracker" becomes a literal explosion on the stage.

The rhythm wells up inside me as they start, my body sensing what's to come. In no time at all, as soon as the first chorus kicks in, everyone's on their feet. And I'm right there with them, dancing and clapping along, mouthing the words as they fire off Jack's lips.

You're my firecracker
Setting my world ablaze
Making my mind a haze
You're my firecracker
You keep me burnin' for days
In a million different ways
You're my firecracker
You're always sparkling;
you're always bold
You're my firecracker
with a heart of gold

I could get swept away by the energy of the band and the audience—it's a perfect symbiotic relationship, feeding off each other. I can only imagine how alive the Gallant Misfits all feel up there with the lights blazing down on them, the sound enveloping them from all sides. It must be amazing.

If he wins this contest—if he places in the top ten, even—things are going to change between us.

I haven't allowed myself to dwell too much on what might happen past the tour. I've concentrated on that six-week span where he'd be away from us; I've mulled over the logistics. But the truth is, if he wins this contest, the tour will be nothing at all compared to the winds of change that could sweep us up in their vortex.

Will he quit his job?

Will he get a record deal?

Will he go out on tour for a hell of a lot longer than six weeks?
And if so, what happens to Mariana? What happens to me?

I know it sounds crazy to think about, but this performance may be the only thing standing between him and that reality, as far-fetched as it might have seemed only a month or two ago. Now it's staring us in the face with its dragon eyes, licking its lips and saying it's time.

I'm filled with all sorts of feelings—I'm *a mass of conflicting impulses*, like Jack would say, quoting *Star Trek*. Because it could be the *best* thing that could ever happen to us—or the *worst* thing that could ever happen to us.

And we have no way of knowing which...until it actually happens. Until this song is over, and the votes are tallied, and the announcement is made.

I won't know for a little more than forty-eight hours, but as he brings down the house with the second chorus of "Firecracker," I know it's these last few strains that will seal our fate.

Claire

13

Can you imagine the stress and anticipation of having to wait two whole days to learn how Jack did at Nationals? Nothing like hanging around in limbo for hours upon end. No wonder my back hurts!

Of course, Jean-Marc pointed out that in *American Idol*, the contestants had to wait a whole week for the results. Thanks a lot, Jean-Marc, for minimizing my pain and suffering.

We came back to Delaware to my cute little house on the Indian River and holed up playing games and watching movies to pass the time. It was like being snowed in during a blizzard—except it's June. Tonight we're watching the second half of the contestants perform, and then the next night, we'll go back to DC for the results show and awards ceremony, which will be taking place in the same theater at the Kennedy Center, and the top ten will each reprise one of their songs.

So we're sitting there watching, and I have my head on Jack's shoulder. Elliott and Jes-sie are curled up on the loveseat, but at least I can see their hands. Mariana has built herself a blanket fort in the corner, and she keeps appearing and disappearing. Who knows what she's doing in there, but at least she's entertaining herself. You know you're a model parent when you spend a lot of time using the words "at least."

We're between two contestants when Jack's phone rings. He glances down nonchalantly as if he's planning to ignore it, but I watch his eyes bug out when he sees the caller. "It's coming from out of the country. I better take this—what if it's Anita?"

I haven't heard the Darth Vader ringtone for a while, so I hope she's okay. Jack scrambles off the sofa and rushes into the kitchen, pressing the phone to his ear and saying hello. My heart is pounding, and I don't know why, but an Ominous Feeling is usurping me, pumping adrenaline through my veins and putting all my nerves on high alert.

I hear him murmuring in a low voice, but I can't make out any of his words. I can't imagine he's talking to Anita, because his volume usually doubles when she calls. She really does seem to push all his buttons. And not in a good way—like I do. *naughty wink*

The next contestant has already taken the stage when he returns, a petite Asian woman with a soulful voice, accompanying herself on a glossy grand piano. I predict she's definitely Top Ten Material as her satiny melody wraps itself around my ears. Then Jack appears by my side, his face drawn.

"What's wrong? Who was that?"

"It was Camellia." He pauses and glances over at the blanket fort, but Mariana is inside, unable to see us. Jack bends down and whispers in my ear, "Anita is really sick."

"What? What's wrong with her?" I gape at him, trying to process what he said.

"Here, come with me." He pulls me up to a standing position, and I realize he doesn't want to talk about this with Mariana around. He guides me into my bedroom and shuts the door.

"What's going on? What's wrong with her?" I look up at him with pleading eyes. I'm not sure I've ever seen him this upset before.

"She didn't go to London for work," he tells me, shaking his head. "That was all a lie."

"What, what do you mean?" I scrunch up my nose. "Why would she lie about that?"

He huffs out a deep breath. "She has cancer."

"What? She's so young and healthy!" I want to add "thin" but stop myself just in time. Even I, the bodypositive expert, almost fell into the trap of equating thinness with health. *I know better than that!*

I swear he's on the verge of tears as he looks past me for a moment, seeming to study the framed photo of Elliott and me on my dresser. When I take his hand, his eyes snap back to mine.

"Take all the time you need." I guide him to the bed, where he sinks into the mattress like his body is made of bricks.

"The type she has—I can't even remember what her sister said now, I was so shocked by all this—it's really rare. And the leading expert in treating it is in London. So that's why she's there. She's been undergoing chemo and radiation."

It's sad that the first thing I think of is all that beautiful hair...gone. *Oh, poor Anita.* He is really going to have to change that Darth Vader ringtone now.

"She had a bad reaction to the last round of chemo, and she's been in the hospital for a couple of days. That's why Camellia called. She said she couldn't keep up the ruse any longer. She felt like I should know."

"Oh my god, Jack, this is horrible. What are we supposed to do about Mariana?"

He shakes his head and stares off across the room again. "I don't know. Nothing yet."

"Well, you know I support your decision no matter what. Do we need to take Mariana to London to see her? Is it that dire?"

"I don't know yet," Jack says. "But if I win this contest, or place in the top ten, I'm going to have to drop out. I can't go on tour. Not with this going on."

I wrap my arm around his shoulder and squeeze him to my body. "In your immortal words, 'let's cross that bridge when we come to it,' okay? There's no sense in deciding that now until a) we know if you won and b) we know Anita's prognosis. The tour is only for six weeks. I'm sure I can manage with Mariana myself while you're gone. Or if I need to take her to London…I have a passport. I can do that."

"Claire, you have a book to write," he reminds me.

"I know. And I'm almost done, I swear." I force a smile because I am at best halfway, but the words have really been flowing lately. I just hope my muse sticks around.

He stands up and pulls me to stand next to him before he sweeps me into his strong embrace. "Claire, you are a good woman." He kisses the top of my head. "You're so amazing. What did I do to deserve you?"

When he pulls back, he lifts my chin up so he can press his lips against mine, shooting warmth throughout my body. I taste the tear that slipped down his cheek, and I don't know if it's because of Anita, Mariana, or me, but it doesn't matter. I want to take care of him. I want to ease his pain.

"I just love you, Jack. I'd do anything for you," I whisper as I break our kiss.

"I love you too, baby," he whispers back before claiming my lips again.

Suddenly, we hear an emphatic, disgusted "EWWWW!" echo through the cracked-open door, making us both jump.

We have a spy.

A cute one with long brown braids.

Poor baby. She has no idea what's going on.

She bursts in singing, "Daddy and Miss Claire, sitting in a tree. K-I-S-S-I-N-G!" She runs up to her dad and pulls on his pant leg, and he scoops her up into his arms. "First comes love… Then comes marriage," she continues. Then a little frown curls her lips. "Are you guys gonna get married?"

Out of the mouths of babes, am I right?

Jack grins and presses a kiss to his daughter's cheek. "Maybe someday!" He grabs my hand and pulls me close so she and I are both wrapped in his warm embrace. I feel safe and content for now…but the future is looming over us even more shadowy and uncertain than before.

This week!

It's been so crazy, I don't know if I need a Xanax, a barf bag, or a celebratory cocktail with a little paper umbrella. I might need all three before it's said and done. Because it's not over yet—far from it, in fact.

We just crossed the Chesapeake Bay Bridge to head back to DC for the contest results. The band is caravanning behind me in a couple different cars, including Sam's Suburban, which is big enough for Luke's drum set. I haven't told any of them about my ex-wife's medical situation. Camellia actually swore me to secrecy and said Anita didn't know she was calling. But of course I told Claire. That's a given.

An hour and a half later, after dealing with the typical beltway and DC traffic, we park in the Kennedy Center garage and make our way inside the venue as a big group. I'm trying not to think too far ahead, but the main thing I've been telling myself is that it would actually be better for me if I don't win. Well, maybe not better for *me*. But it would be better for Mariana, better for Claire, and better for Anita. I would feel selfish for even wanting to win or go on tour at this point.

If I do win, or place in the top ten, it doesn't mean I have to go on tour. I could accept my prize, which I believe comes with some cash if you place, and then decline the tour invitation. I'm sure they could take the number eleven spot in my place. So, if I do get to reprise "Firecracker" tonight on stage, I need to really make it count.

At least I'll still have the gigs I've booked the band for the rest of the summer. We have at least four performances on our calendar. That will have to quench my newfound thirst for the limelight.

We settle into one long row at the Kennedy Center that they've blocked off for contestants. The curtains are drawn, and I feel a little uneasy being in the audience instead of backstage waiting for the lights to come up. Sure, it's nerve-racking as all get out counting down the minutes and seconds till your cue, but at least you have some control. You still have the power at that point—the power to perform to the very best of your abilities and win the audience's hearts. Sitting out here is passive. Now it's all in their hands, the directors and producers, the Support Art Foundation and their bigwigs.

The music starts up precisely at eight PM, and Brenda Monnett, the national director of the foundation, swoops out onto the stage in an elegant black evening gown. She has platinum-blond hair and nearly iridescent skin, and she's glowing with excitement as she waves a thick square envelope with a gold seal in her hands. We're close enough to see it. My future hinges on what's in that envelope.

I have to admit to zoning out a bit as the screen comes down to show a montage of the regional competitions and little bios with each of the twenty-four contestants. Everyone claps and cheers when it's over. From what I understand, they'll announce the ten winners first, and then we'll go backstage at intermission to get set up for our performances.

"And now the moment you've all been waiting anxiously for," Mrs. Monnett says as she scans the crowd, her smile never faltering. She takes the envelope and breaks the seal, her fingers trembling just a little as she opens the card and holds it out to see. Looks like she forgot her reading glasses.

"As I call your name, please make your way to the stage to accept your trophy!" she instructs as two assistants wheel out a cart gleaming with ten golden trophies. "Oh, before I announce the winners, I should first say that we raised over one million dollars for the Support Art Foundation just in audience votes alone over the past two days. That's right, our twenty-four contestants garnered well over one million votes between them, and I can tell you that our winning contestant brought in over 200,000 votes him- or herself. Ooooh, you thought I'd give it away, didn't you?" Her laugh sparkles like the chandeliers hanging over our heads.

There's a drumroll as she straightens the card out in front of her again. She clears her throat and stares at it a little harder, moving it closer and then farther away again.

Oh my god, could she delay this any longer? We're all dying here. Claire is gripping my hand so tight, I think she's about to cut off my circulation!

"I'm so sorry! I seem to have forgotten my glasses, and I'm having a really hard time reading this font!" Mrs. Monnett apologizes, her voice dripping with embarrassment.

I knew it!

A man in a tuxedo rushes out on stage with a tiny case, and when he opens it, Mrs. Monnett reaches in and snatches out a pair of glasses on a long gold chain. "Thank you, Toby," she whispers, but the microphone picks it up anyway.

"Now where were we?" She turns a sheepish smile toward the audience and repositions the card again. "Number ten in our Support Art Foundation Superstar national contest, and eligible for the six-week US tour we'll be embarking upon next month is…" *drumroll again…* "Byron Benson!"

A young man with dark skin and blond dreads leaps out of his seat in the row in front of us and bounds up to the stage. He couldn't be more than eighteen or nineteen, and he has a lot of energy. His smile reveals a mouthful of bright white teeth as he takes the trophy and nods his thanks to the crowd.

"Thank you, Byron," Mrs. Monnett continues, and one of the assistants ushers Byron to a spot on the stage marked with a reflective X. "Next up…number nine, we have Amber Acevito!"

A beautiful young woman with long, wavy highlighted brown hair squeals in the row across the aisle from us, clasping her hands over her mouth in surprise. She carefully teeters on her silver stilettos to the stage to accept the trophy and her spot next to Byron.

"Number eight is Talia McBride! Come on up, Talia!"

Mrs. Monnett continues through her announcements, getting through number seven, number six and number five, and despite having convinced myself I'd be better off not winning, my heart is sinking to the pit of my stomach. I'm sure I didn't make it. Number five, Starr Stevens, was the jazz singer who blew me away. I have a hard time believing I'd get more votes than her.

"Number four is Nick Adebayo," Mrs. Monnett continues. "Congratulations, Nick!"

The young man rushes up on the stage and murmurs his thank yous close enough to Mrs. Monnett's microphone that I can make out his African accent. I'm not sure what country he's from, but he's smiling so brightly, I'm sure they can see his grin all the way from his homeland.

I've resigned myself to the fact that I haven't made it. It's okay. It's all good. I had a ton of fun; I got to meet some really cool people. It was still the experience of a lifetime. This will make things so much easier for me, for Claire, for Mariana. That's what really matters—

"Jack?" Claire shakes my leg.

I'm still ruminating when she grabs ahold of my shoulder. "That's you! Get up there!"

What?

My entire body is vibrating with shock, and my heart that was in my stomach has now shot up to my throat. "She called my name?"

"Yes, Daddy!" Mariana is repeatedly slapping my leg on the other side. "Go up on stage, Daddy!"

Everyone turns around, gaping at me when I stand and work my way through the long row of connected seats. I feel like I'm wading through molasses, both mentally and physically, as I exit the row and make the short trek up the aisle to the stairs leading up to the stage.

"Congratulations, Jack!" Mrs. Monnett beams, and the assistant offers me a trophy that feels like a lead weight in my hands before I'm ushered over to stand next to Nick.

Mrs. Monnett calls Xia Lee to the stage for the second spot, and my ears are now ringing with the applause and my own heartbeat. My blood is rushing through my veins so fast, I feel like I'm on the verge of throwing up or passing out. I finally snap to when the director calls the grand winner, the Number One, and the Support Art Foundation National Superstar.

"Our top spot goes to…Bonnie Scott!"

The crowd noise is almost deafening as the woman I'd met backstage with the lacy skirt and layered necklaces appears from the third row. Tonight she's wearing a short red dress that hugs her figure, and her long, golden hair is swept into a classy updo held by a rhinestone clip. She looks just about as shocked as I probably did a few minutes ago.

Once she takes her spot next to Xia and two spaces down from me, I just stand there absorbing the sounds of cheering and applause, whistles and human air horns (*thanks, Drew*) as it all sinks in.

AFTER THE SEVEN other artists who placed behind me perform their reprise, the band and I head out in the darkness to find our marks on the stage. The lights come up, and I can honestly say I've never felt less nervous to perform before. Now that I already know my fate, a huge weight is lifted from my chest. I'll decline the tour invitation, but just knowing I placed third is an astounding accomplishment. And I'm going to enjoy this performance on a national stage to the fullest.

Nothing like going out on a high note!

14

I don't even remember climbing into bed last night. Things here have been crazy! We got home from DC around two in the morning, and Mariana zonked out as soon as we buckled her into her booster seat. The fact that she's still asleep now when it's eight AM is unprecedented.

I roll over toward Jack, whose back is facing me, and trail three kisses across his shoulder. He stirs just slightly and moans, "Good morning."

"Hey, sleepyhead. Mariana's still asleep…"

"Good. Then we should be too…"

"You don't want to celebrate your achievement last night?" I follow that up with a few more strategically placed kisses.

"I do…" he groans, "but you know what sounds even better?"

"What's that?" I find it hard to believe anything sounds better than morning sex.

He cuddles up against me and rests his head on my ample chest. "Sleeping right here on these magnificent pillows. Mmmm…this is heaven."

As flattering as that is, it isn't exactly what I had in mind. But I guess we've only had six hours of sleep, and he probably needs one or two more to really *rise* to the occasion. I try not to show my disappointment in my sigh, but I'm pretty sure it bleeds through anyway.

"I need to get my fill of you before you leave for six weeks," I remind him, my fingers grazing down his thick mat of chest hair.

He shoots straight up in bed. "I'm not going."

"What? Why not?" I sit up next to him so we're both leaning against my padded headboard. "Why wouldn't you go? I told you I'd help with Mariana, and I'm sure your mother would come help too if you asked her."

He sighs and looks down at his hands, which he folds together on top of the sheet. "I don't feel right about going. Not with what's going on with Anita…or having to burden you with Mariana for that long while you're trying to finish your book."

"Jack…" My voice trails off as I try to formulate my rebuttal. "I already told you I'm happy to do it. What, don't you trust me with her?"

He scoffs, "Of course I do. This has nothing to do with trust. It's more that I feel obligated to stay here. My responsibility is to my daughter."

I grab his hand in mine and squeeze it tight. "What if this is your only opportunity to make a career out of performing? It's not like someone's going to waltz into your classroom at the Delmarva Academy and say, 'so, hey, do you want a record deal? We just happen to have a few extras lying around.' What if this sets you and Mariana up for your entire future?"

I want to say "us"—sets "us" up for our future, but I can't get my lips to make that word. I don't know if there's going to be an "us" after all of this is said and done—what if he goes on tour, and he doesn't miss me? What if he falls out of love with me?

What if he becomes a rock star, and an older, divorced, plus-size writer no longer seems like a good fit?

Still, I can't stand in the way of his dream. I pushed him into this silly contest in the first place, and I'd feel horrible if he didn't see it through as far as he could go. The sky could be the limit...but he won't know unless he goes on tour.

"What if Anita gets worse while I'm gone?"

"Why don't you just call and talk to her about it?" I urge him.

"Oh, right...because she's always been *soooo* reasonable." He scoffs again and shakes his head. "Plus, I don't even know if she's home from the hospital yet. Camellia said she'd update us, but we haven't heard from her yet."

"What does she know about this contest, anyway?" I press. This is a question he's skirted before, and this time, this time I need to know the answer.

He's silent for a moment. *Too long.*

"She doesn't know about it?" I guess.

Ugh. How could he not even tell her? He knew it was a possibility that he'd be asked to go on tour the whole time.

"She never supported my music," he explains. "She didn't even like me to play the guitar, and I could have never gone back to school for my music degree if I'd stayed married to her. She was just about as supportive as my parents—which is basically not at all."

"Maybe it will be different this time," I suggest. "You know, now that you have a real chance of making a name for yourself." I take his hands, both this time, into mine. "Jack...you placed in the top three of a *nationwide* contest. It's like you don't even realize what that means!"

"What does it mean, Claire?" He sounds exasperated for no good reason.

"It means you have fans!" my voice rises. "People loved your music enough to pay money to vote for you. Brenda Monnett said the top person had over 200,000 votes. You probably had close to that many at number three. That's 200,000 people who would potentially buy your album or pay to see you perform live."

He clears his throat and looks back down at his hands again. "I don't know, Claire."

"Will you please talk to Anita?"

When he's still silent, refusing to make any promises, I try another angle. "When do you have to let them know?"

He swings his legs over the edge of the bed and plants his feet on the rug. I guess I'm definitely not getting laid this morning. That pretty much sealed the deal right there.

"I think they just assume everyone will want to go. The tour coordinator is supposed to call us all this week to tell us the arrangements. It starts in two weeks, so there's not much time."

"There's time for you to talk to Anita and to fly across the pond for Mariana to visit with her." I stand up too, feeling an immediate pain shoot through my feet from wearing heels last night to the awards ceremony. *Ugh, great choice, Claire.*

"I'm not sure if I'm in a financial position to just hop across the pond right now," he tells me, his tone clipped. "I am a teacher, you know. I'm not exactly swimming in cash."

"I can help out with that," I offer. "I have some money set aside from my divorce settlement. And besides, I'd love to go to London!"

He starts to leave the room without saying a word.

151

"Jack, please don't close me out!" I follow him into the hall. "Just tell me you'll think about it."

He turns to face me and holds out his arms to me. I fall against his chest, feeling the warmth of his body soak into my skin. As his arms wrap around me, he promises, "I'll think about it."

The phone sat in my hand for several minutes before I worked up the courage to call. I'd finally admitted the truth to Claire: I hadn't told Anita yet about the contest. And now she's sick, and I don't feel like I should tell her at all.

I never thought in a million years I'd actually be invited to go on tour with a national singing competition. I never thought in a million years there'd be an actual chance I could pursue a lifelong dream, even if it was one I've always been too chicken to go after.

But Claire is right—this could be a golden ticket for me. Mrs. Monnett could be Willie Wonka. If I somehow did make an album and earned some money from this whole crazy rollercoaster, it could make a huge difference in my life, and in my daughter's—and in Claire's.

I love Claire, and I do want to marry her, but let's face it, a writer and a teacher aren't destined for wealth. What if we want to travel? What if we want to send Elliott and Mariana to the best schools? What if we wanted to have a baby of our own someday…together? I know the window is closing on that, but hey, if I'm gonna dream, I might as well go big or go home, right?

And I hate, hate, hate that this is even crossing my mind, but—

Mariana has been raised in affluence. I saw the size of Anita's house. I don't know exactly what she does, but apparently it's lucrative enough to pay for that house and for her to take a year off to treat her illness in London. If, God forbid, something were to happen to Anita, I will be supporting our daughter on my income alone.

Don't I owe it to everyone to make the most of this once-in-a-lifetime opportunity?

Then again, if Anita says no, she doesn't want me going on tour, I will concede. I will let them know I can't make it. But the first step is calling and finding out what's going on and what she thinks. I just hope she's well enough to talk.

I press the button for her name and wait for it to connect an ocean away in the UK. It rings four times, and just when I think her voicemail is about to pick it up, I hear, "Hello?"

"Hey, how are you feeling?" I immediately notice how weak she sounds. I was in love with her a lifetime ago, and she's been a thorn in my side for almost as long now as we were together, but I still care about her. I still want her to be healthy and happy. She's the mother of my child.

"Jack…" she warbles. I've never heard her sound like that before. "Sorry, I'm froggy…I was intubated. My throat is kinda raw."

I muster all my strength to get my voice to sound normal. "I'm so sorry to hear what's been going on."

"Yeah, right," she retorts, but it's a lighthearted one. "I wasn't very happy when I found out Camellia called you."

"I bet." Anita has always been a control freak. I'm sure she either wanted to keep me in the dark forever or at least tell me on her own terms.

"I thought I was getting better—that the treatments were working." She coughs, then clears her throat. "But then this last round of chemo, my body just shut down. Dr. Richter said I have to take a break and let myself recover before continuing."

"I don't even know what to say, Anita. I'm so sorry." I try to bite back the stinging tears when a mental image of me having to tell Mariana that her mother is sick flashes behind my eyelids. "What's the…you know…prognosis?" I can barely get the word out of my mouth.

"I haven't had another full scan since I got here," she says. "They wanted to wait until this round was over. I'll know more after that. Typically, this cancer has a sixty percent cure rate, and Dr. Richter's patients are up to seventy-five percent. That's why he's the best. That's why I'm here."

"Why didn't you just tell me the truth?"

There's silence for a moment, and I think she may be biting back her own tears. "I just didn't want you to worry about me, or, god forbid, for Mariana to worry."

I nod, even though she can't see me. "What were you going to do if I said I didn't want to keep her this year?"

"Oh, come on, Jack, I know how much you love her," she chokes out. "I may act like you're not a mainstay in her life, but I know you're a great father and want to be there for her."

I am pretty sure that is the single nicest thing to ever come out of Anita's mouth. And, with that, a rogue tear slips down my cheek. "What can I do for you? Do you want to see her?"

She doesn't hesitate to answer, "No…" I hear a sharp breath whistle down the line. "I don't want her to see me like this, Jack. Maybe in a couple of months. I was hoping

I'd be well enough to travel in September for her birthday…"

"I will bring her to you if I have to," I offer. Though, obviously, I can't do that if I'm still on tour.

Her voice gathers some strength. "So what's this I hear about you competing in some singing contest?"

"What? You know about that?" Of course she does. She always knows everything. "How did you find out?"

"I'm in London, Jack. I'm not on a different planet. We have news here, and television too, believe it or not." Now there's the snark I always expect from my ex-wife. "I watched you on TV the other night."

"You did?" You could literally knock me over with a feather right now.

"Yeah, I was on some pretty high-powered drugs, and at first I thought I was hallucinating, but Camellia assured me it was really you." She manages to laugh, though it comes out more like a squeak.

"Yeah, so about that…"

"Do you get some prize money or something?" She's never been one to beat around the bush. "Didn't you place like third or something?"

"Yeah, I won a little money, but the biggest prize—because it's a charity event—is going on a national tour and having a chance at a record deal," I explain.

"Oh, well, that's pretty exciting too!" And that actually sounded sincere, which is not a tone I'm used to from my ex. It's almost like she's speaking a foreign language. "So when do you leave?"

"What do you mean? I'm not actually going to go," I fire back.

"What?" She laughs in disbelief. "Why not? It's summer…you don't have to teach."

"I don't have to teach, but I'm taking care of Mariana. I promised I would."

"Oh, Jack. I can send Camellia there, or you can take her to my mom's in Texas. Or, doesn't Claire work from home?" she suggests.

I can hardly believe I'm hearing this from her. I expected her to be angry that I didn't tell her, first of all. Then I expected her to rip me a new one for even considering abandoning our child for the duration of the tour.

"Camellia is taking care of you," I argue. "And your parents are old. You know they don't watch her that closely, and they live right on that busy road, and their neighbors have a pool, and they have that mean dog—"

Coming up with a lot of excuses is a special power of mine.

"So, have you talked to Claire about it, then?" she asks. "Surely you're not really considering missing out on this opportunity, Jack. What if you become an honest-to-god rock star?"

My voice goes soft: "I really didn't think you'd be supportive of this, Anita."

She's quiet for a moment, maybe collecting her thoughts. I used to say, when she had these quiet moments, she was gathering up her evil and figuring out how to make the deepest cut, the sharpest stab.

But then she says this: "Having cancer kind of changes your outlook on things, you know? Life is short…and fragile. You should always say yes to anything that might bring you fame, fortune, or happiness. And it sounds like this tour could bring you all of the above."

"I'll think about it…" It's the same answer I gave Claire about calling Anita.

"Don't think too long—you don't want to miss out. Does Claire not want to take care of Mariana?"

"We haven't discussed it at length because I didn't think I was going to do the tour, but she did offer to help in whatever way I need," I share.

I know she will take good care of my girl, though. I'm not worried about that; I'm more worried about being the reason she doesn't get her book to her editor on time. I don't want her to lose a publishing deal because of me. What good is chasing my dream if she fails to reach hers?

"Well, you two discuss it, and let me know what you decide. I am willing to send Camellia to you if need be. I really want you to do this, Jack," she says, sounding earnest once again. "You deserve it."

I never thought I'd hear my ex telling me I deserved anything good.

But I also never thought I'd be going on tour with the top ten singers in a national competition.

I FIND Claire working at her computer and just stand behind her, studying her for a moment. Her auburn hair, which has grown a lot since I first met her, is piled into a messy bun on top of her head, but a few loose strands are curling against her neck. Her freckled shoulders are exposed in the lavender tank top she's wearing. When her head tilts and she leans toward her screen, I clear my throat.

I hate disturbing her while she's writing, but she's just adorable so absorbed in her work. She reads a few lines of text, lips moving, and then her fingers click-clack away at the keys like she didn't hear me. Like she has no idea I'm standing right behind her.

Suddenly, her head whips to the right, and she looks at

me over her shoulder. "What are you doing back there, creeper?"

I lift my hands, palms out. "Just watching you work. I didn't want to interrupt."

"So you thought you'd stare at me like a weirdo? Yeah, that's not disruptive at all." She sighs and stands up, stretching her arms high above her head. When she lowers them, her full breasts bounce, catching my eye.

"I spoke with Anita." I leave it at that, gauging her expression to see how she feels about it. I was worried about confronting my ex-wife, of course, but I'm also worried about saddling Claire with my kid while I go on tour. She said she doesn't mind, but—

"Oh, yeah? And what did Darth Anita have to say about the tour?" She giggles. "Sorry, I shouldn't call her that. She's sick."

"She's all for it." I shrug.

"Wow, well, that's great," she says, but there's no enthusiasm in her words. She steps closer to me. "So, it's settled. You're going." It's a statement, not a question.

I reach out and take her hand, pulling her right into my body. She got some sun when we were at the beach earlier, and her usually pale skin is slightly pink. I can feel heat radiating off her, and, breathing in, I pick up the lingering scent of suntan lotion.

"I need to make sure you're really okay for Mariana to stay here with you," I state. It won't be settled until I'm sure she's on board. And not just because she feels obligated.

"It's really okay. I wouldn't offer if I didn't want to keep her. Jack, she's a lovely little girl. She's sweet and funny and precocious—and I'm having fun with her. Anita really said it was okay for her to stay here?"

I nod. "She offered to send Camellia here, or she said

we could send her to her parents' house in Texas, but I think we both know having her stay with you is the wisest, best choice."

Claire's cheeks slightly flush as her blue gaze pierces into me. "I'm flattered."

"I know it's only six weeks, but that's a long time when you're five."

"I know, but it's summer, and there's a lot to do. Story time at the library. Farmer's market on the weekends. The boardwalk, the beach, the state fair is coming soon…"

"You're absolutely sure it won't interfere with your book deadline?" My eyes drill into hers, looking for any hint of dishonesty.

"I'm absolutely sure."

I can't stop the smile that involuntarily spreads my lips. "Well, then I guess it *is* settled. I'm going on tour."

"I'm so proud of you, Jack." She lifts up on her tiptoes to plant a kiss on my cheek. "This is going to be such an incredible opportunity—"

Even though she doesn't say the word "but," I sense it. There's the slightest reticence on her face, in her words. "What is it?" I wrap my arms around her waist and lean in to whisper in her ear, "Tell me what you're thinking. Don't hide from me."

She sighs and pulls back to look at me again. "It's my old demons…my old insecure demons playing tricks on me," she admits. "The ones that have stuck around after Jeremy, even though I've worked so hard to exorcise them."

"And what demons are those?"

"The ones that tell me I'm not good enough for you." She looks down at her bare feet for a moment, and my eyes follow. Her toenails are painted a glittery blue. "And that if you go on tour and become famous…well, why would you stick with me?"

I wince. I hate that this golden opportunity we keep talking about is triggering her. I know how hard she has worked to become the confident, poised, self-assured woman I've fallen in love with. I know how her ex hurt her. I know how her own family fat-shamed her. I know about her eating disorder recovery, and all the therapy and the growth and progress she's made.

"Sometimes I think *I'm* not good enough for *you*, Claire," I admit.

Her head springs up and she stares at me, speechless.

I smile when I see her incredulous response. "It's true. You're so brilliant, so absolutely lovely, Claire. Sometimes it surprises me that you have no clue how much joy you bring to other people. How much meaning and depth and light to the lives of those you touch." I bring her hand to my lips and press a kiss to it. "This tour might change some things, but it won't change how much I love you. And that's a promise."

She smiles and nods. "Then it's settled."

I claim her lips with my own, then murmur against them, "You're mine now, and you'll be just as much mine in six weeks."

15

I don't know why I'm so nervous now. I've already secured my place on the tour; this is just a formality. I smile at the receptionist as she ushers me back to the Support Art Foundation executive offices. I met Brenda Monnett that first night in Washington, DC, but now I'll be meeting with her and the folks heading up the tour.

"Jack, welcome!" she gushes warmly, taking my one hand into both of hers, which are almost translucent and crisscrossed with turquoise veins. She gives me a firm shake before she gestures toward one of the empty chairs in the sitting area by the windows that overlook the downtown area of the nation's capital.

"I'm so happy to be here." I'm all grins and can-do attitude as I try to relax in one of the leather chairs.

"We're absolutely thrilled that a music teacher won a spot on our national tour," Mrs. Monnett begins. "You really embody the essence of our foundation. We're all about supporting the arts in education and in the community, and we know you are too. We'd love nothing more than to get your music out there so people can see what arts education can lead to."

"I'm thrilled too!" I assure everyone in the room, nodding and smiling in sync with Mrs. Monnett and her co-conspirators.

"I'm Courtney Dawson, the tour coordinator," a petite blonde to my right says, stretching her hand out for me to shake.

I bow my head in acknowledgment. "Nice to meet you, Courtney."

"And I'm Garvey Child, the tour's musical director. We'll be working closely together to build our stage show, starting with rehearsals next week," says the tall man with ochre skin and a closely cropped afro.

"I'm looking forward to working with you, Garvey." I shake his hand as well.

"I'm going to let Courtney tell you a little bit about tour logistics, and then, if you have any questions, we want to hear them. We want to make sure you leave this room feeling comfortable and excited about the rest of the summer," Mrs. Monnett explains.

Everyone is so nice and positive. I feel like I lucked out to be working with such a great group of people. Just the atmosphere and their demeanors are immediately putting my mind at ease.

"The tour will be six weeks long, and in that time, we'll visit twenty cities, so that's about a city every other day. I know it's a rigorous schedule, and this is our first time doing a contest of this magnitude, so we don't really know how feasible the pace is. We just assumed people wouldn't want to spend their entire summers or the rest of the year touring when many of you have families and jobs—"

"—though you might have a whole new job by the end of the tour!" Garvey interjects.

My face must register my surprise, because Mrs. Monnett clarifies, "You may be signing a record deal before the tour is over. We know several recording labels that are interested in our talent, and we expect them to be attending our concerts and deciding who has that, you know, X Factor everyone is always looking for."

"Our tour starts here on the East Coast, heading south to Charlotte, North Carolina, and Orlando, Florida—that concert is actually at a certain theme park you may have heard of."

My heart leaps. I've always wanted to take Mariana. Maybe Claire can meet us there—even if it's only for a day or two.

"That sounds great. What else do I need to know?" I'm so excited, my lungs feel like I can't empty them of air fast enough. My whole chest is puffed out.

"Not much, really," Garvey answers. "There will be two rehearsals here in DC next week, and then we'll leave the next day. I know that doesn't give you a lot of time to prepare, but we're anxious to get out on the road."

"Will we be driving or flying?" I question.

"We have buses arranged for the East Coast cities. I believe there's one, or possibly two legs that would be cutting it close on buses, so we'll be chartering flights for those shows," Courtney explains.

I nod, my excitement still growing. "And my band? What do they need to do?"

The guys are as pumped about this as I am, even if they aren't center stage.

"Oh," Garvey's previously shining face falls, "you won't be able to bring your band along. We'll have a band that tours with us."

It's like a stab to my gut. Ever since I decided I was actually going to do this, the one thing I was looking forward to was having my guys to hang out with. I know I called them all misfits, and that's how we got our band name, but they've really grown on me the past couple of months since we've been rehearsing seriously. I can hardly imagine doing this without them.

"That's too bad. They're all really good musicians." I try to keep my tone upbeat, but I can't disguise my disappointment.

"If you do get a record contract," Mrs. Monnett pipes up, "you can always negotiate to use your own band."

"That's true." I nod, forcing my lips into a smile.

"Do you have other questions?" Courtney asks.

I should have made a list, but at the moment I'm drawing a blank. "I'm sure I'll think of something as soon as I walk away."

"It's fine," Courtney assures me, a warm smile reaching her hazel eyes. "You can call me anytime. Here's my card." She hands me a business card, and Garvey follows suit.

"We're really looking forward to working with you, Jack." He stands and offers his hand again to shake.

Once I've expressed my gratitude and anticipation for the tour and shaken hands all around, I head back down the hall. I can't believe I just drove two hours to DC for a twenty-minute meeting. But I bet it won't be the craziest thing I do in the next few weeks…

I'VE THOUGHT the entire drive home about how to break it to the guys that they won't be joining me on the road. Ice cream and beer were both on the list of possible consolation prizes, but then I realized they're grown men, and they're just going to have to get over it. After all, like Mrs. Monnett said, they might be able to accompany me on any solo album I cut a deal for.

I pull into Sam's driveway, where we're all meeting up for practice, and the first thing I notice is that everyone beat me. They're all there on time. We have grown so much as a band in the past few months. In the beginning, I always showed up on time and had to wait for everyone else to trickle in.

"Hey, guys!" I greet everyone as I head into Sam's garage. They're all in place with their instruments, ready to go. Also a welcome change from the past, where we all seemed to goof off for at least thirty minutes before getting down to business.

Everything's coming together with them—we have another gig this weekend—and then I'm gone for six weeks. I guess that means I either have to cancel the rest of our remaining gigs, reschedule them, or they'll perform without me, and Drew will sing lead.

"How'd it go today?" Luke asks, sitting with his drumsticks in one hand.

"Good, really good." I wonder if we can get a few songs in before I break the news to them.

"So, will we need to reschedule our other shows while we're on tour?" Drew asks.

Look at him being all responsible!

Also, he's not going to like what I have to say. How could I stall a little bit longer?

"Well, that's a good question." My gaze bounces from one bandmate to the next until I've made the full circle. "How do you guys feel about performing without me?"

"Why would we do that?" Russ chimes in.

I sit down on my designated stool and pump my air full of lungs with a couple of sharp breaths. Then I'm going to just rip off the Band-Aid in one swift motion. "They won't let you guys come on tour with us."

"What?!" the four guys shout in unison. "Why the hell not?" Drew adds.

"They're using a house band, so everyone will have the same accompaniment. Besides, I think we're doing mostly group songs on this tour. It won't all be me singing solo. I don't know how they decide all that, but we're having a rehearsal next week, two actually, and then we're heading out on tour. We have a musical director, so I guess he makes all those decisions."

Luke rolls his eyes. "Well, that's not fair. We helped you place at Nationals!"

"I know," I don't hesitate to confirm. "I don't know if I could have done it without you. Especially 'Firecracker.' That song wouldn't be the same without you guys, which is why I sang a different one at the regional competition."

"Well, this blows," Drew spits out what everyone is thinking.

"Trust me, I'm not happy about it either. I really wanted us to share this experience together and come back an even better, stronger band." My tone brightens as I remember the consolation. "Here's the good news, though: if I get a record deal, I can negotiate bringing my own band on board."

"Well, it better be an all or nothing thing," Drew fires back, his volume rising. "If they don't want us, they don't get you. Simple as that."

"Alright," I agree. "All or nothing."

We practice a few songs, and then Sam's wife comes out to say they're having company, and we all need to skedaddle. I wasn't pleased with how it all went, but there's not much I can do now. We'll have to pick up where we left off when I return in six weeks.

Drew pats me on the back as we walk to our cars. "Look, sorry I got upset earlier."

"No, man, it's okay. I get it." I smile at him, trying to show there are no hard feelings.

"I'm disappointed—understandably so. But I really do wish you the best out there, bro. Make us proud, okay?"

My smile can't be contained as I give him a man hug and promise, "I will."

WHEN WE ASKED Mariana what she wanted for a special dinner to celebrate her daddy's performance at the competition in Washington, DC, she said she wanted shrimp. There's no shortage of places to get shrimp in the Rehoboth Beach area, so we went to my favorite seafood restaurant. That's how parenting works, right?

"Hey, it's Mr. Reilly! Congrats on your win in the Superstar contest!" says the hostess before she escorts us through the restaurant.

"Thanks, Cassidy! It was a lot of fun." Jack bends down and whispers in my ear, "She's one of my former students."

A few servers saunter over to congratulate Jack on his victory. He really is a local celebrity now. We can't go anywhere without getting recognized.

And I'm not jealous. I promise. But… apparently having a column in *The New York Times* pales in comparison to being televised on national TV and having a frontpage story about yourself in the *Cape Gazette*, our local paper.

Still, super happy for Jack and not at all jealous.

Maybe if I ever finish writing this book, I'll be back in *The New York Times*, this time on the bestseller list, and then I'll get a frontpage story in the *Cape Gazette* too!

"But you didn't win, Daddy," Mariana points out as we all settle around the table.

"You're right, baby, I didn't win. I got third place, and I've been invited to tour with some of the other contestants for the rest of the summer. We're all going to get on a big bus and travel around the country putting on shows like the one we did in DC the other night," Jack explains.

Her eyes grow wider with every word he speaks, and I have to wonder which part has piqued her interest: the travel part, the show part, or the big bus part. "Oh! Can I come too?"

"Unfortunately, this trip is only for Daddy," he says in an appropriately disappointed tone. "I wish you could come, though." He shoots me a look that seems to say, *that would solve a lot of problems, huh?*

"Will Mommy be coming back to stay with me?" she asks with her long lashes fluttering. "I miss Mommy and Aunt Cammy, and you said I'd get to see her this summer."

It's been a while since Mariana has expressed home-sickness or cried for her mom. The first few weeks she was with us, it was a nightmare at times. But we've always been able to calm her down and remind her of all the times she was with Mommy for months without seeing Daddy. When we told her it was Daddy's turn to take care of her, she seemed to understand.

"Mommy can't come back right now," I tell her because I can sense Jack is getting choked up. Anita didn't want us to tell Mariana that she's sick. She's hoping she can fully recover and be in remission by the time she returns to the States.

"Can I go there? I know she's far away, but I could go on a big bus too maybe?"

Oh my god, she's breaking my heart, this little girl!

"No, sweetheart, it's too far for a bus. You have to cross the ocean," I explain.

"Well, if Daddy's gone, and Mommy isn't coming here, and I can't go there…" It all seems to sink in, and her eyes turn glassy with tears. "What happens to me?"

This may be the saddest conversation I've ever had with a child. I feel like she just shot arrows directly into my heart, so I can only imagine how Jack feels.

"You get to stay with me, kiddo!" I use the brightest, most positive voice ever. "You can be the Princess of Claire's Castle. How does that sound?"

"But I don't have a princess room at your house!" she whines.

"You can!" I assure her. "We can turn the guest room into your own princess room, just like your room at Daddy's." I fight the urge to facepalm myself for making that kind of promise, especially when I'm on such a tight writing schedule. But those big brown eyes are killing me! KILLING ME!

"Are you okay to stay with Claire?" Jack asks, and I shoot him a glare because he doesn't really have a choice at this point.

"I love Miss Claire," Mariana says. "She lets me have ice cream even when you say no."

Hey, I'm Pro Ice Cream, what can I say? I can think of worse things to indulge a kid in. I'm also Team Hot Fudge, Whipped Cream and Sprinkles.

"I'm going to miss you so much," Jack says as he puts his arm around her and pulls her closer to him.

The server comes by and drops off our appetizer, and Mariana doesn't say another word about Jack leaving. It's like once we told her how things were going to be, she was just like, *alright, bring it on.*

She's a resilient kid, that's for sure.

Claire

16

Jean-Marc knows me so well. He asked Mariana and me to meet him for ice cream right after we say goodbye to Jack. He is well aware I'm likely to be a mess. In the past, he would have recommended something with more of a kick than hot fudge—probably vodka—but now with Mariana in my care, I have to rethink a lot of things.

Jack has his guitar and suitcase in the foyer, ready to head out to the car that's been sent to pick him up. I guess he's extra special now because they don't want him driving —and there's also the problem of what to do with his car for six weeks.

He turns toward me with a smirk on his face. "I can't believe I'm actually leaving."

I can't tell if he's trying to subdue his true excitement levels for my benefit, or he's filled with trepidation, but I'm guessing it's a little of both.

"Don't go, Daddy!" Mariana cries out as she rushes into his arms.

He scoops her up and holds her tightly against his chest. "I'm going to miss you so much, Princess."

"Why do you have to go, Daddy?" She hasn't said a word about him leaving since the night we took her out for dinner to explain what was going to happen. But now the waterworks are on, and if Jack is feeling half the guilt I am at the moment, I know his heart is breaking.

"Daddy's going to be a rock star," I tell her. "And I bet he'll get you a special souvenir in each city he visits, right?"

He nods emphatically. "That's right. And I'm sure I'll see you at least once or twice during the tour."

I don't know how he plans to make that happen with the rigorous travel schedule they have, but I guess it's too late to address that now. I'm already telling myself I'm not going to see him for six weeks—so if it's sooner, I'll be pleasantly surprised.

"Here, take this," he says, handing me a white envelope.

"What is it?"

"Some cash, for taking care of my baby." His eyes urge me to take it without asking too many questions.

"I don't need it, Jack…"

"Please?" He smiles. "They're paying for everything. They even said there was no need to bring clothes. I'll have a wardrobe crew."

"Fancy," I snicker.

He sets Mariana back on the tiled floor and pulls me into his embrace. "I'm going to miss you, Claire."

"Don't let the fame change you, okay?" I plead with him. "Please come back the same Jack Reilly I fell in love with."

"I will," he says, choking back tears. "I promise." He presses a kiss to my lips, the most he can do with his daughter standing right there staring at us. He whispers in my ear, "I love you."

"I love you too. Now go break a leg!" I force a smile,

even though my eyes are stinging with my own tears.

"Break a leg?" Mariana shakes her head. "Please don't break your leg, Daddy!"

"It's an expression they use in show business," I explain, patting her head.

She purses her lips like she doesn't know whether or not to believe me. Jack bends down and kisses her cheek again before whispering something in her ear like, "Be good for Miss Claire," I think.

She bursts into tears and rushes into my arms when he turns to leave. And then, just like that, he's gone. I'm left dealing with the aftermath.

I don't even wait another second after I hear the trunk door slam shut, followed by the car door. "Put your shoes on. We're going to go get ice cream with Jean-Marc."

Her eyes light up, shining through the glistening tears. "We haven't had lunch yet!"

"I know! It's a special treat for being so brave when you said goodbye to your daddy. Then we'll take a walk on the beach and look for some shells, so put your swimsuit on and find your sandals, alright?"

Thirty minutes later, we're circling Rehoboth Avenue, trying to find parking. We manage to finally find a space a few blocks off the boardwalk, but at least we found one. Sometimes in the summer, there's not a space for miles. Jean-Marc texts to say he's already at the ice cream place.

We meet him there a few minutes later and buy Mariana a huge vanilla and chocolate twist cone with sprinkles on top, then we head out to the beach. It's going to be another scorcher, and even at eleven in the morning, the sand is filled with colorful umbrellas, towels, and even more colorful people.

"How's the ice cream, sweet girl?" Jean-Marc asks as we stroll along.

I glance down, and it's all around her mouth in a brown ring. *Lovely.* I'd forgotten the messy-face factor of little kids. It's going to take all my effort to keep that cute face clean for the next six weeks.

She marches a little ahead of us as we get to the shoreline, letting the waves ripple over her tiny brown toes with pink nails that I painted last week. Her long, wavy hair is blowing in the breeze and into her face, and into the ice cream, I think. Sigh. I should have tied her hair up. I've clearly never raised a little girl before. These are the things boy moms don't have to think about.

"I can't believe he's really gone," Jean-Marc says in a low voice so Mariana can't hear.

"I know. This whole thing is completely crazy…"

"How's her mom doing?" he whispers, the sound almost swallowed by the wind and pounding waves.

"She's doing better. Jack talked to her yesterday. She's really supportive of him going on this tour, though he suspects there are some ulterior motives. In any case…I'm glad she trusts me with her daughter."

"Why wouldn't she?" my bestie laughs. "You raised a kid almost to adulthood."

I roll my eyes, thinking of Elliott, who conned me out of forty bucks this morning. "Yeah, he seems so close, and yet so far away."

"Look, I know this has been a crazy summer, and you're still trying to finish your book. Then this dropped in your lap, and you couldn't say no. But I just want you to know to please, please ask for help if you need it, Claire. Okay?"

I turn to look at him, absorbing the sincerity in his eyes, which are usually filled to the brim with sarcasm.

"I can help. I'm sure your mom would help. Even your sister would probably help you out if you need it."

"Eliza? Nah, she's too busy with her own kids. Nora would be more likely to help, and she's two-plus hours away."

Jean-Marc gives me a sympathetic smile. "Jack's mom is going to come help out, isn't she?"

I nod. "Yeah, for a few days in a couple weeks, and then maybe in a few more weeks after that. She runs a nonprofit up in Wilmington, so she can't be gone that long at a time," I explain.

He stares out at the sea so he doesn't have to meet my gaze when he tells me, "I see. Well, my point is, we don't know if you need help unless you ask for it, and you're not particularly good at asking for it."

Sometimes it hurts how well this man knows me.

"Why don't we just assume that I need help?" I joke. "I always need help."

He squeezes my hand. "I'm here for you, girl."

"HEY, YOU," comes a female voice as I board the bus. It's Bonnie.

"Hey!" Her warm brown eyes are all lit up when I greet her.

She pats the seat next to her. "Here, sit next to me?"

"Sure." I slide in beside her, then take my phone out to put it on vibrate. I know it's going to be a long bus ride, so I might as well get some sleep.

I've spent the last three days getting to know everyone

on the tour, but Bonnie's been the one I've gravitated toward the most. Maybe we bonded during that wait backstage before Nationals, or maybe we just have more in common. She's a divorced, single mom, and her kid is in her ex's care back in Oregon. It seems like we are two of the older performers, so that might be another reason we've connected.

The set list we're working on is an eclectic mix of pop, rock, and country. I've never sang country before, but they have Bonnie and me singing lead on one of those songs together. It's a duet, I guess you'd call it. I sure hope the record producers don't get the wrong idea about what genre I sing, because I'm rock 'n roll all the way.

"It's not country," Bonnie had told me when I balked at the song choice. "It's folk. Big difference."

I'd rolled my eyes. "I know a twang when I hear it."

"If you're singing it, there doesn't have to be a twang," she teased me.

That conversation is still echoing in my head. I checked in on my girls last night when we were at the hotel in DC, telling them I was leaving for Charlotte in the morning. I wondered if Claire might want to bring Mariana to Orlando when I'm there later in the week, but she said it was early in the tour, and that place would be a madhouse since it's summer.

"Let's go in the off season as a family—when we have more time," she suggested.

Of course, being a teacher, there's really no way I can go in the off season, but I just bit my tongue. The last thing I wanted to do was fight or argue with her when the tour was just getting underway. I already miss them, and we haven't even really gotten started yet.

"What did the stylist say when you met with him?" Bonnie asks, breaking me out of my thoughts.

I glance up at her, the word "stylist" sounding like vocabulary from a foreign language at first. Then I realize she means Frank. Frank is the tour stylist, and he has pretty strong opinions about how we should all look. As hard as I'd tried to eradicate the emotional trauma my meeting with Frank inflicted upon me, the memory was still very fresh:

"You're trending very old with this look," he told me when I went to his makeshift office just a few doors down from my room. Support Art Foundation took over a whole floor of our hotel in downtown DC for the two days we rehearsed. That's probably the way it will be in every city we visit. There's no escaping these people, so I might as well decide I like them.

I tried to keep the smile plastered to my face and not take offense to Frank's assessment. "Well, I'm not exactly young."

His eyes continued to run all over my body, feeling like bugs creeping across my skin. "How old are you?"

"Thirty-four," I told him.

"That's not old!" He clutched at a fake pearl necklace. "Good heavens, son! I've got almost fifteen years on you."

He must have a good skincare routine is all I could think.

Huffing out a resolute sigh, he put his hands on his hips. "Well, we need to youthen you up, for one thing."

I am pretty sure "youthen" is not a word, but he's the stylist, not me. "What do you suggest?" I asked earnestly. *The man's just trying to do his job, right?*

"Take off your shirt," he instructed, his eyes dancing over me in a way that made me feel rather uncomfortable —what's one level below bugs crawling all over your skin?

"Why do you need—"

"Just take it off. I won't touch you." He rolled his eyes

at me as I pulled the garment over my head and tossed it on the desk next to us.

"Now turn," he directed, surveying the situation. "I'm not a fan of the whole hairy back thing, but I do like the tattoo on your arm. You don't have any others?"

The one on my arm is a tribal design a friend of mine sketched for me back when I worked in IT. "Not yet."

Frank's brows quirked. "Would you consider getting a few? And a good wax job." The last part was not a question. It was more of a statement.

Pretty sure getting waxed is not in my contract. "I don't understand what that has to do with the tour…"

"You'll have your shirt off on stage at some point," he sighed. "They all do."

"That's not really in my repertoire," I assured him.

"Look, you wanna be a rock star? Do you wanna get a record contract?" He stood right in front of me and drilled into my gaze with his beady brown eyes. "Then you need to look the part. You need to be commercially viable. So I'd recommend trimming the beard to a nice, sexy scruff, getting contacts, spending some time in the gym, waxing off all this chest hair—" he said it like I'm covered with leprosy, "—and cover up some of that pale skin with tattoos. Chicks dig tattoos. A lot of men do too."

I crossed my arms over my chest. "So, you're basically saying I need to look totally different."

His jaw clenched like he was exasperated when I didn't just immediately nod and agree. "Right now you look like a hipster barista who can't even land a date, let alone a record deal. Like the kind of guy who shows up at open mic and sings the worst kind of song he wrote himself."

"What is that supposed to mean? I *do* write my own songs," I scoffed.

"I'm talking about one of those lame unrequited love

songs. Or even worse, one that blames your parents for all your suffering in life." He copies my pose, folding his own arms over his chest.

I rolled my eyes hard enough to give me a headache. "I'll take what you said under advisement." Claire would probably dump me if I shaved off my beard. And she likes the nerdy lumberjack look.

"Jack?" Bonnie puts a golden-tan hand on the leg of my jeans, and her heat burns into my skin like she's made of stars.

"What? I'm sorry, I zoned out there for a moment." I offer her an apologetic smile. "I haven't slept well the last couple nights."

"What did Frank tell you about your style?"

"Oh, he suggested a few changes." I wave my hand as if to dismiss them all, then I glance over at her, raking my gaze down her body, which is comfortably sprawled in the gray bus seat. I can't imagine what Frank told her—what could he possibly want her to do to look more commercially viable? She's beautiful. "What about you?"

"He just wants me to wear more makeup," she sighs. "Ugh... I hate makeup."

I'm silent for a moment. Why are we never good enough as is? Someone always wants us to change. Maybe that's what I love most about Claire. She loves me for who I am while making me want to be even better. It's a fine line, but she skates down it gracefully—and she'd be the first to tell you she doesn't skate, and she's the polar opposite of graceful.

I miss her. I'm used to being away from Mariana, but of course I miss her too. I can't remember being apart from Claire for more than a night or two for almost a year now.

I should have proposed before I left.

Claire

17

Jack has been gone one week.

My heart aches, feeling like he took half of it with him. I've been FaceTiming with him every day, as has Mariana, but sometimes it only makes the *missing him* pangs worse. Then my mind runs through a variety of mindboggling questions and possibilities that could truly drive me insane if I let them fester.

Let me give you some examples:

-Why didn't he sing the proposal song to me before he left?

-What if I never hear this so-called proposal song?

-If Drew was lying about the existence of said song, I'm going to throat-punch that mother-effer.

-What if Jack isn't missing me as much as I'm missing him?

-What if he realizes I'm not all that?

-What if he becomes this famous rock star and figures out he could do so much better than me?

Now, I know I've come a long way in the past year or two, thanks to therapy and my body image coach. And I think writing the column for *The New York Times* on my reinvention—which was what I dubbed the period of time between my thirty-ninth and fortieth birthdays—taught me a lot about myself and helped me grow in so many remarkable ways. After all, I thought I was going to reinvent my body, but I learned my body is good and worthy of love just the way it is. The only thing that needed to be reinvented was my mindset.

Even after all that and writing a book about it so I can help more people with the same issues, I'm still human. I know, it's hard to believe I didn't sublimate into some higher being, but the truth is, I'm still the same old Claire Sterling, just with better self-esteem.

But no matter how much therapy you undergo, do you ever really, truly get over being bullied as a kid? I was bullied about my weight countless times—hell, even my own mother ridiculed me. Then my husband of almost twenty years cheated on me, so he obviously didn't think I was worth being faithful to. Those are the types of life events that leave scars—deep, everlasting scars. No matter how dramatically I transformed myself, those scars are still there.

Those ideas form the basis for the end of my book. Yes, I'm really writing the end today. I'm reminding my readers to be patient with themselves, that they wouldn't expect to change their bodies overnight, so why would they expect to change their minds that fast?

And I'm also reminding them that self-love isn't a switch that you pull, and then you never regress. It's a choice you need to make every day, and some days that choice is easier than others.

"You're worth it," I remind them. "You're worth other people's respect and love, but most of all, you're worthy of your own respect and love."

And with that, I stop typing and stare at the screen in disbelief. The window where I'm writing says 84,786 words in the bottom righthand corner. I just added the final ones.

My book is done.

Tears fill my eyes, making the screen and all my words blur as I realize the magnitude of this accomplishment. So many people try to write a book or want to write one, but so very few actually do, actually get to the point of THE END. But here I am. I did it.

I scan up the page, and the first thing that catches my eyes is a typo.

facepalm

Well, there's probably more where that one came from.

I want to share this moment with someone, and Jack is the first person who comes to mind. I'm about to pick up my phone to call him—he should be on the bus heading to New Orleans—when Mariana wanders into my office, which is actually just a corner of the living room I have set up with my desk and computer. This is what she does when she wants a snack or she gets bored.

"Hi, whatcha doing?" She studies me with her thick-lashed chocolate eyes. "Why are you crying, Miss Claire?"

I gulp down a breath and wipe my tears away with the back of my hand. "I just finished my book!"

"You did?" She launches herself into my lap. We've been having lots of discussions about why I need quiet to write my book, so she knows how big of a deal this is. "Yay! Good job!"

"Thank you, sweet girl. I was about to call your daddy and tell him, okay?"

I start to reach for the phone again, but it starts ringing. "Oh! Maybe he's calling me?" I flash her a silly smile, and she laughs as I pick it up and press answer.

"Ms. Sterling?" comes a woman's voice.

How does your heart know to kick into a racing beat

from two words? Mine sure did. I feel like it might thump right out of my chest cavity as I answer, "Yes, this is she."

"Hi there, I'm Karma. I'm one of the nurses in the emergency department—"

"Oh my god," I gasp. "What happened?"

"No need to panic. Your son, Elliott, was brought in just a few minutes ago, and he's going to be okay, but—"

"Oh my god, what happened?" I repeat. *Just tell me what happened to my son, lady!*

"It was pedestrian versus bike over on the boardwalk, and he's got some scrapes, cuts, and contusions. Possible broken bones. He's back having a scan right now, but he wanted me to call and tell you not to panic."

"Well, it's too freaking late for that!" I fire back. I'm a mother, for crying out loud. Panic over trips to the ER is in my job description.

"Can you come down here? We need you to fill out some paperwork, and we'll need your insurance cards."

Of course, they don't really care about my son—they just want their damn insurance money. I roll my eyes as I look down at Mariana, who is peering up at me with the most adorable worried look on her face.

What am I going to do with her? I won't have anyone to wait with her, and I doubt they'll let her go back and see Elliott since she's not family. I wish Jack's mom was closer.

"Ms. Sterling?" Karma the Nurse repeats.

"Yeah, I'll figure it out. I'll be there as soon as I can." I hang up the phone.

Well, so much for that celebratory glass of wine I was thinking of having right in the middle of the day—how decadent, right? It's not every day you finish writing a book.

Okay, back to Momzilla Mode.

I dial my mother to see if she wants to play community

grandma today, but there's no answer. That's right, she's at the beach with her real grandchildren. They were going on some boat ride in the bay today.

Crap. What am I going to do now?

"What's wrong?" Mariana asks when she sees me frantically flying through the house.

"Elliott had to go to the hospital," I blurt out.

"Why?"

"Come on, you're going to have to go with me."

"But I don't wanna go to the hospital!"

"I'm sorry, but we need to go now!" My body has been taken over by adrenaline, and I'm not even sure my words are making sense. "Come on. Shoes. Car. Now."

She starts to cry. *Oh, come on, kid, for the love of all things good and chocolatey, not today!*

"Mariana, Elliott needs our help!" I try to appeal to her altruistic side, but that side's possibly a little underdeveloped in five-year-olds.

I drag her kicking and screaming body out to the car, hoping nobody from Child Protective Services happens to be cruising by at the moment. Red is in the yard surveying his bushes and looks over at me like I must be the worst person on earth for eliciting such a reaction from this poor innocent child.

"What's all this racket about?" Mrs. Vandeveer starts in as she crosses her yard into my driveway.

Oh, great, all the neighbors are witnessing me in my finest moment!

"They took Elliott to the ER," I rush out. "I have to get there now, and she doesn't want to go. I guess she has some sort of hospital thing—"

Her dad sure could have mentioned that when he gave me a list of her medical stuff like drugs she's allergic to and which pediatrician she goes to. Seems like a crippling fear of the medical establishment would have made it onto that list.

"We can watch her," Mrs. Vandeveer volunteers.

"We?" I repeat.

"Red and I," she says, casting her gaze in his direction. I can almost see drool forming on her lips.

Good lord. He's shirtless again. My supposedly decrepit neighbor, who is apparently a cat whisperer, has just volunteered herself and Buff Santa Claus to watch my boyfriend's kid. Is she using my kid to nail the neighbor?

Why is my life like this?

"Just go," Red commands in his usual gruff voice. "We'll be fine. Just go to your son."

My body feels like it's being pulled in two directions. I should have left fifteen minutes ago. What if he's really hurt? What if they have to do surgery? The nurse was so vague about his injuries…

"Okay!" I concede. "It's weird, and I don't know if I like it, but Mariana, would you rather stay with the neighbors while I go see Elliott?"

"Yes," she blubbers and nods.

"Fine." I take her out of the car I've just stuffed her into and march her over to Mrs. Vandeveer. "Hopefully I won't be too long."

"We'll be just fine," she assures me with a wink that, in fact, does nothing to assure me.

"Go on. Get!" Red yells after me as I head back to the car.

"Please put on a shirt!" I call out before zooming down my driveway like a bat out of hell.

WE JUST STOPPED FOR LUNCH, and the last thing I want to do is climb back on that bus. I always thought a cross-country road trip sounded fun and exciting, but doing it with your co-workers and bosses has turned out to be the opposite of fun and exciting.

It's not that I have a problem with any of these people. It's just this is work. Way more work than I ever imagined it would be. Teaching high school students is tough, but this takes a whole different level of stamina. We're only on our third city, and I'm already like *wow, we have to do this seventeen more times?*

After we chow down at some weird diner in the panhandle of Florida, I remember I left my phone on silent again. When I grab it from my pocket, I see that Claire has called four times. Panic surges through me as I fumble with the buttons trying to call her back.

No answer.

Better leave a voicemail. She hates voicemails, but what other option do I have?

"Claire, I'm so sorry I missed your calls. I had my phone on silent and forgot. We'll be on the bus again this afternoon, so please call me back as soon as you can. I hope everything is okay."

"You alright?" comes Bonnie's voice behind me as she steps aboard the bus. I turn around and catch the concern in her honey-colored eyes.

"Yeah, everything's fine." I take a deep breath. The narrator inside my head says, "In fact, everything was *not* fine."

"Family problems?" she guesses as she takes the seat next to me again. She always sits with me. There are plenty of open seats on the bus, but she wants the one next to mine.

I hesitate to tell her what's going on, but it's going to be a long tour, and I don't really have anyone here to talk to. Most of our fellow tour mates have paired off by age, gender or genre of music, it appears. I guess that means Bonnie and I have to stick together.

"My girlfriend called several times, but then she didn't answer when I tried to call her back." I run my fingers through my hair. "I hope nothing's wrong with my daughter."

She puts a comforting hand on my thigh. "I'm sure she's fine. Hey, I don't think you ever showed me a picture of your daughter. I bet she's a cutie."

I can't help but smile any time I think of my baby girl. She's not only cute, she's beautiful. She's going to break hearts someday. I pull out my phone and scroll through the gallery till I come across a photo I took of her at the beach before I left. The sun is making a halo around her head, giving her the look of an angel in her white swimsuit coverup.

"Oh my god, this is Mariana?" Bonnie grabs my phone so she can study the photo more closely. "She's absolutely gorgeous! Look at those eyes! That hair!"

My phone starts ringing in her hand. I look down, expecting her to hand it to me, but instead, she puts it on speaker and presses "accept."

"Hello, Jack's phone, Bonnie here," she says with a giggle.

I smirk as I snatch the phone out of her hand. "Hey, Claire, what's wrong?"

"Who was that?"

"It's just one of my tour mates," I tell her, quickly turning off the speaker. "Bonnie. She's probably going to be famous by next week. I'll get to say I knew her when." I add a nervous laugh because I can tell Claire's none too happy about a woman answering my phone, even though it was a completely innocent thing. "What's going on? You called me four times."

"I know. I thought since you were on the bus, you'd be able to answer," she fires back, and her tone is anything but pleasant.

"I'm sorry. I was sleeping on the bus with my ringer off. Will you please tell me what's going on?" I'm starting to grow as agitated as she is.

"I'm at the ER with Elliott," she says, then draws in a deep breath. "He was on the boardwalk with Jes-sie, and some douchebag bicyclist rammed right into him."

"You aren't supposed to ride your bike on the board-walk!" I point out—probably unhelpfully so at this point.

"I know. The dude was high as a freakin' kite. He got arrested. My baby boy is pretty beat up, but he's going to be okay. No broken bones."

"Wow, that's good. I'm glad he's okay." I breathe out a sigh of relief, but then panic surges through me all over again. "Uh, where's Mariana?"

She's quiet for a moment before: "Why do you ask?"

"Because she hates hospitals, doctors, needles, medi-cine, nurses—not necessarily in that order."

"Oh, does she now?" Claire's tone takes a sarcastic turn. "You know, it might have been helpful for you to tell me that before you left, or maybe you could have included it on the list of copious instructions you left me?"

Argh. She's right. "Sorry. I was just hoping you wouldn't have to find out. It's always been a phobia of hers…"

"Yeah, well, I was probably two seconds away from having CPS called on me when I was trying to force her into the car so we could go to the hospital."

I can't help but laugh at how headstrong my princess can be. Heaven forbid any of her peers try to make her to do something against her will someday. She's a little force to be reckoned with. "So what did you do?"

"She's with the neighbors," Claire says. "I'm on my way back now."

"God help the neighbors." I scrub my hand down my face.

"It's only been two hours. I'm sure they're fine."

There's silence between us for a moment, and that's when I realize Bonnie is listening, even though she's looking out the window at the scenery whizzing past and pretending not to be paying attention. But she is.

"Claire, I'm sorry I didn't tell you about her issues. That was wrong."

She huffs out a breath. I'm sure she wants to stay mad at me, but she can't. I've felt the same way toward her a time or two.

"Okay," is all she says.

"Everything else is going well?" Maybe I can turn this conversation around.

She's quiet for a moment, and all I hear is the rumbling of the bus's wheels on the pavement. God, I miss her. It's great to hear her voice, but I want her in my arms. I can't believe I've been gone a week and have so long to go till I'm home.

"I finished my book today," comes her voice down the line, softer than I've ever heard it.

"Oh my god, really?" She doesn't say anything.

"Claire, that's a huge accomplishment! I'm so proud of you."

"Yeah, it's almost eighty-five thousand words. I need to edit it now, then I'll send it to my editor."

"An edit before the editor. You've always been a perfectionist, haven't you?"

"It's standard for the writer to do revisions and edits on her own," she says.

"I'm sure the editor will think it's the easiest job they've ever had." I smile thinking about my girlfriend and all her grammar pet peeves. Elliott and I sometimes use poor grammar just to get her all riled up. It's adorable.

She's still quiet. There's a hint of melancholy in her voice, like the first raindrops before a thunderstorm, and I want to hold her so bad, my body is burning, aching for her to be in my arms. "You okay, babe?"

"Yeah, I will be. Gotta get this kid home. He'll have to take a couple days off work to recover." Her tone brightens like the sun coming out from behind the clouds.

"I hope you're planning to do something to celebrate finishing your book."

"We'll see," she says.

"I'm really proud of you."

She retorts, "Well, I'm proud of you."

That makes me smile. "I guess we're both following our dreams."

"I guess so." She pauses for a second and then, "Jack?"

"Yes?"

"Tell this Bonnie person not to touch your phone—I don't care how famous she is or might become."

There's my girl. "Okay, babe. I love you. Talk to you tomorrow."

Claire

18

Jean-Marc's eyes bounce around my face. "I just think we should commemorate the occasion, that's all."

When I don't say anything and instead stare off at a point in the distance, he lays a hand on mine. "What?"

"Claire, you haven't been yourself since Jack left. I'm worried about you."

I roll my eyes and shrug at the same time. "I probably won't be myself till he gets back."

"He's got, what, another month? Please don't torture yourself the entire time he's gone, okay? You just finished your book. You should be excited!"

"You just want an excuse to throw a party," I accuse. I'm sure he's concerned about me too, but let's face it, Jean-Marc's Party Radar is always fine-tuned to pick up any excuses to celebrate. *Oh, you had your wisdom teeth pulled? Let's have a No More Wisdom Teeth Party!*

"I bet you'll feel better. You could get a babysitter for the night. Isn't Jack's mom coming this week?" He rubs my hand like he's trying to massage away my gloomy mood.

I appreciate his efforts; it's just…

I already missed Jack, but that Bonnie chick answering his phone the other day really rubbed me the wrong way. I haven't been able to stop thinking about it. Why was she in such close proximity to his phone? Were they really on the tour bus?

I know it's crazy, and I trust Jack. I really do. But having been cheated on once—well, there are scars there, like I said before. I trusted Jeremy too. Though, let's face it, Jeremy was always a bit of a douche-muffin. Jack seems to have a lot more integrity than most folks. One of many reasons I fell for him.

But who knows if this rock star business is going to change him? He promised it wouldn't, but the winds of change are some powerful forces.

"Claire!" Jean-Marc's bullhorn voice blares through me, bringing me back to the coffee we're sharing out on my deck. He had to show a house in Millsboro, so he stopped by. Mariana is watching *Frozen* for approximately the forty millionth time, so she's been out of our hair. By the end of the summer, we're going to surpass the world record for *Frozen* viewings; I feel it deep in my bones.

"Yes, Jack's mom is coming next week. I guess she's going to keep Mariana at Jack's house for a few days to give me a break. If you want to throw a party, throw a party. It doesn't have to be for me finishing my book."

His eyes glimmer. "Well, if I throw one, will you come?"

"Yes, dear, of course I will come to your party." I reach out and stroke my hand down his cheek affectionately.

"I don't ask for much," his tone is steeped in self-right-eousness. "Coffee dates here and there and the occasional soirée. I don't think that's unreasonable."

"Anita called to talk to Mariana last night," I share.

"Oh, how is she doing?"

"I think she's doing a lot better. She just had a scan, and they were pleased with the results. I didn't talk to her long—she mostly called to talk to Mariana. I let them FaceTime on my phone. They hadn't done that for a while —not while Anita was in the hospital, so it was special."

Mariana has no idea her mom is sick, and I'm trying to keep it that way. Knowing how Mariana feels about hospitals now further explains why she didn't want her daughter to see her that way. And why she decided to go to London for treatment.

Jean-Marc nods and finishes his coffee. "That's good to hear." He stands up and puts a hand on my shoulder. "Well, I better get back to the office, but I will text you later with the party details."

I give him one more eye roll for good measure. "You do that."

THE CROWD in Houston was amazing! So full of energy. And when Bonnie and I did our solo in that country tune, they almost made me fall in love with the song, they were so into it. After we all have dinner and drinks backstage— don't know if I will ever get used to eating at eleven PM— we head back to the hotel for a nightcap.

We're back on the road tomorrow morning at the crack of dawn, so I promise everyone one drink before I go hit the hay. I guess some of these younger folks don't need as much beauty sleep as I do.

"Jack! Jack! Over here!" Bonnie has saved us a table, along with the other two "senior" members of our party, Talia and Steve. We are the only ones in our thirties, I think. Everyone else is in their twenties, and I think Nick might only be nineteen. The poise that kid has for being so young—it really blows me away.

"Hey, guys. Hold on, let me grab a beer." I signal to the waitress who is circulating between the tables. It's almost midnight, and they're probably ready to close this place down since it's a weeknight.

"I think this was my favorite city so far," Steve says as I join them at the table.

"You said that about New Orleans too!" Talia laughs as she pats Steve on the back.

"I think we're just finally getting in sync with each other," Bonnie speculates. "You know, hitting our stride."

"Well, America voted for us for a reason!" Steve jokes.

They're nice people, right? I should feel lucky to get to hang out with talented and relatively humble folks, despite the adoring, screaming fans clamoring for us in every city. I've signed so many t-shirts and programs in the past two weeks, I think I've developed a permanent cramp in my hand.

Talia leans in close as if it's top secret. "Has anyone heard from a record label exec yet?"

"I heard Xia got a call," Bonnie shares. "I don't think anyone is surprised about that."

We all shake our heads. Xia is this tiny Chinese lady, but when she opens her mouth to sing, the sound that comes out blows you away. She's a vocal powerhouse. Don't judge a book by its cover, and all that.

"Hey, my phone is ringing. I'll be right back." It's not like Claire to call me so late, plus we spoke earlier today before the concert. I hope everything is okay. I hate that I panic every time the phone rings, but I can't seem to stop my body from reacting that way.

I don't recognize the number, but it starts with 302, meaning it's from Delaware. It's almost two in the morning there, which makes me even more panicky. "Hello?"

"Hey, Jack, it's Jean-Marc," Claire's best friend's voice whirrs down the line.

"Hey, man, how are you? Everything okay?"

"Yeah, man, it's great. Did you know Claire finished her book?" he starts in.

"Oh, yeah, of course. She told me the other day. I'm really proud of her. Can't wait to see it in print!"

"Right. Well, I was going to throw her a little party next week to celebrate, and I just wondered if they gave you any time off for good behavior? Could you drop in for like twenty-four hours? I'll buy your plane ticket."

"Wow, that's a great idea." Already, the thoughts are spinning in my head. I would love to see my girls, but I don't know if I can get away. "It's a generous offer, but I'm not sure if I can get the time. We're pretty much in a new city every other day."

"I can fly you here, and then to wherever your next show is. You don't have to miss anything. Even if you're here for four hours, Jack. I want to make it happen," he insists.

"Are you sure everything is okay?" I press because there's a sense of urgency in his voice that's activating my spidey senses—or whatever you call it when a boyfriend and dad feel something is a little off.

Jean-Marc lets out a sigh—not the most dramatic sigh I've ever heard from him, like when his wine glass is empty—but a sigh nonetheless.

"What is it?" *See?* I knew something was up.

"Claire's been really…" He hesitates.

"Really what?"

"Well, frankly, she's not been very Claire-like since you left," he states bluntly.

I hate that, and guilt shreds through me as I realize the sacrifice she's making to take care of my daughter while I'm chasing my dreams and Anita is battling cancer. But, on the other hand...there's a tiny part of me, the selfish a-hole part we all have buried deep inside, no matter how hard we try to keep it at bay, that's a little bit glad she misses having me there.

"It's not that I don't want to be there, Jean-Marc. It's just that our tour coordinator is a real stickler for every-thing. We have our first two consecutive days off next weekend, though. Is there any way you could do the party then? And I'll see what I can do."

"Yes, next Saturday. That's what I was already think-ing," he confirms.

"Okay. Well, I appreciate you being there for Claire. You're a good friend to her."

He breathes out a bored sigh. "Look, I've been there for Claire since long before you came into the picture, and I'll be there for her long after you're gone..."

"The only way I won't be in the picture is if Claire doesn't want me anymore," I fire back, more than a little perturbed he'd think otherwise. He was probably hoping to call and for me to say I'd be there, with no reservations, end of story, and he could look like the hero for getting me there.

"Good. I was hoping you'd say that," he answers. "Let me know as soon as you can."

"I will."

JACK'S MOM, Barbara, is…interesting. I like her, but she's really hard to get to know. She was definitely not what I expected when I first met her. She's very…elegant-looking, always wearing these fitted pantsuits and with her platinum hair perfectly coiffed. And she is never, ever seen without lipstick in her signature coral shade. *Ever.* Jack is so laidback and flannel-y. I guess I expected a feminine version of him?

She loves her granddaughter though; there is no doubt about that. All the way over to Jack's house, which Mariana and I have been stopping by every few days to pick up the mail and water the plants, she is bubbling nonstop about all the things she wants to do with her grandmother.

"I wanna show her the pictures I colored, and I want to play with my Play-Doh. You don't have Play-Doh at your house, Miss Claire. I miss mine. And I want to put on my princess dresses and my tiaras and have a tea party. And I want Nana to watch *Frozen* with me and sing the songs, and we can bake cookies and FaceTime with Daddy. Do you think Nana will take me to the park? I want to go on the swings!"

"Probably, sweet pea. I'm sure you and your nana will have an awesome time. It sounds like someone's just a little excited!"

"Who?" She wrinkles up her little button nose.

"You, silly!"

We pull into the driveway, and Barbara's car isn't there. I guess traffic was bad on Route 1. It always is on Fridays in the summer when everyone from the north heads down to the beach. I tried to talk her into leaving earlier, but she wouldn't listen.

My phone starts to buzz, so I pull it out of my pocket and see it's her calling. It would have been nice if she'd told me she was running late before I drove all the way over here, but whatevs. "Hello?"

"Hi, Claire, I'm so sorry to do this to you, but I won't be able to make it this weekend," she says. "I know it's last minute, but one of our major donors is unhappy, and we have to act now before they pull out their funding. My whole foundation is on the line here. I hope you understand."

"It's the weekend, Barbara," I tell her. "And I'm supposed to be attending an adults-only party tonight."

"I know, Claire, and I'm just so very, very sorry. I will come next weekend. I promise. Please kiss my sweet girl for me and tell my son I said hello." Her voice is firm, unwavering.

"But—"

"Gotta run for now. Thanks for helping out!"

And just like that, she's gone.

Great.

My mother went with Eliza to the Outer Banks this weekend. Everyone else I know in the area is going to the party tonight. Nora is coming down for the party and was all excited about getting an adults-only night. I got the impression she doesn't get too many of those.

"What's wrong now?" Mariana asks as I slide my phone back into my purse. Apparently she's growing a little wary of these crazy phone calls I keep getting. At least it's not the ER this time.

"Your nana can't make it this weekend after all," I break it to her as gently as I can. "She needs to postpone till next weekend." I'm trying to deliver the news without seething the words through my clenched teeth, but I'm pretty sure I'm failing.

I want to call Jack and give him a piece of my mind, but we've already spoken today, and this is one of their first nights off that they're not traveling, so he and his tour mates are enjoying the sights in St. Louis, including the famous arch. I'll have to complain about this later.

On my way home—after I note that Mariana has dozed off in the back seat—I call Jean-Marc. He'll probably be even more ticked off than I am. He went to a lot of trouble for me—even though I insisted he not go to a lot of trouble, but since when does anyone listen to me?

"Hey, it's me," I say when he answers the phone.

"Oh no. I don't like that tone." He picks up on my vibe immediately, of course.

"Well, Barbara just called and canceled, so I don't have a babysitter."

All I hear is an exasperated huff.

"Can Elliott and Jessie watch her?" he asks. "Come on, Claire. You need this! You don't have to stay that long, but you need to come for at least a couple of hours. Please?"

It's not like my best friend to beg. "I think they had plans tonight, but I will find out what they're doing."

"I will pay them a hundred bucks if they babysit, okay?" he offers, desperation dripping off each word.

"A hundred bucks? Are you insane?"

"Yes. And yes."

At least he admits it.

"Fine. I don't understand why this is so important for you, but I'll do my best."

"That's all I can ask!" he assures me. "Call me back."

Okay, fine. I will ask my son and his girlfriend to quit sucking face for two hours so I can go be an adult and make my best friend happy. Okay, three hours, because I need travel time to Rehoboth Beach.

We make it back to my house on the river, and Elliott is in bed. He's fully recovered from the injuries he sustained from his little run-in with the toasted bicyclist, but that doesn't mean he won't sleep all day if I don't go forcibly remove him from his bed.

"Hey, get up." The smell of stinky feet and other foulness hits my nostrils as soon as I step foot in his cushy lair. "Holy crap, Elliott, it reeks in here. Get up!"

He lifts his weary head from the pillow. "What?"

"I need you to watch Mariana tonight for a few hours."

He groans. "What? Why?"

"I have a function to attend," I announce like I've been invited to dinner at Buckingham Palace.

"No, I can't," he says, each word an extension of another groan. "Jessie and I have concert tickets."

"Concert tickets?"

"Delaware State Fair," he tells me. "Her brother is taking us."

I forgot it was fair time.

Is there some sort of conspiracy against me???

I can just see the FBI, CIA and a bunch of covert operatives sitting around a conference table in some secret bunker, passing around manila files stamped with *Top Secret*. Maybe Jean-Marc's boyfriend, the infamous Thor/Tony (not his real name), is involved, I don't know. And inside is a mandate to wreak havoc in one Claire Sterling's life. Then they sit around the table in hushed tones, deliberating ways to make my life unnecessarily complicated. They're probably behind this whole Support Art Foundation Superstar contest too.

'Cause everything seemed to be *just fine* before that started.

(We're going to leave out the part that it was my idea for Jack to try out. It doesn't really fit with my narrative, you see).

Well, there's only one more possible solution that would allow me to avoid incurring the wrath of Jean-Marc Tasse. And possibly the FBI/Tony/Thor. I feel as desperate as Princess Leia in her "Help me, Obi Wan Kenobi" speech when I march over to Mrs. Vandeveer's house next door and beg her to do me a solid.

Mariana was just fine in her care when I made my impromptu sojourn to the ER with Elliott. I know Red helped out too, and I don't know what he's doing tonight, but maybe this is another opportunity for them to *explore their dynamic*?

"Hey, Mrs. Vandeveer?" I knock on her door.

Through the glass on her back door, I see her hobbling my way. She sure wasn't hobbling when she trapped my horny cat under her basket, but whatevs.

"Hello, dear, what can I do for you? I'm heading out to my bingo game here soon," she says.

Oh, crap, it's Friday. She has bingo.

"That's right." I let out the deepest of sighs.

"What's wrong, sugar?"

"Oh, I'm in a bit of a pickle," I confess.

"Why's that, hon?" She opens the door to let me inside. I told Mariana to stay in her room until I get back, and I'm sure hoping this doesn't take long.

"I'm supposed to go to a party in my honor tonight— for finishing my book—and my babysitter bailed. So I'm not sure what to do."

"Oh my. Well, that is a pickle," she agrees, scratching her chin.

"I guess I can go ask Red." I give a little headshake of resignation.

"Red…" she repeats, and I detect a far-away dreamy look in her gray-green eyes.

"Yes, you guys did such a great job watching Mariana when I had to go to the ER the other day. I'm sure he'd watch her solo though—"

"Oh, well, yes, maybe Red and I could do it together?" She sounds nearly giddy at the prospect.

My eyebrows arch as I study the hopeful expression on her wrinkled face. "But…I thought you were going to bingo?"

She totally has the hots for him. It's painfully obvious—and I can't really blame her. For an older guy, Red is in incredible shape. And once you get past the Santa Claus thing, he's downright attractive.

"You know I don't get around too well, and I definitely don't chase men," she leans in like she's telling me a deep, dark secret, "but for a man like Red, a gal might just power walk." When she smiles that wistful grin, she looks ten years younger.

"Wanna go ask him with me?" I'm trying so hard to contain my laughter, but she's too excited to notice.

"Let's do it!"

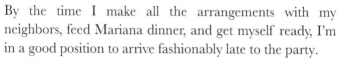

Claire

19

By the time I make all the arrangements with my neighbors, feed Mariana dinner, and get myself ready, I'm in a good position to arrive fashionably late to the party.

"You made it!" Jean-Marc greets me at the door, wrapping me in a warm embrace.

There are twenty or thirty people milling about, and as per usual, half of them are my friends, and half of them have zero clue who I am. It's all good though; I always end up meeting the most interesting people at these things.

"You're the one who's dating the SAF Superstar guy!" a young woman by the food spread gushes as I head over to inspect what kind of goodies my bestie procured for me.

"Yeah," I answer before stuffing a crab ball into my mouth. Party Pro Tip: if you don't want to talk to people, just keep your mouth full. It's foolproof!

I'm normally more outgoing, but ever since Jack left, I haven't been myself. I've felt isolated, trapped inside my own head. And that's not a space I think anyone else would care to venture. There are some pretty strange thoughts circulating in there. I did talk about it with Nora last night, and she said I should harness those voices and make my next writing endeavor a novel. We'll see.

"Hey, Thor, how's it going?" I ask as I approach Jean-Marc's tall, handsome boyfriend. He's employing my full mouth trick and just smiles and nods at me. He's probably wearing a wire.

"Good talk!" I nod back, then glance past him into the kitchen, and my eyes nearly bug out of my head. I race through the open door, almost running smack-dab into a dude who's walking out carrying a tray of hors d'oeuvres.

"Jack!" I scream loud enough that all the other condo-dwellers this side of the bay probably have my voice ringing in their ears now.

He turns toward me, his cheeks lifting as a massive grin overtakes his face. He looks so different! His full beard is gone, replaced with a shadow of scruff, and he's not wearing his glasses. But I don't care because, in a split second, I'm in his arms, breathing in his sandalwood scent and soaking in the warmth of his embrace.

"Oh my god, what are you doing here?" I whisper in his ear.

He doesn't bother to answer, instead lifting my chin with his finger so he can claim my lips in a kiss that makes everyone around us stop to stare. As we reunite, the whole room is as breathless as I am. Literally no one is breathing right now.

I can feel everyone's stares burning into my bare shoulders—they're so hot, I might get a sunburn. I break the kiss and seek the Host with the Most across the spacious living room. "Are you responsible for this?"

He gives me a little innocent shrug, but his eyes hold a devious twinkle. "Oh, I don't know. I may have had a little something to do with it."

"Thank you, thank you, THANK YOU!" I run up to him and plant a kiss on his cheek. "This means so much to me."

"Go on," he gestures toward Jack, "save your kisses for your rock star, mama." He has tears in his eyes that he dabs with his napkin before turning back to Thor, who slings his massive arm around Jean-Marc's shoulders.

Seconds later, I'm back by Jack's side. "How in the world did you get the night off?"

"We have two nights off back-to-back—one of the only times on our schedule. So I flew in this afternoon, and I fly out tomorrow night. I have to be in Phoenix by Monday morning," he explains.

"They made you trim your beard!" I gasp, running my fingers across the rough stubble.

"Yeah, they want to make me look younger." Jack rolls his eyes. "'Youthen me up' is what our stylist called it."

"'Youthen'? That's not even a word!"

He laughs. "I knew you'd say that."

I shake my head at the ridiculousness of it. "If they think you're old at thirty-four, I'm sure they'd find me over the hill at forty!"

"Who cares what they think? How's my baby girl?" He strokes a finger down my cheek.

"She misses you like crazy. So you'll get to see her tomorrow, yes?" My lips curl downward as I remember all the drama that ensued just to make this evening out possible. "Your mom bailed on me this weekend, you know."

"She did?" He huffs out an exasperated breath. "I'm sorry, babe. Who has Mariana?"

"The neighbors," I say. "Don't worry; they're experienced babysitters at this point!"

"Probably better than Elliott and Jes-sie," he agrees,

pronouncing my son's girlfriend's name with the same inflection I use to irritate the poor lad.

"Yup." I nod in agreement. Though with the way Mrs. Vandeveer was leering at Red...

I lose him for a moment while he heads over to greet Drew, Luke, Russ, and Sam. Ah, so that's why they're here. I kept wondering why Jean-Marc thought they'd give a crap about my book. It's all clear to me now.

As much as I want him to catch up with his friends, I need a little more alone time with him first. I stalk across the room, grab his hand and start to pull him toward the bathroom.

He stops talking to Drew mid-sentence, flashing him an apologetic look before turning back to me. "Where are we going?"

I paint a flirty, devious grin on my face before opening the bathroom door and pushing him inside. After I join him, I lock that baby up tight. "I need a proper reunion kiss. One without people staring. One that might get a little handsy..."

He laughs. "I think that can be arranged!"

Jack

I LOOK in on my sleeping angel as soon as we get back to Claire's house. Jean-Marc was the perfect host, as usual, but I was happy to say good night to all the crowds and catch a glimpse of my precious baby girl, even if she was too drowsy to wake up and say hi.

"So, I've managed to keep her alive and well," Claire says, smirking at me as she leads me down the hall to her bedroom.

"Kudos. I can't wait to see her little face when she wakes up tomorrow morning, and I'm here. I just wish I could stay longer."

"Me too, but at least we get a little time with you." She reaches behind her to unzip the dress she wore to the party. It's the cute, summery sundress she wore the night I auditioned for Rehoboth Beach Superstar, the night we went out for drinks with Jean-Marc and Thor and this whole adventure began when she dared me to perform.

"Here, let me help you with that." I put my hands on her shoulders and turn her around, then tug the zipper down until the top of the dress falls to her waist. Then I slide it down her hips and thighs until the fabric pools around her feet.

"Sorry, I didn't wear my sexiest bra and panties," she sighs. "It's not like I thought anyone would be seeing them."

"You could be wearing a burlap sack, and I'd still want you," I assure her as my eyes trail over her divine curves. God, I've missed this woman. I'm completely exhausted from all the touring and traveling, but just looking at her is giving me a second wind. And other notable physical changes…

She moans as I claim her lips, backing her toward her bed until she falls on the mattress. "Oh!" she squeals, not expecting me to launch myself right on top of her.

"Sorry, too much?"

"Never!" she exclaims breathlessly as I fumble with my pants. She helps out by lifting my shirt up and over my head.

Before I know it, my Claire is back in my arms.

Where she belongs.

I PROMISED myself I would get up and make my girls breakfast, but my travel-weary body had other plans. The first of my senses to awake is my nose, tickled by the wafting scents of coffee, bacon and pancakes. It beckons me into the kitchen, and my ears soon join the land of the living when a high-pitched squeal nearly bursts my eardrums: "DADDY!!!"

My little princess bolts across the living room and leaps into my arms so energetically, I nearly fall over. But nothing could possibly beat her tiny arms slung around my neck, hanging on for dear life.

"I missed you, Daddy! I can't believe you're here!"

I look over at Claire, who is flipping pancakes in the kitchen. The look on her face is pure pride and joy. "Good morning, sleepyhead. We were trying to be very quiet so you could sleep in."

"I'm so grateful, thank you both." I give them each a bow with both of my hands pressed together like a prayer. "Now, I want to know everything my girls have been doing since I've been away."

Claire plates the pancakes, eggs, and bacon and carries them to the dining room table as Mariana starts to fill me in on all their adventures. Looking at the beautiful faces of my girls, I feel in my heart the two emotions I witnessed on Claire's face just moments ago: pride and joy. Then two heavy feet stumble down the hall, and Elliott slides into the seat next to me, his hair disheveled and face creased. He's scarfed down two strips of bacon before I can even say hello.

And here we all are, gathered around a table together.
And it feels just right.
Like home.

20

I never thought I'd be invited to appear on the morning news show for a major television station. I would have thought any number of impossible scenarios were more plausible than actually becoming an honest-to-god rock star. Like finding buried pirates' treasure or discovering the cure for cancer—and I'm not even a scientist, you know? But here Bonnie and I are at the TV studios in Los Angeles, and there are hundreds of dedicated SAF Superstar fans gathered outside the building, hoping to catch a glimpse of us.

We've been on tour for weeks now, and it's been an absolutely mind-blowing experience. Possibly the most unbelievable part? Bonnie and I seem to be fan favorites. When we sing our duet together, the crowd goes absolutely wild. When we're all hanging out at the venue after a show, more people seek our autographs than any of the other performers. It's so lopsided, in fact, I think some of our co-stars are a little resentful of us.

She's sitting beside me in the green room as we wait to be ushered on for our segment. It's only going to be like four minutes long. I've already considered all the things that could go wrong in four minutes' time, but Bonnie, with her ever-sunny smile, insists, "Hey, what can go wrong in four minutes? We don't have time to screw up too badly."

We can hear the host introduce us as they direct us which way to walk. They're about to go to commercial when Steve Styers says, "When we come back, we'll introduce you to two of the up-and-coming stars touring with the Support Art Foundation Superstar contest. Bonnie Scott and Jack Reilly join us in the studio after these messages from our sponsors." I look up at the monitor as we step onto the set, and under the picture of the host, it says, "Coming up next: Rock Stars in the Making? The SAF Superstar Tour."

Steve welcomes us to the set, and the assistant ushers us onto the loveseat across from him and his co-host, Gabby. Steve is a very weathered middle-aged white dude, blond and tan, kind of how I'd imagine California surfers looking twenty years past their prime, and he's wearing a ton of makeup. And Gabby is a beautiful Latina woman who reminds me of what Mariana might look like when she grows up.

Speaking of makeup, they dab a little on our faces before they count off the return from commercial break. Bonnie reaches down and grabs my hand to give it a little good luck squeeze right before we go live.

"Welcome back to the program! How many of you have tickets for the sold-out Support Art Foundation Superstars on Tour concert tonight at the Staples Center? If you do, you're among the lucky, and you have a chance to see our guests perform. This is Jack Reilly, who hails from Delaware, and Bonnie Scott, from Portland, Oregon.

Welcome to the show, guys!" Steve animatedly reads the monitor behind us.

We both murmur our thanks, and then Gabby takes over. "Bonnie, tell us what it was like to participate in the contest that secured your spot on this tour. Have you always wanted to be a singer?"

She aims that stunning smile right at the hosts as she speaks—we were told not to look at the cameras, to pretend they aren't even there. "I did always want to be a singer," she starts off. "But you know how life is; it doesn't always give us the opportunities we need to make our dreams come true. I actually work as a dental hygienist back in Oregon, and my co-workers are the ones who pushed me into auditioning for the Portland Superstar contest a couple of months ago. I won that and went on to the Pacific regional contest; then I won that too. Then I was invited to Washington, DC to compete in the Nationals—and I won! I could hardly believe it, and I just want a chance to say thank you to all the fans who voted for me."

"That's amazing, Bonnie, thank you for sharing. Jack, we understand you're a band director and music teacher back in your home state of Delaware. How did that prepare you for competing in the SAF contest?" Steve asks.

I clear my throat and pray to God I don't sound like a moron. "First off, I just wanna say hi to my daughter, Mariana! Hey, Princess. Daddy misses you!" I take a deep breath and wish I still had the full beard to hide the flush that seems to be creeping up my neck. How can I perform in front of thousands of people with no problem but get nervous doing this? "I think teaching band has prepared me a great deal for competing in the SAF contest. High school students are a tough crowd, and I feel like if you can win them over, you can win almost anyone over."

Gabby laughs. "Good answer, Jack. We understand you won the national contest with a song you wrote yourself. Can you tell us a little about that and if we can expect to see more original music from you in the future?"

"Yes, ma'am, my song 'Firecracker' was written about my girlfriend, Claire. And, yes, I have lots more where that came from. I would love to work with a record label to bring all my original songs to airwaves and concert halls everywhere."

"Nice! And lucky woman that Claire is, right, ladies?" Gabby winks at the camera.

"Bonnie, do you have loved ones back home you dedicate your performances to?" Steve asks.

"Yes, sure do, Steve. My son, Corbin, is watching from our hometown in Oregon, and he's always in my heart when I perform. As a single mom, I want nothing more than to show my son that following your dreams and working hard can pay off in a big way. I hope to set a good example for him and other kids, and let them know they should never give up on their art, whether it's music or painting or dance or theater—whatever floats their creative boats."

"That's excellent advice, Bonnie," Steve replies.

Gabby turns her chocolate-brown eyes toward me. "Jack, is there anything else you'd like to add to that?"

"I think Bonnie said it very well. I'd just add for kids not to think of high school band as being the end of their careers as musicians. There are some great college music programs and lots of careers in music they might not even think of such as teaching, librarianship, producing, conducting, composing and lots and lots of technical jobs as well."

"Great points! We've really enjoyed having you here,

and we'll see you on stage tonight at eight PM at the Staples Center!"

"Thanks for having us!" we both say, practically in unison.

As soon as we leave the studios, we're mobbed by fans wanting autographs on our way to the limo waiting for us on the curb. We buckle in and take a jerking stop-and-go ride back to our hotel downtown.

"I hope they're serving something good for lunch," Bonnie laments as we walk through the lobby together toward the conference room our group has taken over for rehearsals and meals. Garvey's been teaching us a new closing routine he wants to debut tonight.

"Tell me about it. The food at our last stop wasn't as good as usual." We head through the doors and are confronted immediately by Brenda, Courtney, Garvey and Frank, who form a circle around us, blocking our view of the lunch table that's set up in the corner. This is the first I've seen Mrs. Monnett since we left Washington, DC, and it raises all the hair on the back of my neck.

"Is everything okay?" Bonnie's eyes dart from our bosses over to me.

"We need to talk to you both," Brenda says before gesturing for us to follow her.

"Uh oh," Bonnie elbows me in the ribs, "guess we're in trouble now!"

She's usually the optimistic one, but I tend to agree with her assessment in this case. The look on Mrs. Monnett's face is the sternest I've ever seen. She marches us down the hall to another room, which appears to be an executive office. We pass a receptionist and waiting area and turn down another hall till we get to a conference room.

She opens the door and silently gestures to our seats

before she takes the one at the head of the table and everyone else takes the others. Bonnie sits next to me, of course.

"What's going on?" I pipe up, not liking what I'm seeing when I glance from face to face. Even Garvey, who once seemed to have a permanent grin etched on his face, looks like he's scowling. This can't be good.

"We need to talk about that little stunt you pulled on the morning show," Mrs. Monnett says, her tone clipped.

Stunt? I'm running through my mental script of everything I said, and nothing jumps out. Was it the part about careers in music? I have no clue.

"I don't know what you're talking about," Bonnie gasps. "What did we do wrong? I feel like we just time-traveled back to the Spanish Inquisition!" She lets out a nervous laugh and then glances over at me to see if I'll join her.

"When you mentioned your girlfriend, Jack," Mrs. Monnett hisses.

"What? How is that a problem?" I fire back.

Garvey sucks in a sharp breath. "Look, we've been monitoring social media, and you and Bonnie are by far our two most popular stars. You're helping us sell out shows and making a fortune for the foundation. The whole single parent narrative and the fact that you're a music teacher—fans are eating it up. But there's another reason they love you both so much…"

"And what's that?" Bonnie jumps in, her tone surprisingly demanding.

"They think you have…romantic potential," Courtney fills in.

Bonnie leans back with a smug smile but doesn't say a word. My eyes bounce between the four SAF folks sitting across from us in disbelief. "You've got to be kidding me."

"Fans create a very specific script in their heads for celebrities," Garvey explains. "That's why we have stylists like Frank, and we're about to bring in a PR specialist to help us spin all this to our advantages. We want to maximize this public obsession with Jack and Bonnie. Did you know they call you 'Jannie' on social media?"

I'm not a social media person, so, no, I didn't know that. And I guess Claire hasn't been following the tour or foundation's social media because she would have flipped the eff out if she'd seen that!

"But it's wrong!" my voice thunders around the room. "It's fake! It's all fiction. Bonnie and I are just friends. We just *met*, for crying out loud!"

"We know what we're doing," Frank adds. "Stylists and PR folks. We're all about creating an image that sells."

"So what are you saying?" Bonnie asks, her voice calmer now and her elbows on the table as she leans in to hear the instructions.

"I'm saying, if you want to continue to sell out arenas and secure record deals, you need to go along with it. Let the fans have their fantasy. It's not that you don't have your own personal lives; it's just that you keep them completely separate from your work life. Except for your kids. The fact that Jack has a little girl, and Bonnie has a little boy...well, fans are eating that up. They want you to succeed so you can create an amazing life for your kiddos, and we're all for that, especially since kids and arts education is at the heart of what we do," Mrs. Monnett explains.

"I don't care about fulfilling fans' fantasies," I insist. "This is all ridiculous."

Mrs. Monnett steeples her hands and aims her sharp gaze toward me. "Do you remember that contract you signed in my office the day you came to DC to get the details about the tour?"

I gulp down a breath but don't say a word.

"Well, your contract specified facilitating any stylistic or PR optics we deem necessary to ensure the success of the tour," she reminds me. "And this certainly falls under optics. If you don't go along with our instructions, you'll be asked to leave."

Courtney adds, "We really don't want to see that, Jack. It wouldn't be good for any of us."

I turn to Bonnie, who's barely said a word in the past several minutes. "Are you okay with all this?"

She shrugs. "It doesn't bother me…but then again, I'm not attached to anyone. I just want to make music and get a record deal. I don't make much as a dental hygienist. I'd love to be able to provide a better life for my son. This is my chance."

I scrub my hand down my face, the stubble scratching my skin. I miss my beard. I miss my woman. I miss my daughter. I didn't realize this was going to be such a pain in the ass.

"Okay, fine." I push my chair back from the table and stand up. "I'll do whatever I need to do." I don't want to ruin Bonnie's chances of getting a record deal, though I don't see how she could possibly need me to do that. And I don't want to screw up the tour for everyone else.

Who am I to throw a wrench in this thing? It's temporary, right? Only a few more weeks, and then Claire will be back in my arms.

Claire

"HEY, COME WATCH DADDY ON TV!" I shout to Mariana once I find a link to the story on the Los Angeles television station's website. She runs into the room with her brown pigtails flying behind her and plops right down on my lap, chasing Figaro, who was settling in on the end of the couch, off to plot some innocent bird or rodent's murder. I press play, and we watch the interview with Jack and his duet partner, Bonnie, the one who answered his phone when I called the other day.

"Oh! Daddy said my name!" Mariana squeals when we get to that point. Then a few minutes later, he cites me as the inspiration for his song "Firecracker." It makes me feel all warm and fuzzy inside. At least Bonnie knows that Jack and I are together. He told her so in front of thousands of viewers.

After the interview, Mariana scurries off to her room, where she spends the next hour hardcore playing. When I don't hear a peep from her, I decide to check in and see what she's doing. Through the crack in the door, I see her twirling around in one of her princess dresses with a pretend microphone pressed to her lips. She's playing her "tunes," as she calls them, a kids' mp3 player Jack loaded with some of his favorite songs. This one happens to be by Dolly Parton, and she's lip-syncing for all she's worth.

One glance over at her little wooden table reveals it's set for tea. "Oh, is it tea time?" I peek my head through the door.

"Shhh! I'm practicing!" she shouts back at me.

I shrug and murmur an apology as I step into the room, my arms folded over my chest as I watch her waltz around. When the song ends, she runs over to the player to shut it off. "What do you think?"

"That was beautiful, Mariana! I especially like your choreography!"

"Chora-what?" She stares at me with big brown eyes and fluttering lashes.

"Choreography," I pronounce more slowly. "Your dance moves."

"Oh, okay. Cool." She puts her hands on her hips and looks around the room. "I'm hosting a tea party tomorrow, and I want to make sure everything is perfect." She emphasizes the word "perfect," and it sounds just like someone else I know. It takes me a few seconds to realize she's imitating Jean-Marc. Wait till he hears about that!

"Tea party! That sounds great. Who's coming?"

I expect her to say her teddy bear or one of her dolls, but she wrinkles up her nose like I should have already known the answer. "Miss Van'veer and Mr. Red," she tells me. "And Mommy on FaceTime!"

"Oh, that sounds great. Do our neighbors know they're invited?"

"Not yet," she tells me, like I should have already known that too. "You need to deliver the invitations for me. Like the mailman does."

I can't help but laugh. "Okay, I can do that. Does your mommy know?"

"I made an invitation for her too," Mariana says. "Can you take a picture of it and send it to her?

"Of course I can, sweet pea."

She stands there for a few more moments, looking at me. Then: "Well, what are you waiting for? You better get those invitations out, Miss Mailman!"

She shoves them toward me, and I take them, trying to conceal my laughter. I wish I could have captured this whole exchange on video so Jack could have seen the adorableness of it. He's missing so much. I can't wait to have him home.

Claire

21

I can't believe I'm currently witnessing this momentous occasion. I've been asked to serve tea at the princess's castle, so I'm doing my best to keep from spilling anything or dropping a whole plate of cookies on the floor. I'm not exactly the most coordinated person on the planet, so it's taking every bit of my effort.

The beautiful Princess Mariana is perched on her chair in a resplendent fuchsia gown with an iridescent overlay. Nestled on top of her long chocolate brown waves is a glittering rhinestone tiara with pink accent gemstones. To her left is my iPad, standing up in its holder with the equally beautiful Anita Sanchez, live from London. Then, rounding out our table, is Mrs. Vandeveer in a spiffy lavender polyester blouse and white pedal pushers, and Mr. Red in a plain white t-shirt—at least it's clean (and on)— and a pair of what appear to be freshly laundered blue jeans. He smells like he might have dabbed on just a little too much cologne.

Even Figaro, who is curled up in the sun taking a nap, looks festive in his "tuxedo." We're quite the sophisticated bunch, though it's been made very clear to me I am nothing but a servant and will not be partaking in the festivities. I sure hope Her Majesty doesn't mind if I snap a few photos for posterity's sake, and to show her father, of course.

And then, the doorbell rings. Oh, yes, our surprise guest! Mariana's grandmother Barbara was kind enough to actually take a day off work so she could come down and enjoy afternoon tea with her granddaughter and her other guests. She's also staying the weekend to make up for flaking out on me last weekend.

"Hi, Barbara," I greet her. "I'm glad you could make it!"

She gives me an air kiss and follows me down the hallway to Mariana's room. When I push the door open, the first thing I notice is that Red and Mrs. Vandeveer are holding hands under the table.

Oh, my heart! I think it's melting as the realization sinks in that I might have actually accomplished my mission of getting those two together. Or maybe I should credit Mariana. In any case, they seem to be happy, and I'm just absolutely thrilled for them.

Someone should be happy, even if it's not me at the moment. I didn't hear from Jack at all yesterday. First time since he left for his tour three weeks ago that he's been radio silent.

I HATE TO SAY IT, but this plan Brenda and associates came up with to play along with our fans' *Jannie* obsession is paying off. We both have meetings today with record label executives and even a Broadway producer to discuss whether or not our talent is a good fit for them.

The first meeting I attend is with a guy named Bryan Adkins from Wheelhouse Records, an up-and-coming alternative rock label. He's a little more grizzled-looking than I was expecting—I guess I thought all these executive types wear suits and ties, but seeing him in his flannel shirt and jeans instantly puts me at ease. It looks like something I would wear. I've got on my Support Art Foundation polo shirt and some khakis, part of my official tour wardrobe. I'm not sure I've even worn any of the clothes I brought along this whole time I've been on the road.

"It's great to meet you, Jack." Bryan shakes my hand and gestures toward the chair across from him.

"It's great to meet you too, Mr. Adkins." I cross one leg over the other and lean forward expectantly.

"Oh, please, call me Bryan, no need to be formal here. We're just one big happy family at Wheelhouse, and we'd love for you to be part of our family too." He steeples his hands together over a manila file folder, presumably containing info about me.

I didn't expect him to be so forward. "Okay, so what do I need to do to make that happen?" I play along.

"Well, we love your sound. We understand you're a songwriter, and we really dig that singer-songwriter vibe here at Wheelhouse. You could say it's 'in our wheel-house,'" he roars with laughter, slapping his knee and everything, "get it?"

"Sure do." I nod along with my best professional smile. "I have a lot more songs besides 'Firecracker,'" I share, thinking specifically of the other one I wrote for Claire.

But there are others too, ready to go. And I have notebooks full of songs I wrote in high school and college that I could pull out and try to do something with.

"We'd love to get 'Firecracker' on an album." He makes it sound like the ball is in my court. "We do want to do a little more work on your image. I know your stylist talked with you about buffing up a bit, maybe adding some more tattoos. We love the tribal one on your arm. We want to give you an edge, really nail that look, kinda hearkening back to 90s grunge. Maybe grow your hair out a little, give you a Chris Cornell-type of look, maybe even Dave Grohl. We think you have that kind of appeal, Jack."

Excitement buzzes through my veins. Foo Fighters has always been one of my favorite bands. We were even working on a cover of "Learn to Fly" with the band before I left. I can't believe I'm having this conversation with an honest-to-God music producer!

"I can do that," I tell him. "I know you want to go for a more youthful look, so I think you'll be glad to hear that my bandmates are in their twenties. In all truth, they're probably a lot more commercially viable than I am." I follow up that observation with a bit of a chuckle. I'm not sure self-deprecation is the best strategy in a meeting like this, but I gotta get my boys' feet in the door.

Bryan steeples his hands together again. "Oh, right. You guys play under the name 'The Gallant Misfits,' don't you?"

"That's right. We're open to changing the name, though."

"Right." His lips purse as his eyes bounce across my face. "Well, we're thinking of you more as a solo act. We have a band you'd be working with in the studio, and for tour, we'd find some seasoned guys with the right look to travel with you."

"Oh…" My face falls as I scramble for something I can bring to the table, something I can bargain with to get him to reconsider replacing my band with complete strangers. *Oh yeah, I have nothing. No leverage whatsoever.*

"Is that a problem?" He leans toward me again and nods like he can't believe I'd be stupid enough to question his authority on something like this.

"Well, I don't know. I promised them I would bring them on board if I got a record contract," I fully admit. "And I don't like to break promises. I'm not a broken promises kind of guy."

"Neither am I," he agrees, now nodding even faster. "I'm definitely not the type to break promises."

"I'm glad to hear that." Though that doesn't really help me, does it? *So where do we stand?*

"Well, here's my card." Bryan places a business card in front of me on the far edge of his desk. "Let me know when you're ready to negotiate a contract."

"So you really won't budge on the band thing?" I check, feeling my stomach sink into disappointment land.

"In our experience, it's just not worth it to sign bands to our label. Too many contracts to negotiate. Too many people to manage. Makes it a lot messier, you know? We do solo acts here, and we have a studio band. That's the way we do things at Wheelhouse." He frowns as he looks me up and down. "I'm sure your bandmates would want you to cut an album—with or without them. Rising tides and all that…right?"

"I'll think about it." I stand up, shove his card in my pocket, and shake his hand. After pivoting on my heel, I march down the long hallway back to the hotel lobby where I see Bonnie talking to Xia and Lilly and bouncing up and down. She must have gotten better news than I did.

As soon as she sees me, she bounds toward me with her

arms outstretched, then leaps on top of me. If I hadn't opened my arms and caught her, she would have bowled me right over.

"What's this all about?" I ask as she slides down my body till her feet hit the floor. "Did you get a deal?"

"Oh my god, YES!" she shouts so loud, everyone in the lobby hears us. That's when I notice a reporter taking notes on a digital tablet while a cameraman films our little scene.

"Come on, let's go talk in private," I whisper into her ear.

"Ooh, private!" she echoes. "Sounds good." She gives me a wink and grabs my hand to lead me to the elevators.

I'm sure they just caught all that on camera, but isn't that what the public wants? I hope I can explain it to Claire without her having an absolute conniption fit. She was married to a guy who was practically a politician—or at least he worked with a lot of them doing god-knows-what in Washington, DC. Surely she understands "optics."

We make it up to our private lounge on the twelfth floor, and I practically kick open the door. I feel like we're being followed, even though I know we aren't. You have to have a key card to access this floor from either the elevator or stairs.

"Okay, spill it, what did they say?" I rush out, absorbing the excitement all over her face. She looks even more radiant than usual; she's truly glowing. I'm so happy for her, even if my own meeting didn't go as I hoped.

"It was Flower Child Records," she says, not bothering to breathe at all before she explodes with, "and they are so excited to work with me! I'm going to meet with their songwriter who'll help me with some ideas I've been toying with. And I'm going to meet with their PR person and their lawyer later this week. Oh my god, Jack, I'm so flippin' excited!"

"That's awesome, Bonnie! I'm really excited for you too. You deserve all this."

"Thank you, Jack," her voice finally calms. She heaves in a deep breath and tosses her long, golden waves behind her shoulder before her honey-brown eyes snap to mine. "How did it go with Wheelhouse?"

I shrug, wishing I had something equally exciting to report. "It went well. They want to sign me, but just me. They don't want my band."

Her lips fall into a frown as her gaze trails across my face. "Oh no. That sucks." A second later, her expression brightens as her lips curl up again. "But you're going to sign anyway, aren't you?"

"Oh, no. I promised my band I wouldn't make an album without them." I shrug. "It didn't work out with Wheelhouse, but there are plenty of other labels that might want to work with us. Wheelhouse is pretty small."

"Jack, you should have gone for it. You deserve to be a solo act!" she argues, moving closer to me. "I'm sure your bandmembers are great, but…"

She's so close to me now, I can smell her wildflower perfume. There's no one in the lounge, and I'm feeling like we shouldn't be this close when we're alone together. For the press and paparazzi, sure. But not when we're alone. There's no reason for it. I take a step back, and she takes another step toward me.

"Jack, look at me." She tugs on my arm to bring my focus back to her. "I want all the good things for you, you know? I don't know how I would have survived this tour and missing Corbin so much if it wasn't for you."

I stiffen as she wraps her arms around me. "I know. I'm glad to have a friend on the tour too…"

She tightens her grip around my waist and rises on her tippy toes, trying to…

WTF? Is she trying to kiss me?

I push her away. "What are you doing?"

Her face falls as her features are captured by a pained look. "I thought—"

"We're putting on a show, Bonnie," I remind her. "Being affectionate in public is for the fans. You know I have a girlfriend."

"I know you have a girlfriend, but she's not here," Bonnie fires back, a glint in her honey eyes. "But I am. I am here."

"Yeah? What's your point?"

She shifts her weight from one foot to the other. "I'm here for you, Jack," is all she says. "And I know you can feel whatever this is between us."

Anger bubbles up in my veins like hot lava as I back away from her. "I love my girlfriend," I blurt out as I turn, march out the door and head down the hall to my room.

Claire

MARIANA IS ZONKED OUT.

The lesson of the day was that playing hostess is exhausting. Red and Mrs. Vandeveer walked out of my house hand in hand, and I'm not sure if they went to her house or his, but I have a feeling it was one or the other. So that left Barbara and me to cook dinner and entertain our sleepy and somewhat crabby princess until it was time for bed. She didn't quite make it that long, though. She fell asleep midway through the four billionth screening of *Frozen*. It's almost like she'd seen it before. *insert rimshot here*

Barbara still looks fresh as a daisy in her crisp suit, and I wish the woman would go put on some sweatpants or something so I don't feel so frumpy. Maybe I need to get a Real Job just so I have a reason to put on Real Clothes every day again. I wanted to send Jack a selfie the other day, and I realized I look like one of those people you see out in public, and you warn your child to stay away from them. How can I get him excited about coming home to me like this?

Okay, that's it. Tomorrow I'm putting on some makeup and doing my hair and snapping a nice pic to send him.

"Oh, did I tell you we went to see Jack perform?" Barbara shares once we're alone.

"We?" What, does she have a boyfriend now too? The Silver Generation is all getting busy, and here I am, languishing in Frumpville.

She takes off her glasses and taps the earpiece on her chin. "Remember that donor I told you about who was getting a little testy with us?"

The reason she didn't come last weekend. "Yup."

"I took him and his wife to see Jack perform last week," she says matter-of-factly.

Hmm, okay.

Why didn't she tell me that sooner? She didn't say anything to Mariana that I'm aware of either. And secondly, why didn't Jack tell me?

Then I realize I've had about a total of fifteen minutes to talk to him since I saw him last weekend. Not only did he have to make up learning some new choreography he missed when he was gone, but apparently some of the performers had meetings with record labels this week, Jack included. I'm still waiting to hear how his went, but he was performing tonight, so I probably won't find out till tomorrow.

Still, you'd think he could have texted me to say, "Hey, my mom is here."

"Well, how was it?" I ask because it sounds like she's already done talking about it.

"Oh," she nibbles on the end of her earpiece for a second before sliding the glasses back into place, "it was a nice show. Well done and rehearsed. Jack sounded just lovely, and that woman they have singing with him is spectacular."

Bonnie. Mmmhmmm. I'm well aware of her talent.

"Have you been following the tour on social media?" Her perfectly manicured brows arch above her blue-gray eyes. Jack must have gotten his father's eyes.

"No," I do not hesitate to reply. I have avoided it, in fact. Him being away from me is hard enough. Seeing it documented in pictures and videos somehow makes it worse.

"All the fans seem to think he and this Bonnie person are a couple," she says nonchalantly. Like it's no big deal.

Meanwhile, rage is building up inside me like pressure in an Instant Pot. I can just imagine a huge, hissing ball of steam erupting when the valve is opened. I hope I can keep that valve locked up tight until Barbara goes home.

"I like what they did with his beard," she continues. "I never liked that scraggly old thing. And it made him look too much like his father. He's such a handsome man. He doesn't need to cover up his face with all that hair. The contacts are nice too. They left the earrings." She shakes her head. "One in each ear; I'll never understand that. Why do men think that's attractive?"

Please. Stop. Talking.

Isn't she going back to his house tonight? Can you please go now? Pretty please with sugar on top?

Elliott walks in from the garage, and I haven't been so happy to see my son in a long time. "Hey, there are some leftovers in the fridge I can heat up for you if you'd like. Say hello to Jack's mother, please."

"Food sounds good, thanks, Mom. Hi, Mrs. Reilly," Elliott says politely. "I miss having Jack here, but it's nice to have meat at every dinner. I think at this point, I'd even get excited over meatloaf, Mom."

"Well, you're in luck—"

"Meatloaf?" His dark eyebrows quirk.

"No, baby. I made a roast."

"Yum! Even better!" He follows me into the kitchen to wait while I heat up a plate for him.

After I get Elliott situated and feed the cat—because he's rubbing up against me as if he actually likes me, and we all know it's just a desperate ploy for food—I pull out my phone and scan the Support Art Foundation Instagram page. There are posts about their regular charity work, but the bulk of the photos are from the Superstars Tour. Yep, there's one of Jack and Bonnie on stage, facing each other, singing with their eyes locked together.

I never thought I'd be a jealous person, but I find myself choking with jealousy. I don't like the way she's looking at him. He's turned so I can't see his expression, but the one on her face is a mixture of lust and admiration.

Yuck.

Claire

22

It's been a month.

Jack left on tour a month ago, and I've seen him once for approximately twenty-four hours. I'm trying to enjoy what's left of the summer and get Mariana ready for school to start back up, but it's been hard. At least my book is with my editor now. That's one giant weight lifted. But my agent is already talking about book *numero dos*. She thinks I should write a book about Jack's music career.

facepalm

Not to sound like a total beeyotch, but remember when I was the famous one in our relationship? Remember when I could brag about having a column in *The New York Times*? Nobody cares about writers when there are rock stars to fawn over. I may have my fans here and there, but I certainly don't get mobbed every time I go out into public by adoring groupies wanting me to sign body parts. I saw a video on Facebook the other day of some lady who asked Jack to sign her boobs. She said he declined her generous offer. I hope so! Otherwise, he's got a lot of explaining to do.

He already has some *'splainin'* to do because of all these posts I see about him and Bonnie. They even have a made-up name for their fantasy couple: *Jannie*. I hate to go all 80s on you, but *gag me with a spoon*. I knew looking at this stuff was opening a portal directly to hell, but remember? I think we've established I'm prone to masochism, and being depressed just buys me a first-class ticket on the Self-Punishment Express.

At least he's on the West Coast, and I have a small window of time to call him between the time Mariana zonks out and when he goes on stage. They're in Seattle tonight before starting to make their trip across the northern part of the country. Two more weeks to go and stops in Minneapolis, Chicago, Indianapolis, Cleveland, Boston and, finally, New York City. I'm in countdown mode.

"Hey," he says, sounding exhausted when he picks up on the third ring.

"Hey, stranger," I try to sound casual, but I'm really excited to hear his voice. We missed our phone call yesterday when his mom was here. "Did you get the pictures I sent today?"

I dressed up in a pretty sundress and did my hair and makeup, then I had Mrs. Vandeveer snap a couple of photos of me by the river. It's amazing that since getting friendly with Red she's a) much more agreeable and b) much more mobile. She seemed downright spry earlier today.

OMG, it's because she ended her thirty-year dry spell, isn't it?

Arrrgggghhhhhh. Did not need to go there.

"I did. You looked really pretty," Jack says. "Thanks for taking those for me."

"So, Red and Mrs. V are a hot item now," I tell him.

"Get outta here! You fixed them up?"

"Well, I put the wheels in motion, and then nature just took its course. Hey, I know a match when I see one!" It's nice to laugh for a change.

And to hear him laugh. "That's awesome, babe. I'll be honest, I thought you were out of your mind, but you knew what you were doing all along."

"Yup, sure did." I pause for a moment, bracing myself for the real reason I called. I have to find out what's going on. Not knowing is killing me, and it's bringing back all sorts of memories of my ex and a certain trainer at his gym he got a little overly friendly with.

"Hey," I start, sucking in a deep breath for fortification.

"Yes?"

"So your mom is here," I remind him.

He murmurs a "yes."

"And she told me last night that she flew out to one of your shows."

"That's right, she did. It was the first night I was back here after being there for the weekend. I forgot to tell you. The Phoenix show."

Okay, that sounds innocent enough.

"She mentioned the whole 'Jannie' thing…"

There it is. The truth bomb. Booooom!

"Right." That's all he says for a moment, like he's searching for the right words to say. I do not like this pause. It does not inspire a lot of confidence.

"Jack?" I wonder if he can hear my heart pounding through the phone. I swear it's all I hear, the blood rushing through my ears and back to my heart. Over and over again while I wait.

"It's optics, Claire," he tells me. "Nothing but optics."

"What the hell does that mean?"

"I know it sounds stupid," he explains, "but the fans

really like Bonnie and me together, and that song we sing. So Brenda and the other folks here at SAF thought it would be better to play it up a little. We're selling out shows in every city, and apparently Bonnie and I are the big draws. I swear to god nothing is going on. We're just letting the fans have their little 'Jannie' moment, and as soon as this tour is over, I'll probably never see her again."

"Why would you agree to that?" I don't like the sound of it one bit, even if it is made up.

"It's in my contract, Claire," he answers with zero hesitation. "Trust me, I don't like it either. But then Mrs. Monnett pointed out that if I didn't follow their PR mandates, I could be kicked off the tour. And that would also affect everyone else on tour. Like Bonnie may not have gotten her record deal."

"What about *your* record deal, Jack?" I'm trying really hard to stay calm and neutral, but keeping my emotions in check has never been my strong suit.

"Hopefully soon, Claire. I told you, I declined Wheelhouse's offer because they wouldn't let me use my own band…and I made a promise to Drew and the guys that I wouldn't do it without them."

I huff out a long sigh. "I hope you know what you're doing."

"I'm doing the very best I can, babe." There's another slight pause, and I envision him scrubbing his hand down his face where his beard used to be. I can't wait for him to grow it back. I'm going to hide all the razors in the house so he doesn't have a choice.

"Hey, I do have a little news," his tone brightens.

"What's that?" I could use some good news. Maybe they're cutting the tour short? Maybe he'll ask us to come to one of his shows now that they're heading back east?

"I'm meeting with a Broadway producer tomorrow," he tells me.

"Broadway? Are you serious?!" I may have gotten a little bit shrieky on that last word. "You know how I feel about Broadway."

"Yes, I do," he answers with a laugh. "I seem to remember you being pro-Broadway. Do I have that right?"

"That's putting it mildly!"

"Right, so it's a new show, and the producer says I'd be perfect for the part. He wants me to read for it," Jack announces.

"Wow, that would be incredible!" It would still take him away from me, but New York is a hell of a lot closer than Seattle. I could spend part of the week up there with him now that Elliott is older…assuming Mariana goes back to Texas with Anita.

"Well, nothing's guaranteed, but I at least wanted to pursue it." I can hear the smile in his voice.

"I can't wait to hear how it goes." My tone drops at the end of my sentence because I know he'll need to go soon.

"I heard from Anita today," he shares. "She's doing a lot better. They want to keep her for a couple more months and do another scan, but she's pretty sure she'll be home in October, if not sooner."

So, not a full year, but maybe she will want Jack to keep Mariana until Christmas, at least? I will sure miss having that little girl around.

"Okay, I hope they got all the cancer."

"Me too."

"Will you call me tomorrow?" I ask.

"Always," he answers.

"I love you, Jack."

"I love you too, babe. Not much longer now…"

WE HAD a late night after the concert, all of us sitting around talking and doing shots. I probably should have gone to bed early since I'm meeting with the Broadway folks, but I have to admit, talking to Claire last night upset me. And that made for a less-than-impressive performance last night. I didn't mess up or anything—I just didn't have my usual energy.

I hate that I'm hurting Claire. I heard it in her voice, plain as day. She loathes this whole thing they're making me do with Bonnie, even if it is all made up. But she knows I want *something* to come of all this hard work—I made it this far, so why wouldn't I? And she's one who originally said I should take it as far as I can.

I head downstairs to the lobby, then turn the corner to the meeting rooms that our group has more or less taken over, like we do in every city we descend upon. I pass Courtney on the way. "Hey, the Broadway guy is waiting for you in Room 100C. Break a leg, kiddo," she shouts out as I pass.

I nod and smile before slipping into the specified room. There's the ubiquitous conference table, this one of heavy oak. The standard hotel chairs circle the table, with a pitcher of water and glasses resting in the center. There are the three Broadway folks: a producer, a director, and some other dude, apparently. And there is Bonnie…

Wait, what is she doing here?

She flashes me an eager smile as the one guy with a sort of jaundiced pallor and thinning white hair gestures toward the seat next to her. I lean across the table and introduce myself to each man in succession. "Hi, I'm Jack Reilly."

"Clark Trenton, the producer," says the white-haired man.

"Jeff Arbuckle," the bearded redhead in the middle greets me. "I'm the director."

"I'm Paul Smith," the gray-haired man on the end says, holding up a pen. "I'm the lawyer, and I need you to sign this non-disclosure agreement before we go any further."

"Standard procedure," the producer adds.

"I signed mine!" Bonnie tosses out.

Great, no pressure. I sit down and glance over the fine print. I'd need my own lawyer to wade my way through this three-page single-spaced document paperclipped on the right-hand corner. Who would put the paperclip there? Only the spawn of Satan, that's who.

"So this just says—" I begin.

Bonnie answers, "It says you can't tell anyone about the project until it's made public."

My brows furrow. "Not even my family?"

"You can tell them you're in a Broadway show, but not which one, what it's about, or who your co-stars are until it's been announced publicly," Paul elaborates.

My brows are so pinched, they might just stay like this for the rest of the day. "Um, alright. Well, I don't even know what I'm agreeing to yet."

"Well, we can't tell you about the show until you sign the NDA," the lawyer retorts.

Sigh. These people are impossible already.

I initial the three spots indicated by little paper arrows and then scrawl my full name across the bottom and date it. "There." I want to add, *Happy?* but somehow refrain.

"Great," Clark says. "So the musical is called *Rock Star*, and it's about a band teacher whose students encourage him to try out for the lead singer role in a fictional band, but it's like a super famous one, and then he does and gets it, but it puts a rift between him and his girlfriend."

"Uh, this is sounding vaguely familiar," I interject. "Almost biographical."

Clark continues, completely ignoring me, "The girlfriend is a fellow teacher, and she's heartbroken about losing her boyfriend to stardom, but she has a secret. The secret is she has an amazing voice, and she somehow manages to land a spot opening for the boyfriend's band. Of course, he already got the part, and yada yada. And naturally it has a happy ending when they're reunited. The kids help her prepare."

"Oookay…" I scratch my head as I glance around the table. The plot sounds like a twisted combination of my life, *School of Rock*, and some cheesy romcom.

"I play the girlfriend," Bonnie chimes in.

Of course she does.

"You'd be perfect for the part of the band teacher. I mean, you *are* a band teacher. And you are now a rock star. It's like it was written for you," Jeff remarks. "You don't even have to audition. I mean, the part is yours if you want it."

"Please say yes, Jack! This would be incredible for us," Bonnie pleads. "Can't you see it now? The Broadway marquis spelling out our names! *Bonnie Scott and Jack Reilly starring in ROCK STAR, an all-new musical!*"

Incredible for us? I want to blurt out. *There is no us!*

"You two are rating like a million on the celebrity couple meter," Clark says. "This would capitalize on your followers' hunger to see you two in a relationship."

"But I'm already in a relationship," I throw back, my

words bitter. I'm getting sick and tired of them throwing this Bonnie woman at me. At her throwing herself at me. What the hell is wrong with these people? There are real lives at stake here. *Real* relationships.

"This is a once-in-a-lifetime chance," Bonnie begs with tears behind her words.

"I have to think about it," I tell them as I stand up. "It's a lot to consider—and it's not even just my relationship with Claire. I'm a single dad too, and right now I'm caring for my daughter while her mother is battling cancer. I can't make decisions like this until I know more about my ex's situation. I'm sorry—I don't mean to disappoint you, and I'm really flattered that you thought of me—"

"Who else would we think of, Jack?" Clark fires at me. "You were born to play this role, and right now you are hot. Hot, hot, hot. People want more of you, Jack. You gotta strike while the iron's hot."

"I'm sorry. I just can't commit right now. Thanks again for the offer, though." I extend my hand to shake, but before I can make contact with any of the men, Bonnie runs from the room crying.

Crap.

"Sorry, I better go after her." I give them a curt nod and head out after Bonnie.

Claire

MARIANA IS out on the porch coloring a picture with Barbara when my phone rings. *Jack.* His meeting with the

Broadway people was this morning, and I'm dying to hear what they had to say.

"Hello?" I might sound a bit over-eager.

"Hey, babe."

Just the sound of his voice—it's like an instant balm. So deep, so smooth. It's like melted butter. *Mmmm, butter.*

"Well, how did it go?" I squeak out, trying to rein in my excitement nodes, but they seem to be shoved into overdrive at the moment.

It's Broadway! What do you expect?

"I signed an NDA, so I can't tell you what the show is about," he explains, "but suffice it to say it hits really close to home."

"What's that supposed to mean?" I balk. "Like…close to our home? Delaware?"

"Close to my personal life story," Jack says.

"It's about an IT guy turned band director?"

He huffs, "I'm not supposed to tell you, but it's about a band director turned rock star and the teacher girlfriend he left behind."

"What?" *That's weird.* "And it was written before this summer? Before the competition?"

"I don't know. It's weird though, right? Kind of creepy." He sighs for like the tenth time, and I can tell he's not happy. "I don't even know if it's fully written yet, to tell you the truth."

"Do you have a stalker?" I tease him. "Because it sounds like the work of a stalker. Do I need to hire a body-guard? How 'bout a hitman? I bet my ex has some connections…"

"Claire, they wanted Bonnie to play the girlfriend," he tells me.

"'Wanted'?"

He's quiet for a moment. "Well, they want her to...but I told them I'd have to think about it."

He has to think about Broadway?

I don't have to think about Broadway. The question is never Broadway. The question is which show to see. And when.

"Jack..." My voice trails off into nothingness as I wish upon every star in the sky that I could wrap my arms around him right now.

"I'm sorry, Claire, I don't even know what to do. I just want to come home at this point, you know? I'm done with this. I don't think this career is for me. There's too much 'optics.'" He mumbles something else that I can't quite hear, and then I imagine him scrubbing his hands down his face like he always does.

"Don't tell them no, honey." My voice perks up—not all is lost. *It's Broadway!* "Negotiate. Tell them you'll do it if they get someone else to play her part. Or tell them you'll do it as long as you can drop the charade that she's your real girl-friend. Let your fans see you act out your relationship on stage—not in real life. That's not too much to ask, is it?"

His tone lightens, "Like if they'll let me go public with my girlfriend, then I could agree with it?"

"You're talking about me in third person now?" I tease him.

"Well, of course I mean you, Claire."

Okay—back to exasperation mode. His moods are shifting on a dime. "So you'll negotiate?"

"I just don't know if the stuff with Bonnie will be nego-tiable. They're putting so much pressure on us," he tells me. "They added another song for us to sing together. And it's a mushy one."

Ugh. I did not want to hear that.

"They practically have us kissing at the end."

"What? Why didn't you tell me—"

I hear a click.

"Jack, why didn't you tell me about this new song?" I demand. "I deserve to know these things."

There's silence.

"Jack?" I can't conceal the panic in my voice. "Jack, are you still there?"

I pull my phone back to look at the screen, but the call has dropped. It's okay. They were getting ready to leave for their next tour stop. He probably had to board the bus. He'll call back…

By that evening, I've been pacing around the house all day. My FitBit registers like a zillion steps. But there's been no phone call from Jack, and no answer when I try to call.

23

I sit, staring at my phone, which is now dead. What the hell just happened? I restart it, wondering if maybe it's just going bad. It boots back up but says "No Service" at the top. *Great*. Where are we again? Minneapolis? Chicago? I don't even know anymore.

My head is killing me.

I recline on the bed, trying to restart my phone again. I can't even call the company to report a problem. My hotel room phone is clear over on the desk, seeming like miles away instead of feet. I guess I could use a landline phone? Sigh. It all seems like too much right now.

Sleep is hovering over me like an angel of mercy when loud pounding makes me lurch to a sitting position, gasping for air. I was settling into a dream with Mariana and Claire on the beach…but I guess that's ruined now.

"What?! Just a second; I'm coming!" I shout toward the door as I wobble to a standing position and make my way over to pummel whoever is causing all the ruckus outside.

When I throw open the door, Brenda Monnett and

Bonnie are standing there, the latter with tear-streaked mascara running down her cheeks, and the former wearing a scowl she may have borrowed from the Prince of Darkness. Pretty sure I saw that look on my ex's face a time or two.

I haven't seen Brenda Monnett since Los Angeles. How does she just keep appearing whenever there's drama? It's like magic. *Black magic.*

"What? I don't feel well," I say from my defensive position behind the door, with just my head peeking around it.

"Let us in," Mrs. Monnett demands.

I suppose that's in my contract too. I had no idea I was signing away all my privacy and rights. I slowly swing the door open as I step out from behind it.

Bonnie throws herself on one of the beds and buries her face in a pillow as loud sobs wreak havoc on her body. Mrs. Monnett sits primly in the leather chair at the hotel room desk. I reluctantly take a seat on the other bed, already bracing myself for whatever nonsense this is going to involve.

She glares at me, her eyes aiming daggers right at my throat. "Why did you dick the Broadway folks around, Jack?"

I scoff, "What are you talking about? I told them I had to think about it." That doesn't sound like "dicking around" to me. Trust me, I work in education. I know the meaning of "dicking around."

She shakes her head and looks at me like I'm a complete moron. "No one tells Clark Trenton no. Do you have any idea who he is? How powerful he is in this industry?"

"I'd never heard of the man before this morning," I insist. "The project sounds interesting, but they could hardly tell me any of the logistics. And, honestly—" I glance over at Bonnie, whose back is facing us as her entire body shudders with tears, "—I don't know if I want to costar with…her."

She seethes the words between clenched teeth, "First of all, you *imbecile*, the reason they didn't divulge logistics is because they're waiting on you to say yes. The entire show was written *for* you. They are willing to cater to *you*. All you had to do was say yes."

I shake my head as I lift my eyes to meet Mrs. Monnett's icy glare. "What? Why would they do that?"

"Clark is an old friend of mine. He wants to support our foundation, and SAF will receive a certain percentage of the proceeds from this show. That's why the story is about a band teacher. That's why the story was written for *you*, Jack. You're the face of this whole thing. It's loosely based on a true story," she explains.

"Well, that's great, but it's *not* a true story. My girlfriend is Claire Sterling, who is a writer and lives in Delaware, and she's not a teacher at my school. And she'd love for me to do the show, but she's not comfortable with the public relationship you're forcing me into with Ms. Scott." I don't even want to say Bonnie's name anymore, let alone have her in the room.

But as soon as I say her name, she launches herself off the bed and lunges at me. "Why are you trying to ruin my life?!" she screams at me. "Don't you realize we can have all this on a silver platter, Jack? All you have to do is play along."

I'm silent as she sinks back down onto the mattress. "I'm a poor single mom, Jack. I barely earn minimum wage. My son has juvenile diabetes and a lot of medical expenses. I can barely afford to feed him. I need this, Jack.

Who the hell cares about your girlfriend? She's old, and she's fat, and you can do so much better than her—"

Oh, now that did it. Now my rage is uncontainable. Completely unleashed.

"What the hell is wrong with both of you? First of all, how do you even know what Claire looks like? Secondly, my relationship with her—or anyone else, for that matter —is none of your business. It has *nothing* to do with you or this stupid tour!"

"I looked her up," Bonnie spits out. "She's not hard to find on social media. She wrote some stupid column for *The New York Times*. Big fat deal. She's nobody, Jack—"

"Quit talking about her like that," I shout, the anger spiking my blood as it surges up my spine. "Don't you dare say another word about the woman I love. You don't even know her."

"Both of you, SHUT UP!" Mrs. Monnett screams, rising to her feet with her trembling finger outstretched toward us both. "Both of you, sit the hell down, and I'll tell you exactly how things are going to be. You are both under contract, not only for the next two weeks, but there is a clause that beholds you to the foundation if you accept any projects that are in any way affiliated with us. It's airtight, and unless you want to have the clothes on your back literally sued off, I suggest you listen very carefully to what I have to say."

I plop down next to Bonnie, far enough away that we're not touching. She's still whimpering, so I thrust the tissue box on the nightstand in her lap, and she murmurs a "thank you" before taking one and blowing her nose at an almost comic volume level. At least, it would be funny if I weren't so livid right about now.

Why is my life so weird? I ponder as Brenda Monnett braces herself to give us a verbal lashing.

"First of all, Jack, you *will* be doing the musical. If you violate that part of your contract, you won't be receiving the $25,000 guaranteed to you for placing third in the national competition and for completing the six-week tour. Secondly, Bonnie, you will also be doing the musical. Failure to do so will result in losing the $100,000 you are guaranteed for winning the national competition and completing the six-week tour. What's more, if Jack drops out of the tour before completing the last show, you, Bonnie, will *also* lose your money."

"What? How can you do that?" I protest through my clenched jaw. My fists are balled up so tight on either side of me, they're burning to punch something—and I'm not ordinarily a violent person at all.

"It's another wonderful clause our lawyer wrote into the contracts. If anyone drops out of the tour before the last show—the grand finale in New York City—no one gets their money. It's $100,000 for the top spot, $50,000 for the second, and $25,000 for the third. Everyone else gets $10,000. We wrote it that way to dissuade anyone from jumping ship and leaving us in a lurch. So far we haven't even had to bring up that clause to threaten anyone to get their act together—pardon the pun. At least not until today."

I suck in a breath so deep, my nostrils flare as they try to collect more air. My lungs squeeze against my ribcage as I scramble for something—*anything*—to say. I thought Brenda Monnett was an amazing woman. I thought she had founded a worthy cause and wanted to do good things with her money. But it turns out she's just a greedy, power-hungry bitch masquerading as a sweet grandmother.

"Furthermore, Jack, you will be taking a break from your phone for the next two weeks. You'll notice it doesn't work—"

"What the hell? You can't do that!"

An evil grin spreads her lips in the most wicked way. "We can, though. It's all in the contract, darling. I guess you should have read it a little more closely. It says we can step in in any way we see fit to control PR matters. And this is a PR matter, my dear. You and Bonnie will continue to be cozy in public. Give your fans what they want. They are going to go wild when they learn about your Broadway show. I don't care what the two of you do in private, but in public—in public we better see the love."

With that, she stands up and sashays out the room, leaving Bonnie still whimpering beside me.

Claire

"WHY HASN'T DADDY CALLED?" Mariana's lip pooches out, and when she adds her hands on her hips, well, it's scientifically proven that no one can resist adorableness of this magnitude.

"I don't know, sweet pea. I think he has an issue with his phone. I've been trying to get ahold of him for two days." And my stomach has been in knots the entire time, but I don't mention that part.

To make matters worse, I've taken to following the tour on their Instagram profile. Big mistake. Like the *worst* of mistakes. I know Jack said the cozying-up-to-Bonnie thing was for show and "optics," but they certainly make it look real. I can't scroll through the feed after eating, not unless I want my meal to make a surprise reprise in the nearest toilet.

When Jean-Marc stops by for coffee, he posits that Jack has probably just gotten busy, and he's trying to get through the last few tour dates. "He'll be home in just over a week," my friend tries to console me. "I'm sure the stress has gotten to him, and he just wants to decompress when he's done performing. Give him some space…"

"But he hasn't called his own daughter!" I protest. "That's not like him. Something has to be wrong. He was so depressed the last time I talked to him."

But what if it's all a ploy? That's what the quiet, dark voices in my head say. The ones that remind me how Jeremy cheated on me. What if Jack is saying it's all "optics," but he's fallen in love with Bonnie and doesn't want to tell me because he needs me to keep taking care of his daughter while he's off gallivanting around the country?

Jean-Marc wraps an arm around me. "Well, he's still performing, and you can see he's alive and well from the pictures on Instagram. It won't be much longer till he's home."

I know his words are meant to be comforting, but they're not. Besides, he has Thor now. And they are so damn cute and happy. I've hardly seen him at all since the party he threw for me.

Plus, watching Red and Mrs. Vandeveer move his stuff across the lawn so he can move in with her is cute and all, but it's not doing much for my mood. They've been fooling around for, what, like two or three weeks now, and they're already shacking up? Jack and I have been seriously dating for a year, and I feel like we're farther away from co-habitating than ever—and don't even get me started on the M Word.

In other words, I'm grumpy. Despondent. And turning it all back on myself like the Old Claire, the Pre-Reinvention Claire, blaming all my flaws for everything that goes bad. My therapist and body image coach would be so disappointed in me.

All that hard work they did down the drain.

Later that afternoon, I get a call from Anita. Well, at least one of the child's parents wants to talk to her. "Hi, there, how are you feeling?"

"Hi, Claire." Her voice sounds smoother and brighter than the last time I heard from her. "I'm doing a lot better. Finishing up what's hopefully going to be my last round of chemo."

"I'm so glad to hear that! Do you want to talk to Mariana?" I offer, not knowing how expensive it is for her to call me—I'm guessing it can't be cheap.

"I do, but I need to talk to you first," she says, her tone growing more serious.

"What's up?" My heart starts to pound, wondering what fresh hell is descending upon me now.

"Jack called me from a different number last night. He said they took his phone and don't want him to communicate with you. I don't know what's going on, but it sounds like she's being held hostage or something," Anita tells me, and she's not joking.

"Oh my god! We got disconnected the other night, and I haven't been able to get ahold of him since. I've been so worried!" A long sigh rushes out as a bit of relief surges through me. Well, it's kind of relief. Part of me is relieved he doesn't hate me, but the hostage thing is scary AF. If he's telling the truth, I mean.

"They gave him an iPad and said he could communicate with me or Mariana, but not you. I didn't probe too much, but he wanted me to let you know. I can give you the number he called from if you want to try to reach him. Maybe you can use someone else's phone so they won't know it's you? I don't know. I just thought it was worth a shot."

"Thanks, Anita. That means a lot to me. I'll see what I can do." My heart rate triples as I think about what they might have told him, threatened him with to keep him from calling me. *These people are nuts!* I don't know what the hell to do, but at the moment I'm feeling a critical level of guilt over getting him mixed up in this whole mess.

"You're welcome," she says, the smile in her voice coming across loud and clear. She rattles off the number, which I copy down. "I'd love to talk to my daughter now."

"Just one sec, and I'll get her." I find Mariana playing with some dolls on the floor of her bedroom. "Hey, sweet pea, your mom is on the phone."

Her whole face brightens when I hand the phone to her. Then I dash into Elliott's room to see if I can borrow his iPhone. He's playing a video game, as per usual.

Well, of course I can borrow his iPhone. I pay for the darn thing, I remind myself as I tap on his shoulder. A split second later, his avatar blows up.

He lifts the virtual reality headset off. "You made me die!"

"Sorry about that. Hey, I need to borrow your phone." I don't feel like answering a lot of questions. I just want to talk to Jack.

"What's wrong with yours?" He scowls at me, the indentions from the VR headset making him look even more irritated.

"Do you want to continue to *have* a phone?" I threaten.

That's all it takes. He hands me the phone and slides the headset back over his head to start a new game.

I hear Mariana on FaceTime with her mom as I open

up Elliott's phone with the code he's obligated to surrender any time I ask for it and punch in the number Anita gave me. I think he's in Chicago today, so there's only a one-hour time difference. And it's afternoon there, so he should be available.

For some reason, I don't expect it to work, which is why I feel a bolt of nervous energy rush though me when he answers the call. His face comes into view just a moment later.

"Oh my god, what's going on?" I immediately blurt out.

He palms his face and then peeks at me through the crack in his fingers. "Everything is royally effed up, babe."

"What do you mean? Why?"

"Shhh...I can't talk for long. They have my room bugged. They're going to figure out I'm talking to you," he whispers, glancing around his room, his eyes filled with panic and paranoia.

"This is crazy, Jack! Why are you letting them treat you this way?"

"They don't want me to talk to you..."

What the hell? I don't know if my boyfriend has gone completely off his rocker, or if these people really are demons in disguise. I know they want him and Bonnie to pretend to be involved, and I'm not okay with that at all, but I'm even less okay with them cutting off communication with me. How can he stand for that?

"Jack, listen to me, this is completely crazy. They can't tell you who you can talk to. You have to demand your phone back. Call a lawyer, do something. This is completely unacceptable!" My voice is rising as fast as my frustration.

I hear pounding on his door, and his paranoid eyes

flash in that direction before snapping back to me. "I've gotta go, Claire. I'm sorry. I'm so sorry…"

That's all he says before the screen goes black.

Now I don't know what to think.

24

I think everyone around me has gone completely insane.

That's really the only explanation I can come up with for this current sequence of events. So, apparently, they're bugging my room in every city. Who knows how long that has been going on? They heard me tell Claire that I'm ready for this to be over. And I guess I'm not allowed to say that.

I think it may be time to call a lawyer. This has gotten completely out of hand. I wonder if I could get away with calling Drew or one of the other guys for help. I stuff the iPad under my shirt and head down the long hallway toward the elevator.

We're in Chicago…I think?

Maybe I'll go walk along the river and do some sight-seeing before the show tonight. They have to allow that, right? They can't hold me prisoner in this hotel all day.

Bonnie turns the corner and nearly runs into me. "Where are you going?" Her face still looks red and splotchy from our earlier encounter with Brenda.

"I just need to get some air." I know I'm being short

with her, but I'm not happy with her at the moment, and it's going to be hard to fake our "connection" when we're on stage tonight if I don't get a little time to myself.

"Maybe I should come with you?" she suggests, her face perking up with the hint of a soft smile.

"I don't think that's a good idea."

"Optics, Jack," is all she says.

Screw optics. I better never hear that word again after this is all over. *Holy crap, I can't wait till this is all over.* If I can just make it through the last show. One more week. Tonight's show in Chicago. Tomorrow night in Indianapolis. The following night in Cleveland. Then we have two days off before our next-to-last show in Boston, and then the grand finale is in New York City.

One more week.

I push past Bonnie, and I swear I hear her burst into tears again. I know I should feel guilty, but I'm getting tired of hearing her cry over every last thing. I am trying to hold everything together, but we are *all* losing it. We are *all* cracking. It's not just me and her. Xia, Lilly, Nick, Steve, Talia—we are all losing it bit by bit. Humans weren't meant to keep up this kind of pace.

I'm staying on board, making myself get through the last show so everyone can get their money. I don't want to be accused of not being a team player, and I do genuinely like my tour mates. I want everyone to be rewarded for our hard work. We all deserve that and so much more.

We should honestly be making a lot more than we are because the Foundation is making a killing off us and this tour. Not only are people paying $80 a ticket to see us live, but they've already released a tour album we recorded when we were in Los Angeles. That album has been in the top ten on the pop charts and doesn't seem to be falling anytime soon.

I thought I was supporting a cause I really believed in, so I didn't care about the money. I do still believe in the cause, I just didn't realize the organization was being run by Cruella de Vil. *Sorry, dad moment.* Mariana loves that movie. And Brenda Monnett does kind of look like that famous villainess other than all her hair is platinum instead of half.

I head down the elevator and start to make my way to the lobby when I'm stopped by one of the SAF security guards. "Where are you going, Mr. Reilly?"

"I need to take a walk, get some fresh air," I tell him with a smile. I try to send out some *nothing subversive going on here* vibes like a Jedi mind trick, hoping he'll buy it.

"Why don't you let one of us accompany you?" His square jaw clenches, foreshadowing that capitulation is the only acceptable response.

"I'm good, really." I try to pass, but he grabs my wrist, stopping my movement with very little effort on his part. Why does he have to be so strong? I'm not exactly a small or weak guy myself.

"It's not safe out there alone, Mr. Reilly. You know how some fans can be…" He makes the gesture for crazy by twirling his finger in a circle around his ear.

That's offensive, but whatever. I just want to be left alone.

However…if I protest, then it's going to get back to Brenda, and then I'll be in even more trouble than I already am. So I just shrug and allow him to follow me out the revolving door and onto the sidewalk outside the Hyatt. I turn onto the Riverwalk, heading toward Lake Michigan, the smell of hot dogs from a nearby food cart wafting into my nose. *Yuck.*

The security guard is wearing a SAF polo and khakis, so I guess I don't look too conspicuous out here strolling along the river on this beautiful August day. The clouds are high in the azure sky, puffy and white, and sunbeams sparkle on the water as it flows toward the lake. It's a gorgeous day that I wish I could enjoy, but my chest feels like it's on fire. Like I'm about two seconds from jumping over the railing and swimming for my freedom.

How can I ditch this guy? I pull my baseball cap down on my head and adjust my glasses. So far no one has recognized me. We don't tend to get recognized unless we're out in a group or coming or going from a venue. When we pull up in this massive tour bus, it's a little hard to go incognito. But just me out here, an average Joe in jeans and a Red Hot Chili Peppers concert tee—I'm not likely to attract much attention.

Unless. Unless I could create a diversion and slip away from the security dude.

It's risky.

But…

Desperate times call for desperate measures. It's something Claire says all the time—usually in a sarcastic way that doesn't involve any desperation whatsoever. God, I love that woman and her crazy penchant for exaggeration.

I rip off my hat and sunglasses, feeling like I'm going from Clark Kent to Superman as I continue to stroll, though the sudden bright sunlight is a bit disorienting, so I nearly crash into a light pole first. Real smooth, huh?

It only takes about two minutes (though my ego would have been happier with something in the thirty-second range) to hear a high-pitched squeal from a group of ladies who look to be part of a bachelorette party. It stops me in my tracks. They also stop and point as the bride jumps up and down screaming, "Oh my god, it's Jack from the SAF Superstar tour!"

In a split second, I'm mobbed by eight or ten bodies,

long hair flying, arms flailing and the scent of perfume almost making me choke. I glance up just in time to notice the Security Dude—forgot to catch his name, so let's call him Bruce; that sounds like a good Security Dude name— stopping to lean against the light pole (different one from the pole that nearly assaulted me) to supervise the encounter.

"Here, can you take our picture?" the bride chirps, handing her phone to Bruce, who grasps it in his bulky hands like it's a fragile baby bird. *Perfect.*

I get in the middle of the mob, devising my exit strategy while the bride attempts to direct her crew on where to stand. We smile for a few normal pics, and then the bride says, "Okay, let's do a silly picture!"

While we're all making funny faces, I make a break for it.

Bruce is left holding the phone and scrambling to give it back to the bride before he can chase after me. My legs are pumping as hard as they will go, and thankfully there's a massive crowd coming out of a building up ahead. If I can just infiltrate that mob of people, I'm golden. I dive between a scowling soccer mom, who's shielding her kids like I'm going to bowl them over, and a man in a business suit who looks seconds away from hauling off and punching me.

Totally worth the risk, by the way.

I elbow my way through the throng and out the other side, ducking down a different street as I search ahead for someplace to go. There's a Starbucks on the corner. *Too easy. Too exposed.* Across the street is a library. *Perfect.*

Now that I'm inside, and it's super-duper quiet—*it's a library, right? Duh!*—I try to act as normal as possible. I slap my baseball cap back on, but I forgo the shades because that's even more conspicuous than leaving them off. I find the stairs and head up a couple of flights to the stacks. Stacks and stacks of books. I've never been more grateful to see books in my life.

There are a couple of empty reading nooks and not too many patrons around, so I settle in where I can keep my eye on the elevator and the staircase. My iPad immediately starts buzzing, but I ignore it. I can't use it. They'll be able to track it. I better turn it off. I wonder if they can still track it even if it's off? Duh, I shouldn't have even brought it. I probably only have a few minutes before they find me.

Of course, there are no pay phones anymore in this part of the universe. But I do spy a bank of computers along the far wall. Heart still pounding from my jog and being out of shape somehow, despite five weeks of shaking my booty on stage every night, I head over and plop down in one of the chairs.

I hate social media, but Facebook has a messenger option, so this is the best I can do.

I message Claire, praying the notification will go to her phone.

Jack: *Hey, it's me, I broke out of jail and am hiding out in the library. I only have a few minutes. Are you there?*

I huff out an exasperated sigh. No answer.

No checkmark to show it's been read.

I suck in a breath as I look up Drew's name. He's a pretty avid social media user, so hopefully he'll answer.

Jack: *Hey, buddy. I wanted to check in and see how you guys are doing? Sorry I haven't been in touch since the party.*

There's the checkmark. He saw it. Three dots. He's typing.

Drew: *Hey, what's up, man? I thought you'd forgotten all about us little people.*

Jack: *No, man, not a chance! I come home in one week. Are you guys still practicing?*

Drew: *Sure are.*

Jack: *I'm looking forward to playing with you guys again.*

Drew: *So, no record deal?*

I'm not going to tell him about the one I gave up because it didn't include them.

Jack: *No, not yet. Hopefully soon. Hey, I need a favor.*

Drew: *Yeah?*

Jack: *Don't you have a buddy who's a lawyer?*

Drew: *A few, yeah. That's what happens when you're a great bartender. *wink emoji**

Jack: *I need some help. Having an issue with my contract, and I need someone to look at it.*

Drew: *Oh okay. Well, can I send his info to your phone?*

Jack: *Uh...about my phone...it's broken. Can you send it here? To Facebook? That's why I'm on Messenger. I haven't had a chance to get my phone replaced yet.*

Drew: *Oh, that sucks, bro. Okay, yeah, I'll send it in a bit. Where ya at right now?*

Claire's message pops up:

Claire: *What do you mean by jail? What is going on there, Jack? I'm getting really freaked out by all this.*

Jack: *I mean figurative jail. How's my Princess?*

Claire: *She's fine. Look, Jack, I don't like this one bit. Can you just come home? I'm starting to worry about you, both your safety and sanity. This isn't right...*

Jack: *I'm fine, Claire. I just have to finish up this last week. Five more shows.*

Claire: *I'm about to call the police. They can't take your phone and keep you from talking to your family.*

Jack: *Don't call the police. Please don't call the police, whatever you do.*

Brenda will probably have me taken out if that happens. I wouldn't put anything past her at this point.

Claire: *I can't do this, Jack. This is too crazy.*

Jack: *Just trust me, Claire. It will all be over soon. I promise.*

Claire: *I saw the headlines, Jack. I saw the kiss.*

Jack: *What kiss? What headlines? What are you talking about?*

There's that stupid *dot-dot-dot* while she types. It stops, then disappears, then starts again. After three more cycles of that, a link appears to YouTube. It's some video from one of our concerts. I have no idea which one because they're all starting to run together now. It's during the mushy song they made Bonnie and I sing.

We're singing, gazing into each other's eyes. It's so creepy, it makes the hair on the back of my neck stand up. And then the camera pans out, only to zoom back in, and it looks like I take her into my arms and kiss her.

What the actual…?

I didn't do that!

When I look back at the messenger screen, Claire has sent an article from some tabloid site. The headline is "Jannie Fans Get Their Wish! Jack and Bonnie Kiss on Stage!"

How did they do that? How did they make it look like that? It didn't happen!

Jack: *Claire, you have to believe me, I didn't kiss her. I promise you. I don't know how they did that, but I didn't kiss her.*

Claire: *I don't know what to believe anymore, Jack.*

The door on the other side of the library flies open, and four men in SAF polo shirts emerge, all scanning the area, obviously looking for me.

Oh crap!

Jack: *I gotta go. I'll call you as soon as I can.*

In seconds, I'm surrounded, and they're dragging me out of the building.

AND JUST LIKE THAT, he's gone again.

I can't do it. This is killing me. I poise my fingers over the keys and type my final message.

Claire: *I will take care of Mariana as long as you need me to, but I can't do this thing with us anymore. If you truly loved me, you would have never let them do this to you. To us. It's over, Jack. I don't even believe you're really coming home in a week. I don't know how I can ever trust you again after this.*

I'm shaking with a mixture of anger and despair. I want to go lock myself in my room for the next decade or so, but Mariana is in the living room watching a movie— thankfully not *Frozen* this time—and she's going to want dinner soon. And then Elliott will come home and want dinner too.

It doesn't matter if your world is crashing around you when you're a mom. You have to suck it up and keep on giving and giving till there's nothing left of you.

If only I had another mom to talk to, one who's been heartbroken but had to pick up the pieces and go on momming. I briefly consider calling Nora, or even Olivia, my college roommate I'm still friendly with. But when I glance down at my phone, my eyes go straight to my last phone call.

Anita.

With trembling fingers, I push the call button, not even knowing what time it is over there, let alone what I'm going to say. But I have a feeling she was heartbroken by the same man who just broke my heart, and she developed a thick, impenetrably bitchy exterior to protect herself from getting hurt by him again.

What would it be like if I took Mariana to visit her? I have a passport. Mariana has a passport. Maybe Anita is feeling well enough for company now?

"Hello?" her voice is a little froggy, but at least she answered.

"Hi…" I can't conceal the sob that wells up in my throat when I hear her on the other end.

Here is this woman I barely know, who is battling cancer across the ocean from me, and I'm bugging her with my petty relationship problems. I shouldn't be doing that. It's a dick move on my part.

"What's wrong, Claire? Are you okay?" Her voice gains an edge of panic. "Is Mariana okay?"

"Yes, yes. She's fine. She's watching *Moana* in the other room."

"What happened? You sound like crap, girl," she says matter-of-factly.

I chuckle at her rather astute assessment. "Yeah…I feel really terrible for calling, but Jack and I just broke up."

"What? What did he do to you?"

I laugh again. I don't know where this laughter is coming from, but it's almost like my body doesn't even know what to do, my heart doesn't know how to feel. It all seems so final and surreal at the same time. I just told him it was over. *Done.*

"Just tell me, Claire. Come on, lady. I can't help you if you don't tell me what's going on," she says, sounding so warm and genuine and caring that I burst into tears at her kindness, which I'm not sure I deserve.

And just like that, the floodgates open, and every single thing that's happened in the last six months or so comes rushing to the surface and gets vomited into the phone like

I'd just eaten a huge meal before riding a rollercoaster that goes upside down.

Anita interjects with questions and heartfelt, "Oh no he didn't!" and "Damn, girl!"

And after it's all over with, she says, "What you need is a distraction."

I laugh because I'd been thinking the same thing before I called. "Yeah, I sure do. I was thinking of bringing Mariana to London to visit. What do you think of that?"

"That would be nice," she says. "Don't make any travel plans yet though, okay? I have a couple of ideas, but I need to make some phone calls first. Alright?"

I nod even though she can't see me. "Okay. I'll wait to hear from you then."

"Chin up, woman," she tells me. "You're gonna get through this. You're a strong person, Claire. I don't think Jack has ever been attracted to anything but smart, strong women, and when I met you, I knew immediately you were just his type."

I don't know if that's still a compliment, but I murmur a thank you.

"Hang in there, and I'll be in touch in a day or two, okay?"

My heart is so full, I feel it whirring and pumping against my ribs. "Thank you, Anita. Thank you so much for listening and being a good friend when you barely even know me."

I hear her voice crack with tears as she says, "It's the very least I can do after you've taken such good care of my baby girl."

25

After a debriefing when I returned to the hotel, I was finally given my iPad back. I logged into Facebook and saw the message Claire left for me.

Claire: *I will take care of Mariana as long as you need me to, but I can't do this anymore. If you truly loved me, you would have never let them do this to you. To us. It's over, Jack. I don't even believe you're really coming home in a week. I don't know how I could ever trust you again after this.*

I asked Mrs. Monnett how they were able to make it look like Bonnie and I kissed, and all she said was, "You did kiss. And someone captured the moment on video. That's how fame and celebrity work, Jack. Everything you do is part of the public spectacle."

I did not kiss her! I would remember doing it—and I'd never do it in the first place. They obviously doctored the footage, and now she's gaslighting me. This whole thing is a crazy and extravagant effort to make me think I've gone insane. I'm surprised they haven't brought out a straight-jacket, to be honest.

That's got to be the next step.

WE DID our shows in Chicago, Indianapolis, and Cleveland. Now we have two days off as we travel to Boston, and when we get there, we'll be working on our closing night's show. It will be our final farewell, so Garvey wanted to mix things up and stage something really special. Boston's show will be sort of a dress rehearsal for the New York closer.

Drew did come through with the name of a lawyer. I was able to borrow someone else's phone, sneak out and give the guy a call. He sounded like a pretentious jerk with a name like Octavius Linderhorn, but I promised to hear him out. I described everything that had happened thus far, and he told me to just lay low for a few days while he did some research.

So that's what I've done.

I haven't talked to anyone back home. I haven't even called Anita or Mariana. And I definitely have not talked to Claire.

I've kept my head down, nose to the grindstone, and just focused on surviving our last five shows. Meanwhile, Bonnie has been all over me. I will only talk to her if other people are around. I'm none too happy about her role in all this. It sounds like she has only helped Brenda and her Flying Monkeys keep me locked down.

"I'm doing it for my son," she told me when we sat down on the bus headed from Cleveland to Boston. "It's all for him. After the Broadway show ends, you don't ever have to see me again."

I didn't dignify that with a response. If my lawyer could work his magic—though I had serious doubts on him actually having any magic, one could hope, right?—then I'd be able to get out of the Broadway show. All I wanted was my $25,000, and then hopefully I could use whatever notoriety I'd acquired in this whole brush with fame to secure a record deal for myself and The Gallant Misfits. And I could beg Claire for her forgiveness and propose to her like I should have done months ago.

When we get to Boston, I ask my handler, for lack of a better term, for permission to call Anita to check in. It's granted, and I'm given a whopping fifteen minutes of privacy to complete the conversation. *Two more days*, I remind myself. *Two more days, and I'm free.*

"Hey, sorry it's been a while since I've called," I tell her as soon as she answers.

"What the hell is wrong with you?" she barks down the line, sounding like the Darth Anita we all know and hate. So much for cancer making her a nicer person, which was Claire's leading theory. I should have known better than to think it would be a permanent thing.

"I'm almost done, that's all. I've had a rough few days, but there's a light at the end of the tunnel," I tell her. "And then I can be with my daughter again. Will you want us to come visit?" I might be able to swing a trip to London once I get my check. And we'll have a couple of weeks before school starts back up.

"What the hell is wrong with you?" she repeats. "I thought you were in love with Claire!"

"What?"

"You heard me," she snaps.

"What did she tell you?" Claire's been talking to Anita? *Oh, this is bad. This is very, very bad.* Now Claire will never want to take me back.

"Well, that you kissed that other woman on stage, for starters. And you've done nothing to inform your adoring fans that there is, in fact, no Jannie—that's a ridiculously *stupid* name, by the way—and now you've lost the best thing that ever happened to you. Besides me and your daughter, of course."

"I didn't kiss her, Anita! I don't know how they did it, but they made it look like we kissed. Did you see how the video panned out and back in? I think they put stunt doubles in and made it look like we kissed. Or it's CGI. Hell, I don't know, but I did *not* kiss that woman!" I seethe. "I swear it on my daughter's life."

She huffs out a breath. "Fine, whatever, Jack. I'm sure it's some sort of conspiracy, but the truth is that you didn't refute the video in public. You haven't said anything about Claire in public since that interview in Los Angeles."

She knows about that? *Geez.* Everything I do must be on the internet. I better be careful next time I go take a dump, or everyone will be tweeting about it.

I'm quiet for a moment because I don't know what to say at this point. I could argue with her, but she's right. I didn't refute it. I tried to keep my head down and play by their rules so everyone could get their money. I couldn't risk getting kicked off the tour.

I can't make everyone happy.

It's the same as when Anita left Texas so many years ago now. I couldn't make her happy and me happy at the same time. It just wasn't possible.

"Do you love her?" comes her voice, stronger than ever.

"Yes. Yes, I do. I hope to win her back when I come home. I'll be home in two days, Anita. Then we can work everything out." *At least I hope so.*

"Two days might be too late, Jack. You need to make a gesture—something big. Something grand. And something public," she tells me.

"I don't know what that might be," I argue. "I'm really

afraid of doing anything before these last two shows are over." I explain the contract to her again, and the talk I had with my lawyer.

"Well, it's your funeral, Jack, but you have a wonderful woman here. A woman who gave up her whole summer to babysit your daughter. A woman who supported your dreams, even if it meant giving up time with you. A woman who put her book on hold to make sure you had what you needed to succeed. If that isn't love and sacrifice, then I don't know what is. Hell, if you don't want to fight for Claire, maybe I'll just try to win her myself!"

"What, you like women all the sudden?" I gasp.

She giggles. "I don't think I'm bi, but for a woman like Claire…I might have to reconsider!"

I do find some amusement in it, but my heart hurts too bad to laugh at the moment. At this point, I don't know if I'll ever laugh again.

"I wish I could talk to her," I lament. "I just want her to understand why I did what I did…"

Anita's quiet for a moment. And then: "When can you talk again? I have something in the works that might help…"

Claire

I'VE BEEN STUMBLING around the house in a stupor for three days now. Maybe four. I might have taken one shower in there, but I wouldn't swear to it. I've managed to keep two children alive, so that's the good news. The bad news is that I feel dead inside.

Jean-Marc has been over. Nora has called. The neighbors have been over to play Chutes and Ladders with Mariana. Everyone is trying to take care of me, but the one person I need and want doesn't even care. I haven't heard a word from Jack since that day on Facebook, and I happen to know he saw my message. I saw the little checkmark to say it was seen, but there was no response.

When Anita calls a few days later, the first burst of hope in what feels like ages bolts through me. All I can think about is hopping on a plane to London. I'm sure Mariana and I would have a blast, even if her adorable little face reminded me of Jack every three seconds.

"Hey there," is all I can muster in the way of a greeting when I answer the call.

"Hey, lady, how are you doing?" the woman I've come to think of as a friend asks.

"I'm hanging in there. How are *you* doing?" When I realize that I forgot to ask her how she's been feeling last time we spoke, I feel like such a dingbat.

"Good news. The last scan I had was completely clear," she announces.

"What? Oh my god, Anita, that's so great!" I gush out, genuinely happy and excited for her.

"Yep! I'm cancer-free, at least at the moment. Dr. Richter still wants me to lay low for a month or two and try to get my strength back up. I got so weak when I was sick during the chemo," she shares.

"Oh, I bet. I know you'll make a full recovery, though," I assure her.

"I hope so. I still have some things to wrap up here before I can return to the States, but I have an amazing opportunity this weekend in New York for us, and I know you were looking for a distraction—"

"Oh, I was hoping to come to London…" My voice trails off, revealing my disappointment. Maybe there's a reason she doesn't want us to come there.

"I know. And that's still on the table sometime before I leave, but this weekend is a once-in-a-lifetime thing, and I think Mariana will love it!" she gushes.

"Okay, I'm game. What is it?"

"I got us a special VIP package to see *Frozen* on Broadway!"

"Oh, wow!" Ordinarily the word "Broadway" sparks nothing but rampant excitement that explodes through me like fireworks, but after Jack's whole fiasco with the Broadway producers, I kind of feel like the whole concept is tainted for me now.

And that makes me so sad.

"Yeah, that's still her favorite movie, isn't it?" Anita asks, possibly sensing my reticence.

"Oh, yeah. She'll definitely love that! When is it?"

"It's the Friday night showing, so we could meet up tomorrow afternoon? My flight gets in at around noon," she tells me.

"Oh, you have it all planned!" I didn't realize this was already a done deal. Well, I can't disappoint her. I know she's dying to see her daughter after all she's been through.

I don't like the fact that I have to go to New York, which is where Jack will also be. His last show is on Saturday. But it's a huge city. I'm sure I can avoid him, and if Anita wants to meet up with him so he can see Mariana, that's fine. I don't have to be there.

"I sure do. I even have a hotel room booked for you. I'm going to text you the address, and all you have to do is meet me there tomorrow afternoon. Maybe three o'clock?

We can walk around the city and grab some dinner before heading over to the show."

"Yeah, of course, that sounds great. Thanks so much, Anita. Do you want to tell Mariana?" I ask.

"No, keep it a secret!" Anita says. "Just tell her you have a surprise for her in New York, and then I'll do the rest."

"Alright. I can do that."

The first glimmer of excitement I've felt in ages sends tingles shooting through my body as I hang up and immediately start thinking of what to pack. I haven't seen a Broadway show in a couple of years now—what to wear?

IT'S no big surprise that Mariana is overcome with joy when we walk into the lobby of the grand hotel in Manhattan only to find her mother sitting on one of the little sofas near the door. The petite woman jumps up and runs to her daughter, sweeping her up into her arms and giving her a million tiny kisses as the little girl laughs in delight. It's such a heartwarming reunion, I forget about my own bitter, jaded heart for a moment and soak up all the joy.

Anita's head is covered by a cute little hat, and an instant pang of sadness filters through me when I realize her beautiful hair is gone. She looks even thinner than when I met her in Texas, but there is a nice rosy color in her cheeks, and her eyes are sparkling as she takes in the sight of her baby girl she hasn't seen in four months now. I'm not sure what she plans to tell Mariana about her hair.

"I never, ever want to go that long without seeing you again, Princess!" she gushes, twirling Mariana around in a circle as people come and go in the lobby and look on with approving smiles. All the sudden she stops and bends down to eye level with the girl. "Did you bring your Elsa dress?"

Mariana looks over at me because I packed for her, and I give her and her mother a little wink.

"Why, Mommy?"

"Because we're going to meet Elsa tonight!"

"What? Really?!" Mariana jumps up and down, celebrating with such a high-pitched squeal that we both have to rush over and beg her to tone it down so we don't get kicked out of this swanky hotel.

The rest of the afternoon and evening is amazing. Anita is so much fun to hang out with, and she knows all the best places in New York. I don't know how, since she lives in Texas, but she said something about spending a lot of time here in her twenties when she first graduated from college.

The show is even more amazing! And our seats are to die for. And when it's all over, we get to go backstage and meet the cast, along with about twenty or thirty other little girls with stars in their eyes. It's fun to be part of a dream come true for all these little princesses. They aren't going to forget this night as long as they live.

When I finally climb into bed that night—alone, Mariana is staying in Anita's room—I feel something like peace rushing over me. My heart still aches, and it's going to be a long time before I feel normal again, but there's a hope there, a hope that someday I'll look back on this year of my life and realize it all happened for a reason.

26

We made it to New York City!

It's our very last show tonight, and I have to say that I cannot wait for it to be over. We've got a whole new routine we practiced in Boston and debuted at our show last night, and it went over really well with the crowd.

Best of all, we're back on the East Coast, only four hours from Delaware. And my daughter.

And Claire.

There's a knock on my hotel room door, and even though I'm only wearing my robe, I figure I better go answer it. I half expect it to be Bonnie, hoping to try one last time to get into my pants—*holy crap*, she's been relentless lately, even if she keeps claiming she only wants to please our fans and get her hundred grand for winning the contest and doing the tour.

But it's not Bonnie. It's Brenda Monnett, and she's standing there with a phone in her hand. My phone.

"Hello, Jack," she chirps, stepping inside my room without waiting for an invitation. "Nice robe."

"Hello, Brenda," I sound a little like Jerry Seinfeld

saying "Hello, Newman," to his diabolical neighbor. "Is that my phone?"

"Indeed it is, Jack." She hands it over with a devious little smirk curling the edges of her lips. "You'll find it intact and fully charged. I'm sorry we had to take it away from you, but it was for the best."

"Whatever." I try to refrain from rolling my eyes, but I only have so much restraint.

"Thank you for being a good sport about all this. Now that the tour is done, after tonight's show, you'll be receiving your check, and we can part ways. Well, sort of. You'll be coming back to New York in two months to start rehearsals for your show, of course."

I narrow my steely gaze on her. I'm not sure I can remember ever hating anyone as much as I do her. "What if I don't want to do the show?"

Her eyelashes flutter with feigned innocence. "Oh, you're locked in now, Jack."

"I have a job, you know—as an *actual* band director," I fire back.

"I'm well aware, and I'll be speaking to your boss next week. I am fairly certain I can negotiate a year's sabbatical for you. After all, it's a real feather in their cap for a private school to have a faculty member who's starred in a Broadway show," she points out.

I roll my eyes yet again. Of course she will "speak with my boss." She seems to get her way with just about anyone she speaks to.

She stands there with her hands folded over her chest, giving me the stink eye as I check to make sure my phone is in working order. After confirming it functions properly, I glance up and purse my lips. "Okay, you can leave now. Thank you."

"Break a leg tonight," she says in that fake pleasant tone she's practically got trademarked.

As soon as she's gone, I try to call Claire. I half expect the number not to connect, but it does, and when her phone rings, my heartbeat ramps up. It rings. Rings. Rings. I get her voicemail.

"Claire, it's me. Please call me as soon as you can. I got my phone back, and I really need to talk to you."

I hang up, wishing I could have reached her. There's still time before the show tonight. I'll text her later, I suppose. *Hell, who am I kidding?* I'm probably going to call her every hour on the hour from now till showtime begging her to talk to me.

The next thing I do is dial my lawyer. He may have a douchebag name, but I'm relying on him to make sure everything goes smoothly from here on out. "Hey, Linderhorn?"

"Yes, Mr. Reilly, what can I do for you?" comes his deep, smooth voice.

"I just wanted to touch base to make sure you went over the contract with a fine-toothed comb. You're absolutely certain what I have planned for tonight won't have any negative ramifications?"

"You're in the clear, Mr. Reilly," he answers. "And when you return to Delaware tomorrow, please get in touch with my office so we can discuss the rest of the plan."

"Sounds good. Thanks."

I hang up and drum my fingers on the surface of the desk in my room in anticipation. I need to go talk to a few other people, then I just need to pray this goes off without a hitch.

I thought Nationals was a lot of pressure. Screw Nationals. That was nothing.

The only show that will ever matter is tonight.

I THOUGHT I'd be leaving the city in the morning with Mariana, and Anita would be flying back to the UK. She had already apologized for it being such a quick trip, but she said she had urgent business in London. This morning at breakfast, however, she told us she was able to get a later flight and had until the afternoon to hang out and enjoy the city.

She touches my wrist slightly before I head up to my room to pack my things. "There's one more thing I need you to do, Claire."

I turn toward her with curious eyes. "What's that?"

She hands me an envelope. "Please take Mariana tonight. It would mean a lot for her to see her father on stage one last time."

"What?" I tear open the envelope and find two tickets to the SAF Superstar Tour at Madison Square Garden. My hands are shaking so bad as I take them out and look at them. I don't even know what to say, let alone how to stop my hands from shaking. "How did you get these? It's sold out!"

"I have a lot of resources at my disposal with my job," she explains. "Trust me, Claire, you don't want to miss this tonight. I know you're angry with Jack...but please...just be patient with him."

"I can't believe you of all people are telling me that." I

can't help but perform an eye roll as she looks on with a knowing smile.

"I know, I know. But trust me, you won't regret it."

"If he kisses that woman on stage again, so help me, I'll—"

"You know that was all fake, right?" She blinks steadily at me.

"He denied it, but how would they fake something like that?"

"Show business," she says. "Trust me. It was fake."

I'd stopped reading all the chatter on social media about *Jannie* a good week ago now. It wasn't good for my health. But their fans were so thrilled their rock stars were "finally together," that I'd convinced myself they really were. That it was real. He'd gone on tour and done the one thing, committed the one sin I asked him not to commit: he let it change him.

But even if it was staged, and the whole relationship was fake, he went along with it. He let them bully him into it. He could have stood up for me. He could have told his fans he was in love with Claire Sterling, not Bonnie.

He could have *also* asked them to buy my book when it comes out, but—

Yeah, okay, maybe that's asking too much.

MARIANA and I are two tiny dots in a sea of humanity as we filter into the arena and find our seats, which are, somehow, in the front row. I don't know how Anita pulls these things off, but, at this juncture, I'm nearly convinced she's my fairy godmother.

"Are we really going to see Daddy?" Mariana asks as she squeezes my hand.

"Yes, baby." He's been texting me all day and left a voicemail asking me to talk, but I'm just not ready yet. After the show, we'll see how I feel. I need to see how they are together in person. I think I will be able to tell if it's real or fake.

Maybe it's because I'm a writer, and making up crazy plots in my head is something I just can't help, but I keep wondering if maybe he was lying about all the crazy stuff they did with his phone and bugging his room and following him everywhere he went. Maybe he even convinced Anita that they'd doctored that video with the kiss. Maybe he was just stringing me along so I'd continue to babysit his daughter for free while he's on this stupid tour and screwing his co-star.

My heart aches knowing that's probably not any more far-fetched than all the crazy stuff being true.

The lights come up on the stage, and ten figures shrouded in darkness are illuminated one by one. I can't remember all their names, but I recognize Nick and Xia, Lilly, and there's Bonnie. And there is Jack over on the other side. They come together to form one group and open with "Dreams" by Fleetwood Mac.

Then Steve—I think that's his name—grabs the nearest mic and starts out "Don't Let the Sun Go down on Me" by Elton John before everyone joins in. They do a fast song after that, which involves some actual choreography, and watching Jack dance might be the funniest thing I've ever seen in my life. He's actually pretty good at it.

He has not been on our side of the stage at all, so he hasn't noticed us. I don't know if Anita told him we were coming or not.

They do a Stevie Wonder song, and then two songs that are current and pop-y that I don't recognize. I feel so old as the mass of teenage girls around me sing along, knowing all the words. In between each song, they introduce themselves and talk about where they're from and what contests they won to secure their spot on the tour.

Then there's a little set change to reveal a grand piano with Jack sitting on the bench, his hands poised on the keys. He plays the intro to "Piano Man" by Billy Joel, and the crowd goes wild. So far, he and Bonnie have been far apart on stage the entire time. *Trust me, I am perfectly fine with that.*

There's one more song I don't recognize because it's country, then another current hit song. After the applause starts to fade, the stage curtains close, and the lights come on for intermission.

"Is it over?" Mariana squeaks out, sounding disappointed. "Daddy didn't see us even though I was jumping up and down and waving!"

"No, baby, it's just intermission. They'll come back on stage in a few minutes. Do you want to get some popcorn or something?"

"Okay. I need to pee-pee too," she says.

"Alright." Flashes of the night at Rehoboth Beach when Jack was singing at the bandstand come to mind as I take her hand and help her weave through the crowd and down the hallway till we exit onto the concourse where the restrooms and concession stands are. The line for the ladies restroom stretches from here to New Jersey, but what are you gonna do? We take our place in line and wait as it creeps closer and closer to the entrance.

We are still waiting fifteen minutes later when we hear the crowd erupt with cheers and applause. There's a monitor across the hall, and I can barely make out the group as they stand together like a gospel choir and sing "A Change is Gonna Come" by Sam Cooke. I'm sad we're missing that one, but we are almost to the restroom doors.

By the time Mariana finally gets to relieve herself, they are on their third song of the second act. I can't believe we missed so much. I help her wash her hands, then we exit into the hallway. I start to return to our seats, but she tugs on my hand. "I thought we were getting a snack?"

"Okay," I agree as the group breaks into "Glory Days" by Bruce Springsteen. We head over to the concession stand line, which is still chock full of people even though the show has started back up again. *Of course it is.* "What do you want, sweet pea?"

"Popcorn and a soda, please." She looks up at me with her irresistible grin.

"Sounds good." We get up to order, but the soda machine breaks. They have to change out the stuff, so they tell us it will be about five minutes. We've already missed five songs now. *Grrr.*

I hear female voices break into some song by Adele. A look at the monitor confirms the guys aren't even on stage. The solo is sung by Bonnie, of course, and she has this sultry, come-hither look on her face that makes me want to puke. Just knowing she probably looked at my boyfriend that way makes me so angry!

My boyfriend.

I can't seem to stop calling him that. Or stop thinking of him that way.

His text said he hopes I will hear him out. I honestly don't know if we can come back from this. What if he does do this Broadway show, and he's gone all the time? And plays opposite her? What if he makes an album, and they want him to go back on the road?

As exhilarating as it's been to date a rock star…I had

no idea it would be this hard. Journey tried to warn me that loving a music man isn't easy. I think they actually said "ain't"... I'll have to look past the poor grammar, I suppose.

I never thought in a million years that this is what I was signing up for when I convinced him to audition for this stupid contest. I just thought it would be fun, and he could help this charity make a few bucks to support arts programs. Who knew it would snowball into this giant thing that has buried us all under an avalanche of hurt?

"Hey, lady, here's your soda," the snippy man at the counter says, pushing the overflowing drink in my direction. Of course, it tips and spills all over the counter —and me!

Oh, you have got to be kidding me!

"Oh, sorry," he says nonchalantly, but it looks like he's trying to suppress a grin.

I want to drop some choice words on him, but, of course, I can't because Mariana is standing right here with her cute little impressionable ears. So I grit my teeth and ask him to make me another drink as I grab a fistful of napkins and attempt to soak up the puddles of soda all over me, the counter and the floor.

Meanwhile, I glance back up at the monitor, and Jack has taken the microphone again. I'm surprised they've given him so many solos, but he is the top-scoring male in the contest, I suppose. He's singing "You Were Always On My Mind" by Willie Nelson.

I know he hates country, so it's a surprising choice for him, but he makes it his own, and I have to admit, he sounds amazing. He looks so handsome up there with his beard starting to grow back in and looking all tall and hot in his tight jeans and his black button-down shirt.

He finishes up the song, but when the music stops, nothing happens. He walks to the edge of the stage and peers out at the audience. "Claire? Are you out there?"

Hearing my name come off his lips shocks me so much that I drop the soda I'd just picked up off the counter, and in a heartbeat, it explodes all over the floor one of the arena employees had just mopped up. The jerk behind the counter yells, "Hey, you did that on purpose!"

I ignore him and zoom in on the monitor. "Claire, if you're out there, stand up. I can't see anything past these lights."

"Oh my god, I'm Claire!" I shout, and everyone around me falls dead silent.

Mariana squeezes my hand, and when I look down at her, she has a huge smile on her face, almost like she knew this was going to happen.

He goes on to speak, "I hope you came tonight, Claire. But even if you aren't here, even if you end up seeing this on the news tomorrow—because I'm sure this will make the news—there's something I want you to know:

He starts to strum the guitar hanging from his shoulder as he continues to speak into the microphone attached to the band on his head, "I'm so sorry, Claire. I'm sorry I didn't let everyone know I'm in love with you. I'm sorry I didn't shout it from the rooftops: I LOVE YOU, CLAIRE STERLING! Is that better, baby? I'm telling you in person in front of a sold-out crowd of over twenty-thousand people, and from what I understand, there are millions of viewers all over the country watching tonight as well. I hope you're one of them, Claire, because I want to sing a song I wrote just for you."

Someone grabs my hand, and I'm still attached to Mariana, so we all go flying toward the doors to the arena.

As we jog down the aisle, the wall of security guards parts. When Jack begins to sing the lyrics to that song he composed for me months ago, the one Drew told me about, we're helped up onto the stage.

He walks toward us, still singing:

> Some say life is a game of chances
> Risk is everywhere you look
> but taking a chance to meet you
> was the best chance I ever took

I look at him with tears in my eyes, then venture a look out into the audience. The lights have dimmed, bathing us in swaths of blue and purple, and all across the arena, silhouettes of people appear, swaying back and forth and holding their phones out with their flashlights on so they look like a twinkling sea of tiny lights.

> I had no idea what I needed
> And it's true I resisted at first
> but now I'm jumping in with both feet
> because my heart's about to burst

His heart's not the only one! *My* heart is about to explode out of my chest as Mariana runs over to her father to throw her arms around his legs. He continues to belt out:

> Life is much too short
> to not admit that this is real
> Life is much too short
> to not tell you how I feel
> Life is much too short
> to deny what I know is true

Life is much too short
to not spend every
minute with you
Life is much too short
to not have you in my life
Life is much too short
to not ask you to be my wife

And then, the song winds down, and he lifts his hands from his guitar before sinking down onto one knee and pulling a tiny box out of his pants pocket. My hands fly to my face as a gasp hits my palms.

"Claire Sterling, I want to spend the rest of my life with you. None of this—none of the fame or fortune, or any of this—matters to me if you're not by my side. I don't want any of this if I can't have you. I've proven to myself over the past six weeks that I'm completely miserable without you. I can't live without you by my side every day. And I will do everything in my power to make sure we are never apart like this again—if you'll just say yes to marrying me."

He opens the box and, sparkling under the stage lights, is the biggest rock I've ever seen.

It's not too often that Claire Sterling is rendered speechless—just ask anyone who knows me. But the only word I can manage to fire off my lips at the moment is "Yes."

Mariana lets go of Jack and stands back as I walk toward my man, my rock star. He lifts the guitar over his head and hands it to his little girl. It's almost as big as she is, but she takes it, holding it like it's made of gold. And then this man, this man I've missed so much over the last six weeks, slides the ring on my finger before taking me into his arms and promising me he will never, ever let me go.

"Not ever?" I verify, glancing down to see how the lights are bouncing off my ring.

"Never ever."

Epilogue

I finish explaining to Claire how I managed to pull off my now infamous concert hijack in Madison Square Garden. It involved getting both Bonnie and Garvey on my side, not to mention a plethora of technicians and stage crew. And someone to distract Brenda Monnett to keep her from pulling the plug on the entire thing.

My lawyer assured me they had to honor their contract as long as the last show was completed, and that's why I waited till the very end to do my thing. After my proposal, the rest of the group sang the closing number and rocked it before being invited back for an encore number. I joined them for that, fulfilling my very last obligation to Support Art Foundation. Linderhorn was able to find a clause that released me from the Broadway deal, and I even have Thor/Tony/FBI Dude on the case if I need him. They've already opened a preliminary investigation into SAF on suspicion of money laundering.

"So, everyone gets their money?" she asks, her eyes glassy with tears. *Happy ones, this time.*

"Everyone gets their money."

"And Bonnie isn't going to bother you anymore?"

"Once she realized I was truly in love with you, and there was no way I'd ever be with her, even if you were out of the picture, she finally decided that having the money was good enough. Besides, she got a record contract. She's going to be just fine," I assure my beautiful fiancée.

"That's good. But I guess the Broadway show is off?" I detect a hint of disappointment in her tone.

I shrug. "Yeah, that was definitely a casualty of my actions at the concert. But there could be other opportunities. You never know."

"I didn't like Bonnie, but I really wanted you to do a Broadway show," Claire admits. "I guess I'll get over it."

"You know…" I use my index finger to tilt her chin back to look at me.

"What?"

"I do have kind of a crazy idea…"

"Oh, no…not sure I want to be part of any more crazy ideas!" she says. "Wasn't this whole thing crazy enough?"

"It was pretty darn crazy." I trail my finger down her cheek before pressing a kiss to her lips. I've missed those beautiful, luscious lips so much. Heck with talking, I could just sit here and kiss her all night long. Though my daughter may be forever traumatized if I did that.

"Well, are you going to tell me or what?"

That's my Claire. She hates not knowing stuff.

"What if *we* wrote a Broadway show?" I ask her.

Her brows scrunch. "We have zero Broadway connections." She laughs. "I mean, it sounds fun, but I think you burned the bridges you had with a Broadway producer."

"Yes, okay, maybe not Broadway…but we could write a musical. What if we wrote a musical to stage here in Rehoboth Beach? That would be fun, right? You write the lyrics; I write the music."

"Sure, okay," she plays along. "We'll just write a musical. No big deal."

"I knew you wouldn't take it seriously!" I give her a fake pout.

She strokes her hand down my back and leans in. "Oh, I can see it now. A musical about pirates invading Rehoboth. We'll call it Yo-Ho-Rehoboth!" She laughs so hard, she nearly starts coughing.

She might have something there. *My girl's so freaking smart!* "Actually...I think that idea has some merit."

"Oh, right!" She slaps her hand against my chest and shakes her head.

"They were basically going to write a musical about my life. Pirates sound way better than that!"

"Pirates do make everything better," she agrees with a nod.

I clear my throat before changing the subject entirely. "So, what do you say, Ms. Sterling, should we pull out the calendar and choose a wedding date?"

She looks over at Mariana, who is engrossed in something on the television. She'll only be here for two more weeks. Anita has made a full recovery and will be coming to pick her up just in time to take her back to start first grade in Texas. I'm sad I missed so much of our summer away on tour, but we're going to spend the next two weeks doing every single fun thing we can think of to try to make up for it.

And I couldn't really argue with The Ex Formerly Known as Darth Anita for wanting to take Mariana back to Texas early. And not because I was afraid she'd pull the old Vader chokehold on me. In reality, I owe my ex everything. She saved my relationship with Claire. It was a completely selfless act, one I didn't know she was capable of. I guess we've both grown and changed a lot since we were married. I don't know how I could ever repay her.

Claire grabs her phone off the coffee table and scrolls to her calendar app. "You're awfully eager, aren't you, Mr. Reilly?"

I take her hand into mine and bring it to my mouth to press a kiss to it. "I want us to be a family more than anything, Claire. The sooner the better."

"Then I wonder if we should do it before Mariana leaves for Texas?" she suggests, and at first I don't know if she's serious, or she's calling my bluff.

"Do you think you can really throw something together that fast? We only have two weeks!"

She scoffs, "Do you know who you're dealing with here?"

"Um…no?" I shake my head, not understanding what she means. "You?"

"Jean-Marc, the King of Parties, duh!"

Her radiant smile is contagious. "If we can pull it off that fast, then, by all means, let's do it!"

There's a knock at her door, and she excuses herself to go answer it. She comes back a few seconds later with her neighbors, Red and Mrs. Vandeveer, in tow. Mrs. Vandeveer looks a decade younger than the last time I saw her, and she's standing there holding a cake with fancy piped frosting roses.

"Hi there! Welcome home!" Red says, his voice only sounding half as gruff as it usually does.

"They baked us a cake to welcome you home, Jack!" Claire says. "Isn't that sweet?"

"That's wonderful. Thank you, guys, that's so thoughtful. It looks delicious!" I take the cake into the kitchen and set it on the counter before rejoining the group in the living room, immediately noticing two people are missing. "Where did Mariana go?"

"Oh, she went to show Red the new pictures she colored," Mrs. Vandeveer says. "She just loves him so much. You know, it was watching the way he interacted with her that made me fall in love with him. And I also have you to thank, Claire, for bringing us together. If you hadn't needed us to babysit that beautiful little girl, I'd have never ended my dry spell!"

Before we can cut her off, she continues, "You know, it'd been almost thirty years since I had a man—"

Claire lunges forward to cut her off. "Oh, we know, Mrs. Vandeveer. WE KNOW!"

She laughs. "I better go look at these pictures too. I don't want Frederick to hog all the attention from our sweet little angel!"

"Frederick!" we both exclaim in unison. So *that's* where "Red" comes from.

We watch Mrs. Vandeveer sashay down the hall, all signs of her usual hobble completely vanished. She's made an incredible transformation. I can hardly believe she's the same woman.

"Doesn't she look different? I think she even colored her hair," Claire says once she disappears into Mariana's bedroom.

"Yeah, it's amazing what a little sex can do, isn't it?" I joke.

"I wouldn't know," she fires back. "It's been six weeks since I've had a man between these legs!" She throws her arm over her forehead in dramatic fashion. "Any chance you're up for some *intercoursing* tonight, Mr. Reilly?"

"I hoped to never hear that word again," I say, laughing at the memory of that day on our porch, the day this whole crazy journey began. "Tell you what, never say that word again, and I'll give you all the D you want."

"You got yourself a deal." She starts to shake my hand, but then she leaps into my arms and captures my lips with her own instead.

Read how Claire and Jack met in
Fat Girl
Read the real-world version of the bodypositive book
Claire wrote:
The Fat Girl's Guide to Loving Your Body
Continue the Romance in Rehoboth series with Drew &
Sonnet's story in
The Flip
Read about the musical that Jack and Claire wrote in
Plot Twist
Get the first boxed set here:
Romance in Rehoboth Boxed Set 1
Get the second boxed set here:
Romance in Rehoboth Boxed Set 2

About the Author

K.L. Montgomery writes bodypositive sweet romance, cozy mysteries, and romcom. A librarian in a former life, she now works as an editor and runs the 6000-member Indie Author Support group on Facebook in addition to publishing under two names.

Though she remains a Hoosier at heart, K.L. shares her coastal Delaware home with some furry creatures and her husband, who works in law enforcement (and is also somewhat of a furry creature, to be honest). She has an undying love for her three sons, Broadway musicals, the beach, Seinfeld, the color teal, IU basketball, paisleys, and dark chocolate.

Learn more at www.klmontgomery.com or follow her one of the following social media sites:

facebook.com/GreenCastles

twitter.com/klmontgomery8

instagram.com/k.l.montgomery

bookbub.com/authors/k-l-montgomery

Acknowledgments

Since this book is all about a rock star, I thought it would be appropriate to mention who has been a total rock star in helping me write and prepare this book for publication. First off, my PA, Jared Gallant. He always takes on any task he's given so cheerfully, and I really appreciate that. Secondly, my proofreader, Tina Kissinger. I think she set a world proofreading record with this one! And because of her, my ARCs will go out on time and all sparkly clean!

I need to send a serious shout out to my two favorite promo goddesses: Colleen Noyes of Itsy Bitsy Book Bits and Natasha Carrere of RRR Promotions. They deal with my utter flakiness on release dates and forgetting to send them stuff, and frankly, I don't know how they put up with me. They must love me, that's all I can think.

Finally, a huge thank you to my husband, Mike, and my son Kadan, who bore the brunt of my panic and bitchiness when I was so behind schedule on this book. I holed myself up in my office for too many hours to count the last two weeks, and I think they were even more relieved when I typed THE END than I was. And I've promised them not to do this kind of crazy (self-imposed, mind you) deadline ever again. Oh, boy, do I hope I can keep that promise!

Hope you enjoyed this rock star romance—even if it's a lot different than most rock star books out there. As far as I'm concerned, Jack and Claire are still rock stars—and always will be.

And so are you, for giving me your support! <3

Hugs,
   Krista

Also by K.L. Montgomery

Nonfiction

The Fat Girl's Guide to Loving Your Body

Do you wonder if you'll ever be happy with your body?

It's a choice, you know.

This book is one part humor, one part journal, one part recipe for self-love. Mix it all together, and you'll come out the other side with a greater appreciation for both what's on the outside AND what's on the inside.

The Guide tackles:

-how to deal with bodyshamers

-how to dress for your body

-relationship and sex advice

-365 #bopo meditations

Plus, strategies for learning to love the skin you're in now and forever.

Have you ever struggled to love your body?

YOU NEED THIS BOOK. NOW.

Romance in Rehoboth Series

Welcome to the Romance in Rehoboth Series, where the ladies are strong and independent and the men are actually nice guys. These delightful romantic comedies are set against the backdrop of Rehoboth Beach, Delaware's top vacation destination. The books can be read as standalones.

Music Man, Romance in Rehoboth #1

You're never too old to fall in love with a rock star. Or chase your dreams.

Every girl dreams of dating a rock star--even a girl who just turned the Big 4-0. Is it the beard? The flannel? The guitar? Claire isn't sure, but Jack is simply irresistible.

Music was Jack's first love. When life got in the way of him making it big as a singer/songwriter, he settled for teaching music--which included giving piano lessons to a certain stunning redhead named Claire.

He's fallen head over heels for her--just in time for his big break to finally arrive. But do you ever really give up on your first love?

The Flip, Romance in Rehoboth #2

Andrew and Sonnet hated each other in high school. Always rivals for the best grades and top academic honors, there was no love lost between these two nerds after graduation.

Ten years later, they've both been named heirs to property in Bethany Beach, Delaware, after the passing of its owner, Penelope Vaughn. Ms. Vaughn was Andrew's Great Aunt and Sonnet's beloved next door neighbor growing up.

The quaint beach cottage needs serious work before going on the market. Andrew and Sonnet are both willing to bury the hatchet in exchange for drills and saws, especially since they stand to make a pretty penny with the beachfront property, which will finance Drew's dream of opening a business and Sonnet's plan to earn her doctorate in astrophysics.

But when they face a multitude of home improvement obstacles, will these two former adversaries be able to pull off a successful flip? Or did Great Aunt Penny have something else in mind with her bequest?

Plot Twist, Romance in Rehoboth #3

If you think what's happening on stage is entertaining...you should see what's happening BACKSTAGE!

A brand new show is coming to Rehoboth Beach! Jack and Claire (yes, THAT Claire) Reilly have written an original musical, and they have the perfect cast. Plus, there's pirates. Who doesn't love pirates?

Meric Chandler is a neurotic, introverted accountant by day, but at night he transforms into a magnetic leading man whose voice makes all the girls swoon. Just getting over a divorce, he has sworn off backstage romances. After all, that's how he met his EX wife.

Lindy Larson prefers to stay behind the scenes, but her girlfriends convince her to audition for a new local theater production. She has a stunning voice but plans to blend in as much as possible, which isn't easy to do when you're the awkward plus-size girl with two left feet.

While backstage romances are to be expected, they don't usually shut down the entire production. But you know what they say: the show must go on!

Badge Bunny, Romance in Rehoboth #4

Chris Everson has a pretty sweet life: a great job as a state trooper, lots of buddies to hang out with, and living at the beach. What could be better? But he's harboring a secret--a secret that doesn't fit with his whole tough guy cop persona. He's gone to great lengths to keep his secret from his guy friends AND the women he dates.

Brynne Miller's job as an ER doctor means she's always meeting cops. In fact, she's dated so many that her friends call her "Badge

Bunny." But she will never date Chris Everson. Nope. Not a chance. He managed to piss her off within two seconds of meeting him...and first impressions are everything.

Aren't they?

Wedding War, Romance in Rehoboth #5

All's fair in love and war...and this is war.

Jason Friday's family business has kept the grooms of Delmarva in style for over forty years. Hannah Robinson's family has been doing the same for brides for nearly thirty.

A squabble over twenty years ago turned the two families into mortal enemies. As their businesses grew, their rivalry only became more cutthroat...until Über Brides sets up shop in Rehoboth Beach. This bridal superstore chain is known for slashing prices, squeezing every drop of discounts from their vendors, and running family-owned shops out of business.

The days of the Fridays and Robinsons serving the brides and grooms of Delmarva are numbered unless Jason and Hannah can band together to run Über Brides out of Rehoboth Beach. Can they manage to work together and ignore their growing attraction to each other? Or will they lose both their jobs and their families when they succumb to their desires?

Stage Mom, Romance in Rehoboth #6

A mom who'll never give up fighting for her special needs daughter...

A "nice guy" who finally learns to take a stand...

Larissa and Mateo's worlds collide in Stage Mom!

Everything about Larissa Emerson is strong.

Her personality.

Her snark.

Her aversion to men after one too many disappointments.

Her unwavering fight to ensure her special needs daughter is treated like any other girl--a fight that ramps up when she begs to compete in a beauty pageant.

Mateo Flores is in his first year of heading up the Little Miss Rehoboth pageant, and he's not about to screw it up. He knew he'd be dealing with stereotypical pageant moms, but he never saw this one coming. She hits him like a hurricane, all strength and beauty and attitude.

How can he say no to a force of nature like Larissa Emerson?

Shark Bite, Romance in Rehoboth #7

You've heard of second chance romance, but what about third time's the charm?

After being divorced three years, Megan Adams is desperate for marriage and a family before it's too late. When she tries to help her friend Shark upgrade his rugby team's reputation in the community, her attraction to him is rekindled all over again. Could he ever think of her as more than a friend--or is she risking one heck of a shark bite?

When you score in rugby, it's called a try. When it comes to scoring with the ladies, Shark Kelly usually doesn't have to try. But when the captain of his rugby team takes a liking to his friend Megan, he tries to stop the jealous feelings he never expected to have. And there might be a lot of other things he'd be willing to try--if Megan is brave enough to swim with a shark.

The Light at Dawn

No matter how dark the night, hope is reborn at dawn.

It wasn't just her marriage that crumbled in the wake of unspeakable tragedy, it was her entire life. Even though five years had passed since she lost Evan, Angelia White was still picking up the pieces. Getting involved in a cause she could pour her broken heart into was just another part of the healing process.

The wounds were too fresh for Mark Lyon to keep his grip on reality. Everything he thought he knew and believed was obliterated when he lost Ashleigh, along with his heart. The only way he could pick up the pieces was to fight for a way to prevent any other parent from ever suffering such merciless pain.

Two heartbroken parents enduring the darkest of nights.

Two wounded souls waiting for the light at dawn.

Given to Fly

Can you break your vow if it's the only way to save yourself?

Annelise Lowe was taught that if she was a good enough person and Christian, all life's puzzle pieces would simply fall into place. God would bless her with a happy marriage and children of her own. But those promises were shattered when she came face to face with her husband's infidelity and her own infertility.

The one unbiased friend she can lean on is the widowed father of a little girl in her preschool class. His own wounds still healing, Trek Blue needs Annelise as much as she needs him.

Annelise discovers that Trek is another path to happiness…but can she turn her back on everything she's been taught?

Green Castles

Inspired by true events, Green Castles tells the story of three former high school best friends; Jennifer, Kat, and Michelle; who are reunited in their small Indiana hometown when Jennifer's daughter loses her battle with mitochondrial disease. Through a series of flashbacks to their teen days in the late 1980's/early 1990's, the three women learn about resilience, forgiveness, and just how strong the bonds of family and friendship truly are.

K.L. Montgomery Cozy Mysteries

Made in the USA
Middletown, DE
30 September 2023

39840749R00184